Praise for *Mending Fences*

"Fisher gently unpacks the challenge that making peace with others brings after a fall from grace."

Publishers Weekly

"Suzanne is Queen for writing about the Old Order Amish. I have learned so much from reading her books. She has a way of evoking all of your emotions."

Interviews and Reviews

"Fans of Fisher's Stoney Ridge books will be delighted at this return to familiar characters and story threads introduced in previous books that now get a chance to shine."

Hope by the Book

"A funny, heartwarming story of friendship, love, and the possibility of happily ever after."

Amy Clipston, bestselling author of *Seat by the Hearth*

"A warm story of community, forgiveness, and acceptance, this will resonate with a lot of readers."

Parkersburg News & Sentinel

"There's just something unique and fresh about every Suzanne Woods Fisher book. Maybe it's the characters that are both flawed and endearing. Maybe it's the unexpected bursts of humor that make me smile just as I start to tear up. Whatever the reason, I'm a fan. *Mending Fences* features Luke Schrock, an Amish hero like no other. It's a wonderful contemporary Amish romance full of hope, love, and fresh starts. It's also, well, it's also just a really good book."

Shelley Shepard Gray, *New York Times*
and *USA Today* bestselling author

"Suzanne Woods Fisher has written a sweet and poignant story you won't want to put down. As the title suggests, *Mending Fences* is a journey of healing and redemption, a reminder of God's grace and mercy. Definitely a must-read!"

Kathleen Fuller, bestselling author
of the Amish of Birch Creek series

TWO STEPS FORWARD

Books by Suzanne Woods Fisher

TWO STEPS FORWARD

SUZANNE WOODS FISHER

Revell

a division of Baker Publishing Group
Grand Rapids, Michigan

Published by Revell
a division of Baker Publishing Group
PO Box 6287, Grand Rapids, MI 49516-6287
www.revellbooks.com

Printed in the United States of America

Library of Congress Cataloging-in-Publication Data
Names: Fisher, Suzanne Woods, author.
Title: Two steps forward / Suzanne Woods Fisher.
Description: Grand Rapids, Michigan : Revell, a division of Baker Publishing
    Group, [2020] | Series: The Deacon's Family ; 3
Identifiers: LCCN 2019027618 | ISBN 9780800727536 (paperback)
Subjects: LCSH: Amish—Fiction. | GSAFD: Christian fiction. | Love stories.
Classification: LCC PS3606.I78 T96 2020 | DDC 813/.6—dc23
LC record available at https://lccn.loc.gov/2019027618

ISBN 978-0-8007-3774-0 (casebound)

Published in association with Joyce Hart of the Hartline Literary Agency, LLC.

20   21   22   23   24   25   26   7   6   5   4   3   2   1

To Reagan, Madeline, and Bryce Fisher,
for all the love and joy you have brought to our family.
I can't imagine life without you!

We can't fix the whole world, but we can do what we can. One by one.

DEACON LUKE SCHROCK

Cast of Characters

Sylvie Schrock King—cousin to Luke Schrock, widow of Jake King

Joey Schrock—Sylvie's four-and-a-half-year-old boy

Jimmy Fisher—second son of Edith Fisher Lapp; recently returned to Stoney Ridge after a four-year absence. Originally introduced in *The Keeper*, book 1 of the Stoney Ridge Seasons series

Luke Schrock—deacon for the church of Stoney Ridge; originally introduced in The Inn at Eagle Hill series, his story continued in The Bishop's Family series; main character in *Mending Fences*

Isabella "Izzy" Miller Schrock—wife to Luke Schrock; introduced in *Mending Fences*

Fern Lapp—owner of Windmill Farm; surrogate mother and grandmother to all; originally introduced in the Stoney Ridge Seasons series

David Stoltzfus—bishop of Stoney Ridge; originally introduced in *The Revealing*, book 3 of The Inn at Eagle Hill series; main character in The Bishop's Family series

Hank Lapp—uncle of deacon Amos Lapp; originally introduced in the Stoney Ridge Seasons series

Edith Fisher Lapp—wife of Hank Lapp; originally introduced in the Stoney Ridge Seasons series

Grace Mitchell Miller—mother of Izzy and Jenny; a woman with a very messy past; introduced in *The Lesson*, book 3 of the Stoney Ridge Seasons series

Juan Miranda—newly appointed fire chief at the Stoney Ridge Fire Station

Jesse Stoltzfus—son of bishop David Stoltzfus; introduced in *The Revealing*, book 3 of The Inn at Eagle Hill series; his story continued throughout The Bishop's Family series

Jenny Stoltzfus—wife of Jesse Stoltzfus, half-sister to Izzy Schrock; introduced in *The Lesson*, book 3 of the Stoney Ridge Seasons series

Teddy Zook—carpenter, jack of all trades, church Vorsinger (music leader), husband to Alice Smucker Zook

Sam Schrock—younger brother to Luke Schrock; trains young horses from the racetrack for buggy

Mollie Graber Schrock—niece to Fern Lapp; married to Sam, Luke's brother; originally introduced in The Inn at Eagle Hill series

*O*NE

Growing up is hard on a man. If he'd done well for himself, coming home again should be one of his finest days. The kind of a day that kept him buoyed up with hopeful visions to survive his lowest moments: A mother peering out the kitchen window, eager for the first sign of her returning son. A sweet aromatic cinnamon cake baking in the oven. A loyal dog, muzzle now gray, sitting by the mailbox.

Unfortunately for Jimmy Fisher, he hadn't done terribly well for himself since he'd left Stoney Ridge. Years ago, he'd left home to chase some big dreams, but those had fizzled out like smoke up a chimney. As for a mother waiting anxiously for her son's return—Edith Fisher Lapp wasn't the type to hover or to wait. And she never did let Jimmy have a dog.

Jimmy stopped at the bottom step of the Bent N' Dent store, stalling. He recognized the beat-up buggy and tired old horse in the parking lot as belonging to Hank Lapp. That meant that Hank would be inside and, to be honest, he was not the person Jimmy wanted to see first upon returning to town. Closer to the last. He was still baffled that his mother had married Hank. Of all the men on earth, she chose wild-haired, wild-eyed Hank Lapp.

Jimmy pivoted on his heels, wondering if he should just turn tail and flee. If he had a dollar to spare in his pocket, he would do just that. Sadly, he didn't. And he was hungry too. He hadn't eaten since yesterday morning, when he came across an orchard filled with withered, wormy apples. He rubbed his stomach, still regretting that indulgence.

A buggy driven by a stunning white horse pulled into the parking lot. Intrigued by the horse's unique facial features, he felt himself drawn to it. Horses had always captivated Jimmy. They were the theme of his life, the very reason he had left Stoney Ridge in the first place. He'd been lured to Colorado to work on a ranch with the promise that he'd receive a few colts or fillies to start his own stable. So sure was he that he had landed on a gold mine that he'd even put a temporary long-term hold on his romance with girlfriend Bethany Schrock.

But Bethany got tired of waiting. She up and married a fellow who she said could actually make up his mind. Jimmy was disappointed but not completely heartbroken. That came later, when the ranch went belly-up, the horses were sold off, and his only option to receive back pay was to sue the rancher, but he couldn't do that. He had plenty of character flaws, more than most men, but he was true to his church's teachings. The rancher knew it too. Alas. So here he was, back and broke.

He ran a hand down the slightly concaved nose of the buggy horse and the horse jerked its head away. Jumpy. This was not a horse typical of the Thoroughbreds or Standardbreds that pulled Amish buggies.

"Prince don't like you."

Jimmy looked around the horse's head to find a solemn boy peering up at him. He was just a small boy, with a mop of curly hair under his black hat, but he stood with spread legs, his fists stuck on his hips and his chin jutting out. You'd have thought he was David the Shepherd Boy facing down Goliath the Giant.

"Joey, honey, it's all right. He's just saying hello to our fine horse."

Jimmy turned. A young woman stood by the buggy door. Under the brim of her black bonnet were violet eyes—not just blue but truly violet. Pansy purple. The woman wasn't smiling at Jimmy but at the horse, with genuine admiration. For the briefest of seconds, Jimmy felt a spark of interest in a female, something he hadn't felt for a long time. But then he realized she was the boy's mother. *Lord-a-mercy!* The spark fizzled like someone had doused him with a bucket of water.

He swallowed down a gulp and lifted his eyebrows in a greeting. "If I'm not mistaken, this horse is Arabian."

Her face registered surprise. "You're not mistaken. How'd you know that?"

"I've been out in Colorado, working on a ranch. Mustangs, Arabians. Hardworking horses." He cocked his head. "So you use an Arabian"—he glanced underneath the horse's girth—"*stallion* as a buggy horse?" This little gal had guts.

Dark brows flared over indignant violet eyes. "Whoever wrote the rule that there's only one kind of horse to use for buggies?" She ran a hand down the horse's neck, straightening his mane. Calmer now, she added, "If there's a job for a horse, there's a horse for a job. And I happen to think that nearly every job can be done by an Arabian."

Jimmy was more than a little flabbergasted. It wasn't every day you found someone who understood horses, especially not a female someone. "Interesting notion, to expand what's used for the buggy. The Arabian and the Thoroughbred are both efficient movers. They share that daisy-cutter action, keeping their feet low to the ground." He could keep going on, as he considered himself something of an expert on horses, but he didn't want to show off.

She tipped her head up to study him for a long moment. "Any chance you're looking for work?"

He felt a little dizzy from those twinkling eyes of hers. Positively bedazzled. Or maybe he was just hungry.

Lord-a-mercy. Jimmy Fisher, what is wrong with you?! He was getting all jelly-kneed over somebody else's woman, and a stranger to boot. She waited for him to respond, but before he could gather thoughts into words, the door opened to the Bent N' Dent and out walked Hank Lapp.

"SYLVIE SCHROCK KING! THAT BOY IS NOT AVAILABLE!" Hank roared at them from the top of the Bent N' Dent stairs.

Jimmy sighed. "That's Hank Lapp."

"Everybody knows Hank," the little boy said.

The woman, Sylvie, gave the little boy's hand a tug. "Let's get our shopping done." She gave Jimmy a courteous nod and turned to head into the store.

Hank held the door open for her, then came down the steps, arms flung wide to embrace Jimmy in a bear hug. Hank squeezed him so tight that he practically jolted some of Jimmy's molars loose.

"Hank, let me go," Jimmy gasped.

Hank released him but slapped him on the back. "YOUR

MOTHER IS GOING TO BE TICKLED PINK THAT YOU CAME HOME FOR HER BIRTHDAY."

Oh boy. Jimmy had completely forgotten his mother's birthday.

"SON, YOU OWE ME A THANK YOU. I JUST SAVED YOU FROM THE CLUTCHES OF A WIDOW LADY. YOU KNOW WHAT THEY SAY ABOUT WIDOW LADIES. ALWAYS ON THE HUNT FOR A NEW HUSBAND." Hank tried to lower his voice to a whisper and it came out at normal volume. "Jake King. Remember him?"

"Jake the Junkman?"

"THAT'S HIM. Always trying to COBBLE things together to make a living."

"So Jake finally got married." Jimmy shook his head. He remembered Jake, a neighbor, as a strange guy. He would head off to tag sales or auctions, lugging home odds and ends. And old. Why, Jake must've been forty or fifty years old. Or older. Everyone considered him on the shelf and there to stay, a lifelong bachelor. It was hard to see a match with Jake the Junkman and the twinkly violet-eyed beauty.

"She's the one who got him tangled up in that horse-breeding business. NO ONE WANTS THOSE FUNNY-NOSED HORSES."

"They're Arabians, and they're probably the best horse anyone could ever have."

"WHAT?" Hank stroked his wiry beard, if you could call it a beard. More like stubby whiskers. "YOU DON'T SAY."

"Maybe she's got some good reasons for the decisions she's making."

Hank looked all around, before leaning close to Jimmy to shout, "SOME SAY SHE MIGHT BE THE REASON

JAKE DIDN'T LAST LONG." He wagged a bony finger in Jimmy's face and tempered his voice to a low roar. "Some say she brings BAD LUCK wherever she goes."

"You've got to be kidding. Hank, even you don't believe nonsense like that."

"OF COURSE NOT. BUT . . . SHE'S A SCHROCK, YOU KNOW."

"Why would that matter?"

"DON'T YOU KNOW ABOUT THOSE SCHROCKS?" He slapped his knees. "OF COURSE NOT! You've been off playing cowboys and Indians."

Jimmy frowned at him. Ranch work could hardly be described as playing cowboys. It was backbreaking work; long, hard days in the saddle. There were times he thought he'd always walk like he was holding a barrel between his knees.

"I'll fill you in later on the SCHROCK SAGA. Sylvie is a cousin to LUKE SCHROCK. AND YOU KNOW ALL ABOUT LUKE SCHROCK."

"Hank, is it possible for you to stop yelling?"

"I'M NOT YELLING. I'M JUST TALKING." But then he did drop it a tidge. "And then there are some that say Sylvie might be a LITTLE BIT . . ." He whistled a note up and down, while whirling his finger around his ear like a clock. "As for me, I just figure some folks are down on their luck. Permanent-like."

"No such thing as luck, good or bad." To be honest, Jimmy had wondered now and then if he might be prone to bad luck. Things never seemed to end up the way he'd planned. "Besides, that's no way to talk about old Jake. Or his widow."

"I'm only repeating what folks are KNOWN TO WHIS-

PER." Hank shrugged his thin shoulders. "MOSTLY YOUR MOTHER. She's had some run-ins with Sylvie."

Jimmy rolled his eyes. His mother was legendary for her disapproval. "How did Jake die?"

"ROPING A DEER."

"He did *what*?"

"Jake figured it would be easier to just CATCH IT that-aways."

"So what happened?"

"A sharp HOOF to the head." Hank thumped his forehead. "Deer reared up and KICKED him. A trapped deer can be a SAVAGE BEAST. Did you know that?"

"The deer attacked him?"

"Yup. A severe blow to the head, Dok said."

"Huh. That's sad."

"MAYBE YOU SHOULD MARRY HER." He gave Jimmy a sharp jab with his bony elbow. "Nice piece of property she's got from Jake. You like those funny-nosed horses. And that boy o' hers needs a daddy."

No way. No way! *Change the subject, quick.* Jimmy squeezed his eyes shut. Why had it ever seemed like a good idea to return to Stoney Ridge? His stomach rumbled and he remembered why. Hungry and broke, in that order.

The door to the store opened and out came Sylvie Schrock King, now with a bulky package added under an arm. Jimmy walked over to help her, but she shook her head and said crisply, "I can manage just fine, thank you."

She swept right on past the two men, which only proved to Jimmy that Hank was dead wrong about women—widow or single or anything in between. She wasn't husband hunting; she paid him no mind.

After getting her boy settled into the buggy, she untied the horse's reins and turned to face Hank. Her voice became sharper. "Neighbors shouldn't go telling tall tales on each other. That's written in the Good Book." She shifted her gaze to Jimmy. "And just so you know, I am not on the hunt for a new husband. Consider the job offer withdrawn." Just before hopping into the buggy, she winked at him, then shut the door.

Jimmy's eyebrows shot up. "Did you see *that*?"

"SEE WHAT?"

"Uh, nothing." He must've imagined it.

"IS it really in the GOOD BOOK for neighbors to not tell tales? I never heard it."

"I don't know. Probably. Sounds like it."

Sylvie's horse stepped backward gingerly, as if on tiptoe, then gracefully shifted forward into a smooth trot. Lord-a-mercy, that stallion was a fine specimen. Jimmy watched the horse, enchanted. "You know, I wouldn't mind being around that."

"Son, if you want to marry her, then go right ahead. BUT DON'T SAY I DIDN'T WARN YOU."

Jimmy felt a stitch in his stomach—those bad apples were catching up with him. So was Hank's foolish waffling. Warning him about widow ladies in one breath, suggesting he marry her in another. "I was talking about the horse, Hank. I wouldn't mind working with horses like that." He rubbed his sore stomach. "And I sure do need a job. Why'd you have to go and ruin it for me?"

"RUIN IT? Not hardly." He untied his old weary-looking horse's reins. "Hop into my chariot and I'll take you home."

The bad apples poked at Jimmy again, higher up, and he winced.

Hank was already backing up the buggy and waving for Jimmy to jump in. As he climbed in the passenger side of Hank's beat-up buggy, Jimmy thought he might know how that roped deer felt. The noose felt tight around his throat, and he could feel a panic rise up. The closer the buggy got to home, to his mother, the tighter it felt.

Naturally, Hank didn't notice Jimmy's discomfort. All the way home, he nattered nonstop, catching Jimmy up on news and gossip, as if he'd been gone weeks and not years. As they passed the property that belonged to Jake the Junkman, Jimmy spotted Sylvie Schrock King at the mailbox. The buggy rolled past, and Sylvie looked over at the last minute. Her violet eyes caught Jimmy's and she winked at him, as if they shared a private joke. This time, there was no mistaking it. Jimmy knew all about winks and what they meant.

Hank, who generally noticed nothing, noticed *that*. "HA! I TOLD YOU SO! Boy, she's already SET HER SIGHTS on you. She's got the FISH ON THE LINE. Now she just has to REEL HIM IN."

Jimmy's stomach did a slow, sickening turn.

Sylvie Schrock King was a pretty good judge of people. She knew who to offer a job to and who to send packing, and that was why she spent the rest of the afternoon regretting how she'd snapped at that poor pathetic homeless man who was patting her sweet Prince at the Bent N' Dent. It shocked her that he recognized an Arabian horse, shocked and intrigued her. It seemed like he knew a lot about horses. When she pushed a little more, he sounded both supremely confident and totally vague. That she understood as a way to keep people at arm's length. She wished she hadn't been so quick to withdraw her job offer from the homeless man. She might not see him again and she sure needed help around this place.

It was all because of that loudmouthed Hank Lapp. Whenever Hank or Edith Lapp were involved, mostly Edith, Sylvie's hackles rose, and she felt like she had to ready herself for battle. Sharing a creek as a boundary line with Edith Lapp had created all kinds of headaches, especially after the heavy storms they'd had this last year, and Hank didn't help. He made a mess of everything.

She checked on her napping boy and went outside to fill Prince's water bucket. As she made her way down the grass path to the paddock, that familiar swirl of anxiety began, and she tried to push it down. She thought of all the endless chores that needed to be done around Rising Star Farm, and she still hadn't had any success with Prince as a stud for buggy horses—and then she remembered it was the horse's name that rankled Edith Lapp most of all. She had accused Sylvie of being prideful, despite how many times she explained it was the name the stallion came with, and you just didn't change a horse's name. That was how things were done in the horse world, Sylvie had told Edith.

"This isn't a horse world," Edith had crisply replied in her stone-faced way. "This is an Amish world."

Well, to Sylvie's way of thinking, the two didn't have to cancel each other out. Besides, Bishop David Stoltzfus didn't mind the name of her horse. Sylvie's cousin, Luke, was a deacon. If the bishop and the deacon didn't object, why did Edith Lapp think she was judge and jury of Stoney Ridge? Who wrote that rule for her?

Sylvie had pointed out to Edith some might consider the

name of the property to be a smidgen prideful: Rising Star Farm. She was well acquainted with the history of the farm, and that Edith's grandfather, the original owner, had been the one to name it.

Edith huffed. "That's entirely different."

"How so?"

Edith's sparse brows came together in a V. "It just is." She had pivoted and stormed home.

Up from his nap, Joey called out to her from the porch, and she waved to him, then turned off the water spigot and pushed the bucket under the bottom rail. By the time she finished, Joey had joined her. "Mem, the crabby lady from across the creek is waiting for you on the porch."

Sylvie dried her hands on her apron and went out to greet Edith Lapp, feeling cornered. What now? Edith's visits were never social calls. She had yet to have a conversation with Edith that ended well.

As they walked up the path to the house, Edith looked Joey over from head to toe as if seeing him for the first time. She clicked her tongue in mocking reproof. "He must take after his daddy, because he sure doesn't look like you."

Stung, Sylvie smoothed Joey's flame of hair where it tufted on top. "He takes after himself, that's who." She bent down to talk to him. "Go on down to the barn. Prince told me he's been wanting a carrot for his afternoon snack."

Edith sniffed. "Horses don't talk. You shouldn't fill the boy's mind with silly tales."

"Prince talks," Joey said, his chin jutted out. "But he just talks to Mem."

Sylvie gave Joey a gentle push toward the barn before he could say anything more to annoy Edith.

"I've come to make you an offer on Rising Star Farm."

"It's my farm now and it's where we plan to stay. Me and Joey. Jake left it to us."

"Oh?" Her sparse eyebrows lifted. "Is that in Jake's last will and testament? I'd like to see it."

Sylvie hesitated just a moment too long. She had no idea about Jake's will, if there even was one, and Edith read her thoughts in her hesitation.

"You certainly can't run this place all by yourself," Edith continued, sweeping the yard with a disapproving glance. "I'll pay you this amount for it. Cash." She handed Sylvie a piece of paper. "It's more than fair." She grinned and it was so unnatural-looking on her dour face that it gave Sylvie the shivers.

Sylvie's eyes flickered to the amount on the paper, then she took a second look. "Fair? Edith, this property must be worth a lot more than that."

"No, it isn't. Not in the condition it's in." The odd grin slipped off Edith's face and the frown returned. "Besides, I've had to look at this junkyard for years now. Seems like I should be getting a discount. Plus it's my birthday today. That should count for an extra discount." She crossed her arms over her ample chest. "This property belonged to my grandfather. Used to be the prettiest farm in Stoney Ridge. Now look at it. Years of neglect have taken a toll. And then in you come with your silly idea of breeding horses." With a grimace, she added, "You'll only ruin this land."

"Ruin it?"

"You heard me. It's high time that piece of property returns to family instead of going to an outsider."

"Outsider?!" Sylvie slapped her palm against her chest.

"Outsider? You make me sound . . . like I'm English. Hardly that!"

"That church you came from is just about as far from Old Order Amish as the English." Edith clapped her palms together. "I'm making you a very fair offer. Very fair." She wagged a finger at Sylvie. "If you're smart, you'll take it. A bird in the hand is better than two in the bush."

Sylvie was so angry her knees shook. She tried to keep her voice as calm as she could. "Edith, thank you for your offer. I'll give it some serious consideration." *Just long enough to toss it in the trash.*

Edith didn't look at all happy to be dismissed, but she did take her leave. Sylvie felt her eye twitch wildly as she watched her make her way home. That woman! She'd been a thorn in Sylvie's side since the day she married Jake. Sometimes, she could almost feel Edith Lapp's disapproving eyes on her from wherever she happened to be on the farm. She quickly learned to take care to avoid her, even to the point of standing at the doorway and watching, waiting until she saw Edith's buggy's dust trail disappear before she went out to the garden. The fewer interactions with Edith Lapp, the better.

Calm down, Sylvie, she told herself. *God doesn't give you more than you can handle.* She didn't know exactly where that phrase was in the Bible, but she'd heard it repeated so often that she was sure it was true. It didn't always feel true, though. She squeezed her eyes closed, to shut out the sight of all the work to be done around the farm—stalls to muck out, horses to exercise, animals to feed—and she felt a weariness clear to her bones. She hated the feeling of helplessness that was always lurking nearby, a feeling that had been with her long, long before Jake died. Overwhelmed by all that needed to be done, she opened her eyes, blew out a puff of air, and rubbed her forehead.

Just thinking about Edith's request to take a look at Jake's last will and testament made her chew on her fingernails, already bitten down to the quick. His last will and testament? Where in the world would Jake have kept something like that? She had no idea. He was the most disorganized man in the world.

She saw Joey wander from the barn, up the path, and over to the creek to pick up sticks and throw them in. She sat on the porch steps, watching him. The sticks landed in the water with a satisfying *plunk*, only to have the rushing current bring the sticks back. He couldn't understand why the same stick kept returning to him.

That was exactly how Sylvie felt. As hard as she tried for a fresh start, the same thing kept coming back to her.

Must everyone think the worst of her, of Joey?

Two

The October sun was sinking low in the afternoon sky when someone knocked at the door at Rising Star Farm. Sylvie sent Joey to open it, then heard the door slam shut. He ran back to the kitchen, eyes wide. "Mem, it's the cowboy."

Sylvie wiped her hands on her apron and went to open the door. Standing a few feet in front of her was the poor pathetic homeless man from the Bent N' Dent.

"We met a few hours ago."

The tramp had a gentle voice, polite, and his eyes were hopeful, though sort of sad. "I remember," she said, nodding. "What can I do for you?" Her voice, even to her own ears, sounded flat, wary.

"I was wondering about that job you mentioned. Before Hank got you riled up." He scratched his temple, pushing the cowboy hat askew. He took it off and raked a hand through his bushy sun-streaked brown hair. "Hank has that effect on folks."

"Oh my stars, don't I know it. You should try living next

door to him and his cold-natured wife. Why, that woman couldn't melt ice cream on a hot summer day."

The homeless man's eyes crinkled at the corners. "I've had a dose of that once or twice"—his grin spread from ear to ear—"seeing as how I'm the second son of Edith Fisher Lapp. Jimmy Fisher's my name."

Sylvie gasped. "Oh dear. I shouldn't have said that out loud."

He chuckled, lifting a hand to wave off her worry. "Why do you think I spent the last couple of years in Colorado? Trying to find my own footing in life."

She knew all about that. She softened and crossed her arms behind her back. "So, did you do it? Find your footing?"

He took his time answering. He swallowed once and his Adam's apple bobbed. "Seems it's a bit harder than I'd thought."

When their eyes met, Sylvie thought she saw a shine in his eyes. In that one poignant line, the cowboy had given her a glimpse of himself. "Life can be funny that way. The things we keep trying to get away from keep finding us." Well, she had a child to tend to and animals to feed. "So you're not a pathetic homeless fellow, after all."

He glanced over at Edith Lapp's house. It was a small but tidy home, nestled against a hillside. "My mother turned my bedroom into her scrapbook room. My only option is a sagging couch in the basement. But I'm not homeless." He looked down at his clothes. "Do I look so awfully pathetic?"

His clothes were certainly pathetic looking. Patches on his knees, scuffed boots, threadbare cuffs on his sleeves, and a worn collar. Plus he smelled a little ripe. But his face—it was not such a pathetic face. Now that she thought about it, it was a rather nice face, scruffy whiskers and all. And those blue eyes—they were kind eyes, as blue as a summer sky. She noticed he was shivering in the brisk wind and she felt a little sorry for him.

"Why don't you come inside and have a cup of coffee to warm up?" Sylvie said. "It's too cold to stand around out here."

He didn't move. "Thank you, no. I'd better get home. It's my mother's birthday. I just wanted to see if the job's still open."

She pondered that momentarily, studying him in silence. It seemed ludicrous to have the second son of Edith Lapp working for her. On the other hand, it might be just what was needed to take the frostbite off that woman. Didn't the Good Book say to extend the olive leaf to your enemies? Something like that. "Job's still open."

"Are you really trying to introduce a new buggy horse?"

She pulled her shawl tightly around her shoulders and shrugged. "I haven't quite figured out all the plans yet, but I do believe Arabians are the best horse in the world."

"They're fast. I'll grant you that."

"Not just fast. They're hardworking, sturdy, tough as nails." Her eyes followed Prince as he shook his head in the paddock, tail and mane lifted by the breeze. He'd picked up some scent in the wind that made his nostrils flare. The sight of him, standing at full attention, took her breath away. "I'll be honest with you. What I'm doing here, well, at times it does seem a little crazy. Like I'm swimming upstream, fighting the current." She wasn't sure why she felt she needed to tell him so much, but it always seemed best to get things out in the open. She glanced at him. "Doesn't it to you?"

He stared at her hard with a frown between his eyes, as if she were a puzzle he was trying to piece together. "Well . . . maybe a little." He fingered the brim of his hat, giving Sylvie the impression that he might be anxious to put it back on and run for the hills. She didn't blame him. It was crazy! She sensed that he was too kind to give her a flat-out yes.

Then Jimmy Fisher grinned—a full-blown smile that revealed endearing deep-set dimples in both cheeks. "Seems I've always been a little partial to crazy."

Sylvie's eyes burned suddenly, as if smoke had gotten into them, and she blinked fast to clear them.

Something must have surprised him, because his eyebrows shot up to the top of his forehead.

Luke Schrock set the newspaper down with a sigh. The front page had a story of a newborn baby found dead in a gas station restroom. It was the second time such a horrific event had happened in Pennsylvania in the last two months. The article stated abandoning newborn infants was not uncommon, linked to a rise of teen pregnancies.

His eyes lifted to see his wife, Izzy, stirring a bowl of cookie batter with one hand. Their little one-year-old daughter, Katy Ann, rested on her hip. Izzy was talking to Katy Ann in a soft voice, explaining the intricacies of cookie batter to her. Katy Ann was more interested in trying to grab the dangling strings of her mother's prayer cap.

Luke felt a swirl of emotions. Little Katy Ann could have been one of those horrible stories. Her birth mother was only fifteen, in the foster care system, and had successfully hidden her pregnancy from everyone. And that meant *everyone*. She'd been living at Windmill Farm for a few months during her third trimester. Even Fern, savvy to the ways of teens, even she had missed signs. Who knows what Cassidy, Katy Ann's birth mother, might have done, had she not been placed with them?

God's providence intervened, and Cassidy wanted Luke and Izzy to adopt her baby. They jumped at the chance, as they had yet to be blessed with a child of their own.

And now Katy Ann belonged to them. She'd made them a family. Luke didn't think it was possible for the two of them to love their daughter any more.

His eyes dropped to the newspaper article. He picked it up and folded it, tucking it under his arm to toss before Izzy or Fern saw it.

"Too late."

Luke practically jumped out of his seat at the sound of Fern's voice coming from behind him. She was always doing that, appearing out of nowhere, silent as a cat.

"We already saw it," she said.

Izzy looked up. "We've already talked it over."

That was another thing that happened a lot. Fern and Izzy were usually a step or two ahead of him, and they were always in cahoots. He felt a little outnumbered by females.

"Luke," Fern said, "we think you need to do something about it. Not let it happen again."

"Me?" His voice rose an octave.

Izzy hitched the baby up on her hip. "After all, you are the deacon."

He cleared his throat. "These aren't Amish babies that are getting abandoned." No chance of that ever happening.

"It seems to me," Fern said, sliding into the chair next to him, "that the promise you made to Amos about emptying out the foster care system in Lancaster County—"

"And I'm doing my best with that. Slow and steady, we all agreed, Fern. You said it yourself. Don't let your branches grow past your roots—"

"You're doing fine, Luke. Two more families this year have gotten licensed to be foster care families. I'm talking about going a step farther. Let's make sure those babies aren't abandoned in the first place."

"How in the world do I do that?"

Fern and Izzy looked at each other.

"That's the part we can't figure out," Izzy said. "But you'll find a way. You always do." She set a plate of warm-from-the-oven cookies in front of him and smiled, and Katy Ann smiled, and life felt full of possibilities.

The door to the kitchen opened to a blast of cold air. "YOU WON'T BELIEVE WHO'S BACK IN TOWN."

Hank Lapp. Making the rounds.

"Who?" Fern said, as she rose to fill a mug with coffee for Hank.

"JIMMY FISHER. DOWN ON HIS LUCK."

Fern stopped midpour. "Jimmy's back? You don't say." A fond look filled her eyes, relaxed her face. "So, he's finally come home."

"Who's Jimmy Fisher?" Izzy said.

"Edith's youngest," Luke said. "He courted my sister Bethany for a long time."

"BETHANY GOT FED UP WAITING FOR HIM."

"There's some truth to that. Jimmy went off somewhere—"

"COLORADO."

"Colorado. That's right. He was doing something with horses."

"HE WAS A COWBOY."

"Huh," Izzy said thoughtfully, as she fed bits of cookie to baby Katy. "An Amish cowboy."

"LUKE, YOU HAVE TO DO SOMETHING."

That was the second time in the last fifteen minutes that Luke had been told he had to do something. "Why?"

"JIMMY SAYS HE IS GONNA WORK FOR SYLVIE. YOUR COUSIN." He circled his ear with his finger and raised his sparse eyebrows.

"Hank Lapp"—Fern pointed a finger at him—"there's nothing wrong with Sylvie and you'd better stop that nonsense. I've heard you say something mean each time her name is brought up."

"I'M ONLY SAYING WHAT EDITH THINKS."

Luke scowled at him. "What's wrong with him working for Sylvie? She could use help. And Jimmy knows horses."

"TWO REASONS. HE'S ONLY DOING IT TO RILE HIS MOTHER. AS SOON AS HE HEARD THERE WAS A FEUD BETWEEN EDITH AND SYLVIE, HE HIGH-TAILED IT OVER THERE."

Fern frowned at him. "What's the second reason?"

"SYLVIE'S GOT HER CAP SET FOR POOR UNSUSPECTING JIMMY."

Izzy rolled her eyes. "Why in the world would you say such a thing?"

Hank started winking one eye, then the other. Luke thought he looked like he was having a seizure. "Oh, Hank. Come on. She has an eye twitch, that's all. Dok told her it was due to stress. It started when Jake died."

"WHAT?" Hank sank into a chair. "So she wasn't making come-hither eyes at him?"

"No, Hank."

"OH boy." He took a long, noisy sip of coffee, then another and another. When the cup was empty, he jumped out of his chair. "I BETTER GO TELL JIMMY. Just in case he's misinterpreting those WINKS. You KNOW that boy." He tapped his high forehead. "Not a lot of SENSE up here." He started to the door, pivoted, and turned. "Mind if I TAKE SOME COOKIES to EDITH? It's her birthday and I FORGOT A CAKE." He didn't wait for an answer. He grabbed the cookies on Luke's plate and off he went, leaving the door wide open.

Luke closed the door behind him.

Izzy looked at him with puzzlement. "So Edith was married before Hank?"

"Yup. She had two sons, Paul and Jimmy. Edith and Hank married a while ago."

"Interesting," she said, feeding a bite of cookie to Katy Ann. "Sounds like this Jimmy is more like Hank than his own mother."

Luke and Fern exchanged a surprised look, then they shared a slow, wide grin.

⌒

Near dusk, Izzy wandered through the garden rows, looking for any chili peppers that might have dried on the plant this fall so she could save the seeds. Next summer, she wanted to try even more varieties—Fresno, habanero, serrano, and of course the ubiquitous jalapeños. Edith Lapp told her about a ghost pepper that sent a chill down her spine. It was reported to be the hottest known chili pepper on earth. A little went a long way with all chili peppers—imagine how minuscule an amount she would need with a ghost pepper.

It figured that Edith would enjoy ghost peppers, Izzy thought, as she yanked her skirt free from a hacked-off dried cornstalk. A little bit of Edith went a long way too. Izzy admired Edith and had learned much from her, but she was still frightened to death of her. For some reason, Edith had been kind to her. For most everyone else, especially Luke, she had an effect on them like an unexpected cold snap in the month of May. Just when you thought spring was finally here, winter would blow back in.

Her thoughts traveled to the conversation Luke and Fern had this morning, about the return of Jimmy Fisher to Stoney Ridge. She hadn't heard his name mentioned very often, only in context of being one of Fern's wayward teens. He sounded like he'd been a character as a teenager, a con artist. Not like Luke, who had sounded more like a criminal-in-the-making. She wondered how old Jimmy had been when his father died, and if that had affected his upbringing. Made him a little off-kilter. Luke thought his own father's death when he was a boy had a lot to do with why he wanted to lash out at others, to make them hurt like he hurt. He told Izzy once that he missed his father every single day of his life.

Fathers were important. She knew that because she'd grown up without one.

The kitchen door squeaked open and out came Luke on the porch, carrying their baby, Katy Ann, close against his chest. "She wanted to see you," he called out.

Izzy stayed where she was in the garden, watching the two of them. Luke held Katy Ann up in the air and tickled her tummy, and she giggled, waving her chubby arms. She adored her daddy, and he was thoroughly smitten by her. Luke's devotion to their baby constantly surprised Izzy. It's not that she had doubted he'd be a good father, but she hadn't expected him to be the doting type.

Early in their marriage, he hadn't even seemed all that

eager to be a father, not in the urgent, almost desperate, way she had felt about becoming a mother. But the minute Luke had laid eyes on Katy Ann in the hospital, he was enchanted. Those first few months, he got up in the night to feed her a bottle and still stopped in the farmhouse or the yarn shop throughout the day to check on her. Those two had a special bond, and Izzy found she didn't mind one little bit. She was so grateful that their little girl had such a tender, loving father, that she had chosen a fine man as a husband. Luke was the best of men, and he was an excellent father to Katy Ann.

But right on its heels was a bone-deep ache that Izzy had missed out on something she never had. Watching them, she felt a catch in her heart for the father she'd never known, the arms that had never held her, the stories she'd never been told. Every child should have a father like Luke.

She'd had the strangest sense of loss lately, almost overwhelming at times. When she shared it with Luke, he reacted with hurt. "Aren't we enough for you, Izzy? Katy Ann, me? Can't we be enough? Will happiness always be around the corner?"

Yes, of course they were enough. And no. The emptiness she felt from her upbringing might not ever be filled. She decided she would never mention her sense of loss to Luke again; he didn't understand.

Folks around here always said that you don't miss what you never had. But she didn't think that maxim rang true, at least not when it came to missing out on a father.

⟡

Oftentimes Sylvie would go into Joey's room at night and watch him sleep, marveling at the fact that this child was hers, yet he wasn't. Not really. She felt overwhelmed by the measureless love she felt for this little boy, by her desire to protect him.

Tonight she checked on Joey, closed the door to his room, and sat down at the kitchen table to make a list of everything that needed doing or fixing on the farm this spring. She'd lived at Rising Star Farm nearly a year now and had a general idea of where she wanted the farm to go, what she hoped it could look like with time and proper attention, but getting there was a whole different story. She had a vision of a thriving, tidy, and well-kept horse farm, using Prince as the stud. She believed in that horse, knew that he had the genes to make a positive impact on other breeds. That horse could make a difference.

She set down her pencil and walked over to the kitchen window, admiring the long expanse of grass that gently curved downward to the creek. This place—it was the most beautiful spot on earth to her. Outside, night peepers started their chirping. Their sound had grown quieter this spring since the creek had moved. The light from the full moon lent a velvet richness to the yard, disguising its rusted junk and chicken dung and tall weeds.

She remembered the day she'd first seen Rising Star Farm, really seen it. Her cousin Luke had urged her to come visit, to consider making a move to Stoney Ridge. Luke and Sylvie were the same age. Their fathers were brothers, oldest and youngest in a large family, and were much the same men. The same kind of father. Despite the fact that Luke always had a wayward bent, Sylvie had felt an inexplicable concern for him, an unbending affection. Once her cousin had been her worry; now she was his.

"You need a fresh start," he urged. "Trust me. This town is good for that."

"Luke, it's not just me anymore," she had reminded him. "There's also Joey."

"Bring him," Luke insisted. "Stoney Ridge is different, Syl. Come and see. Come and find out for yourself."

The church Sylvie was raised in was far more conservative than the church of Stoney Ridge. Hillbilly Amish, Luke called them. No indoor plumbing, no kitchen sink, no paint on their houses or barns. There were times, after Sylvie had left and come back again with fresh eyes, when she wondered if the people in her church, including her father—especially her father—were downright proud of a lifestyle committed to voluntary poverty. Still, it was the world she knew, and she was willing to return to it, had she and Joey been welcomed back. But they weren't. Not with Joey there to remind everyone why she had once left.

Luke kept on asking, and finally Sylvie agreed to come visit Stoney Ridge. On the very first Sunday church, after hearing David's sermon on Christ and the Samaritan woman at the well, how he knew all about what a terrible person she was and offered her that good living water anyway, she discovered that Luke was right. This church, these people, for the most part, they were different. Not Edith Lapp, but most everyone else.

Sylvie had been staying at Windmill Farm for a week or so when she thought she might take a walk around the area. Joey was napping, Fern was reading the *Budget* in the kitchen, and the autumn day beckoned.

"Go," Fern said. "Explore. I'm here if Joey wakes up."

She remembered it had been a warm September afternoon,

a day of brightly colored leaves and endless blue sky. Around the bend she noticed a white horse running in a pasture, kicking up its heels for the pure joy of living, and she stopped to gaze at him for a while. "My stars," she said aloud as the horse galloped past her. Her heart raced. "Oh my stars. An Arabian stallion!" On an Amish farm, of all places.

She had walked farther down the lane until she found the farmhouse. She realized she'd seen the house from a distance on buggy rides, but approaching it then, on foot, cast in the golden afternoon sunlight filtered through a canopy of trees, gave it charm.

It was a large structure, three stories, clapboard covered, the roof bookended with two huge brick chimneys. On the porch hung a cracked pot filled with a bright red geranium. Hanging between two trees in the yard was a sagging rope, full of laundry. Men's clothing only, she noted. Behind the house was a large old barn, with wide pastures all around it, and far in front of the house was a running creek.

Charming, yes, but the closer she got, the more she saw. This place was a mess: shingles curled off the roof, the porch looked like it was ready to drop right off the house, there were two broken windows, and one of the green shutters was hanging precariously, like it wouldn't last through the next winter. In the yard between the house and the barn was a weedy remnant of a garden. There were piles of trash and rusting tools, a stump with an axe in it, and firewood stacked helter-skelter all around the stump. And then there were chickens. Everywhere there were chickens! Picking and strutting their way around the yard. She sniffed the air and wrinkled her nose. Their sour scent was in the breeze. The barn looked like a big gust of wind might tumble it right over. The whole place was sorry looking, shabby, but that didn't scare her. Maybe that was a gift from a Hillbilly Amish upbringing.

There was something about this place that spoke to her, deep in her heart. Even the geranium touched her. If she had to compare herself to some kind of object, it might just be that cracked pot with the red geranium. Still blooming, despite everything.

The white horse whinnied to her from the pasture, as if he had something to tell her. The closer she got, the more excited he got. She walked over to him slowly, thinking he'd bolt away from her, but he didn't. He stuck his nose over the fence rail, a horse's way to exchange hellos, and let her stroke his velvet muzzle. When she dropped her hand, he nudged her with his nose. Sounded crazy, she knew, but it seemed the horse wanted her as much as she wanted him. It felt like the sign she needed, the one she'd been looking for. This was where she belonged. She and Joey. Somehow, she knew that she'd found the home she'd longed for all her life. She fit right in.

On the walk back to Windmill Farm, Sylvie's longings had transformed into desperation. She'd always been a terrible one for bargaining with God. It might be wrong, she wasn't really sure, but she did it anyway. *Lord God, I want that house. I want that horse. I need them, both. For me, for Joey. For both of us.* She begged God to let her find some way to have those two things . . . but what could she offer God in return? She'd work on being a better person and try to live a straight and narrow life. *Lord God, if you could just get me those two things, I'll never ask for another thing.*

Later that night, she quizzed Izzy about the horse's owner. Izzy filled in the details: a bachelor named Jake King, who was considered as odd as a cat with feathers.

"Odd, in a mean, spiteful way?" Sylvie asked. Like her father?

"No, not mean. Real nice, in fact. Just . . . peculiar."

The next morning, Izzy pointed Jake out in church. He was quite a bit older than Sylvie had expected, and not much to look at—flabby compared to the well-muscled farmers, eyes that drooped like a cocker spaniel's, and a head full of frizzy hair.

During the fellowship meal, Sylvie finagled things to make sure she was serving the table where Jake was seated and gave him an extra coffee refill.

Edith Lapp noticed and gave her a tut-tut scolding. "One cup of coffee per person," she said gruffly.

Sylvie paid her no mind and gave Jake a third refill, just as soon as Edith's back was turned. She smiled at him, twice, and he blinked at her as if he was a bear woken too early from hibernation.

When had a man ever looked at her like that? As if she was the answer to his prayers. Never. And suddenly she knew that this odd old bachelor who owned that magnificent horse and beautiful farm was the answer to *her* prayers.

They married a few months later, and Sylvie moved into that big white farmhouse. Jake was kind to Joey, and he was gentle and caring to her. Throughout their brief year of marriage, he remained a little dazed that she had ever wanted to marry him. She had to do the asking, because the timid man wasn't able to muster enough courage to even hold her hand on a moonlit night. One evening, scooting her rocker close to his on the porch of Windmill Farm, she asked if he might like to marry her. For one full minute, Jake looked like he'd been hit by a lightning bolt, and then he let out an expletive, apologized, thumped his hat on his head, and stammered, "I sure do!"

It might not have been the kind of marriage that Sylvie had hoped for as a girl, but it was enough for her now. More than enough. Romantic love, she had decided long ago, was a lot like swirls of meringue on the top of a lemon custard pie. It looked pretty and appealing, but there wasn't much substance to it. With Jake, Sylvie had found the life she wanted. He let her do whatever she wanted and didn't object to her idea of starting a horse-breeding farm with his Arabian stallion. He might not have helped her with it, but he didn't stop her from trying, and for that she was grateful.

Then Jake up and died on her, and she was left on her own again.

Outside, a screech owl hooted, jolting Sylvie back to the present. A bobbing light caught her eye. Across the creek, someone was walking across the yard at Edith Lapp's house. Her thoughts turned to the pathetic homeless man who offered to work for her. So, he wasn't pathetic, nor was he homeless. He was the second son of Edith Lapp, Sylvie's cantankerous, unpleasant, cranky neighbor who was making such a fuss over the creek. So what if it was shifting and moving onto Edith's property? That wasn't Sylvie's fault. That creek had a mind of its own. Nor was it her fault that the property deed clearly indicated the creek was Rising Star Farm's boundary line.

She wasn't at all sure it was wise to hire Edith's second son, but the man did know his horses, and he wasn't averse to her notion of creating a Partbred. Still, she couldn't shake the feeling that she might've just made a terrible mistake. Well, tomorrow, she'd find out.

THREE

Jimmy Fisher had to admit that he would enjoy the stunned look on his mother's face when he told her about his new job at Rising Star Farm. Assuming he hadn't blown it by oversleeping this morning. He polished off a plateful of scrambled eggs and hash browns while his mother ran down a list of possible employment opportunities.

"Start with Teddy Zook. He's looking for a carpenter's apprentice."

"Thanks," he said, after a big swallow, "but I've got plans of my own."

As usual, his mother ignored him. "After Teddy, go talk to David at the Bent N' Dent. If he doesn't have a job open, try volunteering as stock boy."

"NOW YOU'RE THINKING, EDDY-GAL!" Hank bellowed. "That store could SURE use a stock boy."

Watching his mother over the brim of his coffee cup, Jimmy let her continue on down the list. When she finished, he loudly swallowed the last of his coffee and rose to his feet. With the back of a hand, he smeared the drips from the corners of his mouth. "I'm starting a job over at Rising Star Farm today."

She stilled, and Jimmy wondered what was running through her mind. He wasn't used to speaking his mind to his mother. He'd only done it a few times in his life and it had never gone well. At a very young age, he had learned that the way you got along with Edith Lapp was to go along with her. "I'll be off then."

Hank's eyebrows lifted his forehead. "HOO-EE! Didn't I TELL YA? Sylvie Schrock King is REELING YOU IN." He pantomimed the reeling in of a fish on a line until Edith, annoyed, made him stop.

She raised her head and her voice. "Just what do you think you'll be doing over there?"

"Working with horses, mostly. Some farmwork. A little of this and a little of that." Jimmy didn't let his smile waver while his mother looked like a storm cloud about to rain down.

"For *that* woman," she said.

"What's wrong with Sylvie?"

"I NEARLY FORGOT." Hank's brows wrinkled at a thought. "SOMETHING ABOUT *THAT* WOMAN. SOMETHING LUKE told me." He rubbed his chin whiskers thoughtfully. "But I can't remember."

Jimmy knew then what he had to do. "Stop calling her *that woman*. Both of you. Her name is Sylvie. She's your neighbor." He started for the door and opened it, then glanced over his shoulder. "Don't expect me for dinner. Or supper. I'll be taking my meals over there." He hoped so, anyway. Sylvie hadn't said anything about food. A gust of wind whacked the door shut behind him.

As Jimmy went down the porch steps, he heard Hank's loud cackle. "MEALS! HOO-EE. THAT WOMAN IS LAYING A TRAP FOR YOUR BABY BOY, EDDY."

Hank was always wrong about women, about everything. Surely, he was wrong about Sylvie. Those winks though, they did nettle Jimmy. He liked to be the one to wink at a girl, not the other way around. Besides, Sylvie Schrock King was no girl. She was a woman. A mother. Mothers shouldn't wink at men.

He was just about to hop over the creek when he stopped abruptly to gaze at it. Forgotten memories of childhood came to mind.

When they were boys, Jimmy and his older brother Paul would climb the big old willow tree to get a bird's-eye view of the world, then jump down in the creek to cool off. They spent hot summer afternoons wading in the water, catching toads and bugs and small fish. They used to have such fun together. Now Paul lived in Canada with his wife and children, and the brothers hardly talked anymore.

Jimmy looked up and down the creek, puzzled. Seemed like it used to be farther away from his house, quite a bit of a distance. Out of sight of his mother's kitchen window, as he recalled. And now the willow tree was nowhere near the creek. He scratched his head. Had something changed? Or maybe it was him. He'd been warned that when you go home again, everything would seem different. Smaller.

And it sure did.

Sylvie had tossed and turned all night. She wondered if she'd made an enormous mistake asking Edith Lapp's second son to work for her, partly because he was Edith's son. The last thing she needed was to add him to her list of worries along with Edith.

Normally, Sylvie relied on her intuition. It hadn't failed her yet. Edith's son—what was his name again? Jerry? Jeffrey?—the way he looked at her horse, the way he knew Prince was an Arabian, something about the look on his face as he gazed at her horse spoke to her. She trusted him instantly.

But could he *work*? That's the only thing she wanted from him. A steady, solid, hard worker. Someone who could finish what he started. Not like Jake.

As fond as she'd grown of Jake, that man was not blessed with ambition. He meant well, but there was always something that came along and distracted him from finishing anything.

Prince had ended up with Jake only because an English fellow had driven his car too fast around a corner and careened into the pasture, knocking down the fence. He offered the horse in exchange for replacing the fence. Unfortunately, that meant the fence never did get replaced. Prince spent his days in a paddock.

That horse was itching to work. Arabians weren't meant to spend their days running around a small paddock. Jake and Sylvie hadn't been married long when she brought up the notion of using the stallion as a stud, to create a Partbred. "Seeing as how you aren't using him for anything in particular."

Jake raised his chin and nodded wisely, as if he'd been thinking the same thing, which he hadn't. He tilted his head to one side and gave her his puppy-eyed look. "Sounds like a plan to consider."

That was Jake's way, she had quickly come to learn. He entertained all kinds of ideas, but very few ever came to be. Sylvie was a doer more than a thinker, and she took his passive response as permission granted. She posted an advertisement for the Arabian stallion's stud fees down at the Hay & Grain. So far, there'd only been a few bites of interest, none among the Amish. Jake told her to be patient, and that was something she appreciated about him. He was easy to be with and gave her free rein on the farm. She wished that she had felt about Jake the way he felt about her. She was fond of him, genuinely sorry when he passed on. But she didn't love him. The guilt of not loving him scratched at her heart.

She shrugged off her melancholy. It came at odd times, when she least expected it. There were moments when her head still spun with all the changes in her life since Jake had died.

There wasn't much time to grieve because worry about the future came along fast and pushed regrets away. She had a child to care for and a farm in truly terrible condition. What in the world was she going to do? Out of the chicken coop and into the stewpot, her father would say. It did feel as though she'd been wrung, plucked, and scalded.

But if there was one gift she'd been given in Jake's sudden passing, it was the discovery that she was stronger than she thought, capable of coping with some very trying experiences. She had a vision for Rising Star Farm, anchored on Prince, and she was a determined woman. Fueling her focus was the fact that this was her only hope to give Joey the life she wanted to provide for him. She refused to return home to her father, tail between her legs. She absolutely refused.

Something out the window caught her eye. Edith Lapp's second son was hopping over the creek, heading her way. She moved toward the window to watch him. *Jimmy.* That was his name. Jimmy Fisher.

As he drew closer to the house, she blinked, rubbed her eyes, and blinked again.

This new Jimmy Fisher looked like an altogether different man than the shaggy and downtrodden tramp whom Sylvie had spoken to yesterday. Why, he was all spiffed up. He had shaved that stubble of whiskers off, gotten his hair cut, and wore clothes that weren't patched and cobbled together. He even had a black hat on, not that oily misshapen cowboy hat he'd worn. He looked much more presentable today than when she'd first seen him at the Bent N' Dent. His hair had been standing on end, and his eyes had looked anything but calm. He wasn't as old as she had figured him to be, but surprisingly young.

Turned out, he wasn't bad looking. Not so bad at all. Jimmy Fisher had a lean, oval-shaped face with a strong, square jaw, and a deep cleft in his chin. Thick, wavy, dark brown hair, a high forehead and curved brows that might have come from his father. Certainly not Edith's brows—hers were sparse and pointed.

Sylvie knew he had been hoping to marry Luke's sister, Bethany, but heard she'd gotten tired of waiting for him and married someone else. She only knew that fact because Hank Lapp had been sure to tell her so, just last night as she was bringing Prince in from the paddock. He'd always taken liberty to show up around the farm, uninvited, even after Jake had passed. Last evening, he said he wanted to remind Sylvie that Jimmy was an eligible bachelor, available for courting. "FREE AND CLEAR," Hank had bellowed, loud enough to scare a flock of black crows right out of their roost.

Joey sidled up beside her. "The cowboy sure does look different now, don't he?"

She smoothed down the topknot on Joey's head, only to watch it pop up again like a rooster's comb. "He sure does. He looks just like one of Izzy's newly shorn sheep. Nothing like that shaggy old tramp who was patting our Prince at the Bent N' Dent."

"Prince don't like him."

"Prince is hard to impress. He's slow to warm up."

If Sylvie were interested in finding a husband, which she wasn't, her new farmhand had transformed into a mighty fine-looking man.

As Jimmy stood on the bottom steps of Rising Star Farm, he eyed the sorry-looking house, then turned in a half circle. The closer he got, the more he saw that the yard was truly pitiful. There were junk piles here and there, like winter corn shocks dotting a farmer's field. A rickety trellis on the front stoop. Grass choked the front steps. A derelict appearance covered the entire house like a moth-eaten blanket.

Jimmy had never paid much attention to Jake King; he just thought of him as the odd old bachelor who lived across the creek. Not the type you'd borrow sugar from in a pinch. His mother had always warned Jimmy and Paul off his property—she worried they'd step on a rusty nail and die of lockjaw. The place looked like it always did, run-down and shabby, though everything was in far worse condition than Jimmy—or his mother—could have seen from their home. He had a rare and fleeting moment of sympathy for his mother, living across the creek, seeing and smelling this raggedy farm from her front windows for most of her adult life.

He glanced up and discovered Sylvie was watching from the door with a wry smile. She was wearing a blue dress that made her violet eyes an even brighter hue. "You're late. It's nearly nine thirty."

"Sorry. I overslept." She didn't look too happy and it took him off guard. He hadn't thought she'd be a stickler for something small like showing up on time. "It won't happen again."

"I figured you might've changed your mind." She tipped her head. "Having second thoughts?"

"No." *Yes.* "Should I be?" He cleared his throat. "Having second thoughts, that is?"

"Probably." She came down the steps, and the little boy stood by the doorjamb, eyeing Jimmy suspiciously. "Might as well show you what you're getting into. Then you can decide about staying." She folded her arms against her chest. "Or maybe you'll decide to run back to Colorado."

She said it as a dare, and for a moment neither of them knew what to say next.

She was the first to glance away. "I thought we should start with a tour around Rising Star." She glanced over her shoulder to call to her little boy, inviting him to join in. "Come on, Joey, you lead the way."

Joey whistled, clapped his hands, and a three-legged dog hopped out of the house to join them. They made a curious group, those three. Jimmy let them pass, then lagged behind, watching them saunter along the path. It gave him the opportunity to study Sylvie covertly. Hank's warning that she was husband hunting swirled in his head, though she'd given him no cause for alarm. Not yet. But there were those unsettling winks.

She stopped and pointed. "Here's the barn."

Hands on hips, he gazed at the barn a long moment. It wasn't much to look at, definitely not by Amish standards. The paint job was probably the original one, back when his great-grandfather had built it. Planks were missing off the sides and shingles from the roof.

At length Sylvie sighed. "Needs some work," as if there was any question. "Well, let's go inside."

Inside, Jimmy could see that someone was paying attention, or trying to. There were two mares in clean box stalls. The horses nickered as they saw Sylvie and pushed their noses through the stall bars to say hello to her. She patted their noses and gave each one some sugar cubes that must have been in her apron pocket.

"They're due soon?"

"Next spring. Gestation is nearly a year for a horse."

Sadly, he should've known that, but he didn't.

"They're Prince's first heirs. That's my plan here, to start a horse farm. I just have to get the rest of the place cleaned up a bit."

A bit? Jimmy nearly laughed out loud. All the other stalls were filled with junk. It was like Sylvie could manage just a small part of the barn and closed her eyes to the rest of it. In a way, he sort of admired her for that. She was doing what she could and trying to move forward with her plan for the property. But the farther along they went on the tour, the more overwhelmed Jimmy felt. How in the world did Sylvie manage to live like this? How had Jake?

She pointed a hand toward the hillside. "And that over there is the old barn."

"Old barn?" He turned her way. Behind the band of woods

lay the old barn, a sagging roof nearly hidden in long weeds. He'd never even seen it before, never even knew it was there. It was leaning to one side, so far to the right that it looked like it would topple over in a strong wind. "So that"—he pointed back to the other barn, which looked like something to knock down and start again—"you consider to be the new barn?"

She nodded.

"What's inside the old barn?"

"I don't really know."

"You never went inside? Never thought to ask?"

"Jake would tinker in there a lot, but I never bothered him."

"Mind if I take a look?"

"Not at all." But she stayed where she was.

Looking at this old barn from the outside, Jimmy couldn't tell what kept it from falling over. Now he knew. The junk held it up from the inside. He tried to make his way in, but it was crammed with everything from soup to nuts. Furniture, tools, cowbells, kettles, brass lanterns, an old buggy. Dusty spiderwebs coated the place. Who knew what else was buried in this close-packed building?

He came back outside, blinking in the bright sunlight. "Well, a little bit of everything is in there, and then some."

"Anything valuable?"

"Hard to say." Jimmy pivoted to look back inside. "Though there did seem to be a lot of copper." A whole lot, if he wasn't mistaken. Pipes, lawn ornaments, teakettles. "All in serious need of polishing."

"Well, then I'm especially glad I never ventured in."

"Why do you think Jake collected so much . . . um . . . ."

"Junk? You can say it. That's what I call it. He would

head off to tag sales and auctions in his wagon and bring home all kinds of junk. I would say to him, 'Jake, what're you planning to do with all that stuff?' But he'd only say that one man's junk is another man's treasure. And he just kept going to sales and hauling back junk."

They moved on, reaching the far end of the property, turning back toward the house on another path. They passed stubbled fields and patches of woods, and suddenly they'd come nearly full circle, back to the new barn, which looked old and rickety to Jimmy.

"Well, that's the grand tour. Now you can make a fully informed decision." She looked him square in the eyes. "I'll be honest, Jimmy. I have a hard time thinking your mother wouldn't have something to say about you working here."

"Oh, she has plenty to say about it. She's never been one to avoid sharing suggestions."

"You sure you want to cross her? Maybe she's right. I wouldn't blame you if you tucked tail and ran for the hills. Things are a real fright around here, I know. But I guess you can see that for yourself."

Jimmy tugged his hat brim clear down to his eyebrows— a habit from ranch days—folded his arms, and tucked his hands, scanning the property. Everything was far worse than he'd thought. But all he said was, "Well, the place could definitely use a little cleanup."

Sylvie scoffed. "I'll say. I don't even know where to start."

Frankly, neither did Jimmy. He felt like he was at the bottom of a mountain, looking straight up, with no idea which path would get him to the top. And even if he did scale the mountain, what might he find at the summit? More of Jake's junk?

Why was he getting involved with this, anyway? All he wanted to do was to work with horses.

"If you don't want the job, now's the time to say so."

Hands on hips again, he turned in a circle. He saw possibilities. It was the way his mind worked—he'd always been able to see opportunities, even if no one else could. He eyed the front yard and saw the grass mowed and trimmed. He eyed the chickens and saw them in a tidy coop. He eyed the new barn and saw its roof repaired, its sides painted. As he pivoted, he eyed that beautiful white horse, and nothing could make him turn his back on that horse. "I'll take it, if you still want me."

"I do," she said without hesitation. "But on time each morning." And then she winked.

Lord-a-mercy.

Down in the Fix-It Shop, Luke Schrock had finished screwing holders on a new sign for Teddy Zook's carpentry shop. Teddy's old sign had been knocked off the post in a late summer storm that packed a punch. By the time he'd realized it was gone, cars had driven over it and smashed it to smithereens. Time for a new sign.

It was turning into a nice little side business. Teddy made the signs, Izzy did the lettering, Luke did the finish work. The waiting list was growing and Luke knew it wasn't due to him or Teddy. His wife's talent with a paintbrush made each sign stand out.

The door opened and Luke glanced over his shoulder to see David come in. "I didn't hear your buggy come up the driveway."

"You look pretty absorbed in your task. Should I come back later?"

"No, no. Let me just finish up and then you've got my full attention." He pointed the screwdriver handle toward a thermos on the workbench. "Hot coffee, if you're interested."

"I am." David rubbed his hands together. "The wind has a bite to it."

Luke turned a screw tightly into the wood, making a sound like a honking goose. "Winter hasn't even arrived and I'm ready for spring." He tightened the last screw and set the sign against the wall.

David poured a mug of coffee and held it between his hands. "Funny you should mention spring. That's why I'm here."

Luke grinned. "You've got a way to hurry spring along?"

"I wish I did." David settled on a stool. "All in good time, though. But Easter's been on my mind."

"What happened to Christmas?"

"That, too. Can't have one without the other. But I want to toss out an idea I've been mulling that concerns Easter."

Luke relished this side of being a church leader. Most of it was hard, gut-wrenching work, but this part . . . it was a joy. To think that David Stoltzfus, the bishop, would seek him out to share his thoughts. *Me. Luke Schrock. The juvenile delinquent of Stoney Ridge.* He corrected his thinking: former juvenile delinquent, now reformed. "I'm all ears." And he was. "What do you have in mind?"

"Luke, the way you set about making amends to others in the last few years—that's had a big impact on folks."

"Uh, David, that was you pushing me to do it. You and Amos."

"At first, yes, we encouraged you. But then you took it

seriously for yourself. And the results have been life changing. Look at Alice Zook's healing."

Alice had been the victim of one of Luke's worst pranks, and it triggered a reaction of crippling anxiety in her. Luke had apologized, sincerely, and Alice had forgiven him. Little by little, the chains of anxiety and fear had been broken in her.

"David, where's this leading?" This kind of talk made Luke nervous, like maybe David was insinuating there were even more stones he'd left unturned. It wouldn't surprise him. A lack of awareness for others continued to plague him.

"I think that we should ask the entire church to consider doing the same thing. To search their hearts, to make amends with those they have tension or problems with. To prepare their hearts for Easter."

"Isn't that what's supposed to happen?"

"Supposed to." He took a sip of coffee. "This year, let's raise the bar."

"How so?"

David pulled a list from his pocket. "I was reading through Scripture this morning and found some examples of fence mending: paying back what you've borrowed. Forgiving someone for what they've borrowed and haven't returned—"

"Hold it a moment. You're talking about money, right?"

"Not just money. Folks around here borrow all kinds of things from each other and never settle their accounts. Money, tools. Time, too."

"Time?"

"Think of the recent harvest season. Neighbors help each other out all through the harvest."

Luke paused. His brother Sam had helped him harvest the orchard in August and Luke had promised that he'd return the favor. Two months had passed and he'd completely forgotten. Knowing Sam, his brother would remember but never say anything. It would just kind of fester, until Luke did something else, something small and insignificant, and his brother would blow up at him.

"And then there's words."

"Whoa. Wait just a minute. Words?"

"Absolutely. Words can do more harm than arrows and swords."

Luke rolled that around in his mind. He'd had a generous dose of arrows aimed at him since he'd become deacon. There were some folks whom he couldn't please and they didn't mind telling him, or telling others. The one that still smarted was when Freeman Glick told him that he might be the world's worst deacon. He couldn't quite forget that jab. Whenever he felt insecure about deaconing or was facing a new dilemma, Freeman's words returned to him. David was right; words could do a lot of harm.

David was staring into his coffee cup with such intent that Luke wondered what was running through his mind. As bishop, he received plenty of arrows too. David glanced up. "And then there's grudges. I want folks to think seriously about the grudges they carry. About the relationships that have wedges between them. Friction, problems, buried grudges—they only grow bigger. Little things become big things. They wear like a pebble in a shoe."

"I see where you're going with this," Luke said, and he did. "But, David, do you really think people will be honest with themselves? It's not easy, this fence mending. It takes a lot to acknowledge what you might have done to hurt someone. And even more courage to make things right again."

"True. But Paul admonishes us to live at peace with everyone, as much as we are able. In other words, we're all responsible to clean up our side of the street. The healing part, that's the work of God's Spirit." David swallowed the last of his coffee and rose to his feet. "Just wanted to run it by you. I'm going to do some more praying on it, and if the Lord gives me the go-ahead, next Easter our church is going to take making amends seriously." He set the cup of coffee on the counter and patted Luke on the shoulder as he passed by him toward the door.

He paused at the door and turned back. "So then," he said with a smile, "better get prepared."

For what? Luke walked to the door and saw David climb in the buggy. He ran outside and stopped him. "For what, David? What should I be getting prepared for?"

One foot in the buggy, one foot out, David turned toward Luke. "'If my people, which are called by my name, will humble themselves, and pray, and seek my face, and turn from their wicked ways; then will I hear from heaven, and will forgive their sin, and will heal their land.'"

Luke figured the look on his face was as confused as his thoughts, because a broad smile covered David's face. "It's a verse from 2 Chronicles. Hearts will change, Luke. Watch and see."

FOUR

A *wicked way.* Luke couldn't stop thinking about that Bible verse David had quoted. He'd never really thought of some things, like not remembering to repay his brother with time, as a wicked way. But in a sense, thoughtlessness was sort of wicked. It was definitely self-centered. He'd gotten the help he'd needed with his orchard harvest and then blown off any concern for his brother. That was wrong. Maybe not wicked, but definitely not right.

As soon as he finished up the project he'd been working on, he drove over to Sam's to talk to him. Mollie, his wife, was hanging laundry on the clothesline. She waved to him when he climbed out of the buggy. "Hello there, Luke. What brings you here on a workday?"

When she turned sideways to hang a towel on the line, he noticed her belly bump. *Oh wow.* Talking about the coming of babies just wasn't done, especially by men, but that didn't mean others weren't aware. Mollie was a small woman too, and wouldn't be able to hide that belly much longer. He tried to swallow his smile but couldn't, so he tipped his hat down over his face and stayed where he was. "Looking for Sam."

"He's in the barn."

Luke went straight toward the barn, relieved. He knew he couldn't be around Mollie without saying something about the coming baby. Izzy always reminded him that he needed to tighten the filter on his mouth, but he wasn't sure he had one to start with.

He found Sam in the center aisle of the barn, wrapping a horse's leg. "Sammy!"

Sam glanced up at him. "Folks call me Sam." It was their customary greeting. He finished wrapping the horse's leg, made a small tie to the ends, then rose to his feet. "What brings you by?"

"It occurred to me that I haven't repaid you for time you gave me during the harvest."

A corner of Sam's mouth quirked. "Let me guess. Mollie talked to Izzy. Izzy talked to you."

"Nope. I realized I'd neglected to offer you payback time. It was wrong of me to forget about it."

"You've always done that kind of thing to me."

"I do?"

"Sort of a big brother thing, I figure. My life isn't that important, not compared to yours. Especially now that you're the deacon."

"But, Sam, that's not true. I don't think I'm so important. I just forget stuff a lot." Luke took his hat off. "I'm being entirely truthful. David stopped by today to talk about preparing the church for Easter. About making amends. I realized I had completely forgotten about paying you back with time. So I'm offering now."

"Now?"

"Now, if you need help. Or next time you need an extra hand."

Sam's gaze shifted to the horse stalls. "I wanted to get to an auction this afternoon, but I'm behind on exercising some horses."

"Go. I'll do it. Just tell me which ones."

He shrugged while humor lit his face. "Well, actually"— his grin spread—"all of them."

Ah. That meant Luke's Fix-It Shop projects were going to have to wait. That meant he wouldn't have Edith Lapp's broken flashlights fixed, like he'd promised, and that meant he would have to swallow his pride and risk a tongue lashing. "Brother, you go," he said, with a touch on his hat brim. "I'll handle the horses today."

Sam's taut look melted into relaxed lines. "Thank you, Luke. It means a lot, you doing this. You making amends."

Luke watched him stride toward his buggy with Saucy, his favorite horse. Sam waved as he drove down the driveway, and Luke felt a sweeping sense that all was well between them.

Typical. As usual, David was right. Little things became big things.

It worked both ways. And big things, if properly handled, could become little things. It worked both ways.

There was enough work at Rising Star Farm to keep a man going nonstop for a solid year. Maybe two. That, Jimmy thought, was the good news. The bad news was that he had no idea where to start. As he crossed the creek, he sniffed the air. Yes, he knew where to start. Those stupid chickens. Get them penned. If not today, then soon. They'd never been one of his favorite animals. The smell, even from where he stood, was horrendous.

No wonder the chickens kept leaving the yard to head across the creek.

One of the things that irritated Edith the most about Jake was that he had always let his chickens run free. They would cross the creek and end up in Edith's flower beds until she'd shoo them away with her broom. Whenever she warned him to cage those chickens before the foxes and hawks could snatch more up, Jake would say that no creature on God's green earth should be caged.

On this issue, Jimmy leaned somewhere in the middle. Chickens needed a good solid henhouse, safe from foxes and hawks and cars and brooms. But he wasn't entirely unsympathetic to Jake's point of view. He thought they should be allowed out in the day, into the henhouse to roost at night.

He saw Joey trot down the porch steps with an empty coffee can in his hands. "Hey! Where ya going?"

Joey stopped and gave him a suspicious look. "Feeding the chickens."

"Can I help? I'd like to know where you keep things around here."

The little boy shrugged. "I guess so."

Jimmy followed him around the house to find a metal garbage can with a brick on top of the lid.

Joey pointed to it. "In there. Two scoops."

Jimmy yanked off the lid to find a sack of chicken food. "Two?"

Joey nodded. He filled the can, but as he pulled it up, he couldn't lift it. Jimmy reached in to help, but the boy stopped him. "I can do it myself." And so he did.

As they walked back toward the yard, Jimmy said, "Do you feed the chickens each day?"

"Yup. And while they eat, I hunt for eggs."

Jimmy whipped his head around the yard. "Where?"

"Everywhere."

"Everywhere?"

"They have secret places. But I know their favorite laying spots. Most, I think."

Jimmy had to wonder how old some of those eggs might be by the time Joey found them. "Do these hens give many eggs?"

"Some do, some don't."

Jimmy bit down on the corner of his lip to keep from smiling. He was a funny little guy. Tried to look and sound like he was the boss around here. Well, Jimmy would handle his tender pride with respect. He knew what it was like to be henpecked.

"Joey, something I aim to do is to build a henhouse for these birds."

Joey squinted at him. "What for? They like being free."

"Have you ever noticed that something is stealing those eggs?"

"Raccoons."

"And have you ever come out in the morning and found a bunch of feathers?"

Joey nodded.

"That's because those hens need to have some kind of shelter to keep them safe at night. From raccoons and foxes."

"Mem says that your mother's broom has caused more chickens to lose their feathers than anything else. She says they get stressed by your mother."

Jimmy struggled not to smile. "Well, there's that too. So I want to build a big, strong, solid henhouse for them. It'll make egg gathering a lot easier for you."

"Today?"

"Not sure I can get to it today, but soon. First thing, I need to get the day's chores done. Your mem said she plans to take Prince into town this morning, so I want to get him hooked up to the buggy."

Haltering a horse was something Jimmy had done thousands of times, but this darn horse wouldn't stand still for him. It was like Prince was playing games with him—Jimmy would slowly walk toward him, the horse would snort and prance, and at the last minute, Prince would gallop off to the other end of the paddock.

"He don't like you."

Jimmy spun around to see Joey grinning at him, sitting on top of the paddock gate.

"Prince don't like you."

"Not yet. He will, though, soon as he gets to know me." He hoped so. "Horses don't have feelings like people do."

"Mem says they do. She says that horses have a way of speaking but most folks just don't understand them. She says you got to listen to what the horse is trying to tell you."

"She knows a lot about horses?"

"Lots."

"So what does a horse tell her?"

"Like, when a horse flattens both ears back on his head, he's mad. Like Prince is doing now."

Ears pinned. Prince did that a lot with Jimmy.

"But you gotta watch out," Joey said, hopping off the gate to walk toward Jimmy. "If his leg is cocked and his ears go back, that means he's getting ready to kick you. It's just like the ocean. Mem says you're never supposed to turn your back on the ocean." He scrunched his small face. "I've never been to the ocean. Have you?"

"I have."

"Is it big?"

"Very big. Big as the sky."

Joey jerked his head up to look at the sky so sharply that his hat fell off. "Wow."

Jimmy grinned and swept down to pick up the small black hat. He could get used to this little guy. "What else?"

Joey shrugged and plopped his hat back on his head. "I don't know exactly." He pointed behind Jimmy. "There's Mem. Ask her."

Sylvie had slipped into the paddock through two rails and walked toward them. As soon as Prince noticed she had come in, he stopped his snorting and prancing and came toward her like a sheep to a shepherd. "Ask me what?"

"Joey says you can understand horse language."

Sylvie grinned. "I suppose so. They let you know what they're thinking about."

Prince lowered his head as he drew close to Sylvie and stilled. He let her stroke his forehead. She rubbed his ears, then ran a hand down his nose to his velvety muzzle.

Whoa. Prince was not at all relaxed around Jimmy.

She lifted Joey up to stroke his muzzle. "Horses are herd animals. They like to be around those they trust."

"When Jimmy Fisher comes around," Joey said, "Prince runs off."

Jimmy frowned at Joey. "The horse is trying to act like he's the boss."

"I don't think so," Sylvie said. "Horses run off when they're frightened or worried."

"Why would he be afraid of me? Yesterday I cleaned out the best stall in the new old barn and filled it up with sweet fresh straw, and I fed him and gave him plenty of water. What's he got against me?"

"I don't know why he's afraid of you," Sylvie said. "Horses are full of fear."

Joey tilted his head. "Why?"

"It's instinctive," Sylvie said. "In nature, they get chased a lot, by wolves and mountain lions and other predators. Remember how that saying goes, Joey? Eyes in front, an animal hunts. Eyes on the side, they hide."

"What's he thinking about now, Mem?"

"Well, his ears are forward now. Ears are the first thing a person needs to notice about a horse. Ears can tell you a lot. They'll tell you if he's interested, happy, bored, angry."

"They're always pinned back when Jimmy Fisher is in the paddock."

Hadn't Joey ever heard the saying that children should be seen but not heard? Jimmy grew up hearing that saying just about every single day.

"Next thing to look for is the way a horse carries his head. See how Prince's head is high, and his tail is up? He's showing off a little, feeling all relaxed and happy."

"He didn't look that way when Jimmy Fisher wanted to put the halter on him." Joey hopped off the fence and did a little jig. "He was prancing and dancing and stomping his feet."

Jimmy couldn't help but laugh as he watched the little guy try to dance, so clumsy and goofy. Sylvie was grinning too.

Joey enjoyed the attention he was getting. "And then Prince does this, too, when Jimmy tries to get his halter on him." He swept his neck from one side to the other in a big exaggerated motion.

"That's his way of trying to tell you: 'No sir. No halter on me.' Whatever you want to try and sell him, he's not buying."

Jimmy leaned an elbow against the fence post. This was fun. He admired how patient Sylvie was with her son, answering his questions, teaching him about horses in a light-hearted way. She had a way about her that appealed to a child. To horses too.

Joey stopped and pointed at Prince. "What's he telling us now? Is he about to kick Jimmy?"

Jimmy took a step back, just in case.

Sylvie watched the horse for a moment. "No, no. When a back leg is cocked like that, it just means he's relaxed."

"I thought it meant he was about to kick him."

"You have to look at the whole horse, Joey, not just one part of the body. See Prince's head and ears? He's interested in what we're saying. He doesn't look like a horse who's upset or angry, does he? Just look at his eyes. They're blinking. That means he's thinking things over."

"What's he thinking now, Mem?"

Sylvie glanced at Jimmy. "I figure he's trying to decide if Jimmy Fisher is going to be a friend or foe."

Sylvie whispered something and Prince lowered his head as if bowing to her. She spoke so softly that Jimmy had to lean close to hear her. "Try to be nice to Edith Lapp's second son, Prince. He's nothing like his mother. He's trying to help us and fix things up around here. So go easy on him, sweet boy."

Prince kept his head bowed, blinking his huge dark eyes as if he really were listening to Sylvie's words. The contrast between this small woman and the horse couldn't have been greater.

"That's a good boy. You're my good boy, aren't you, Prince?"

By the time she gave Prince's shoulder a final pat and turned to Jimmy, the horse was standing so still, he might have been a statue. Slowly, Jimmy showed him the halter and slipped it over his head, calm as could be. He led the horse out of the paddock and into the buggy traces, and slipped him a carrot after he got the bridle on without a problem. Prince nickered in response. First time Jimmy had gotten a nicker out of him. He knew what a nicker meant—a contented horse.

Hmm. He'd been around horses most of his life, wrangling, breaking, training. He knew a lot about horses, even how to rehabilitate them after injuries. Frankly, he considered himself something of an expert on horses. But he'd never thought of talking to them the way Sylvie did. And he sure never thought of listening to them.

⌒

The first week Jimmy Fisher was there, Sylvie hardly saw him. He worked and worked, with a practiced ease, like he was accustomed to hard labor. It surprised her, considering he'd overslept on his first day on the job. As dawn lit each morning sky, she'd see him hop the creek to head straight to the new old barn. He'd feed the animals, lead the horses out to the paddocks for the day, and then set to work cleaning out the new old barn. She saw him haul wheelbarrow after wheelbarrow of manure and dump it on the garden to decompose before winter hit. He cleaned that barn, top to bottom, better than Sylvie thought possible—cobwebs swept, windows shined, gutters spread with lime. Even the abandoned birds' nests in the rafters were gone, tossed into the compost pile.

After the new old barn was cleaned out to his satisfaction, he dragged some lumber from the old barn and started to build a henhouse. First, he took the trouble to sink posts in cement. As the cement dried, he made a run for the chickens to peck around in during the day. As the foundation, walls, and roof of the henhouse got underway, he added a ramp that led to the enclosed run.

Joey sat nearby, close but not too close, watching him warily, until Jimmy started painting the henhouse. He didn't directly ask Joey to help him, but he did have two paint-brushes and made a show of leaving one near the paint can. Joey couldn't resist, and soon the two of them were slapping red paint all over the henhouse. Sylvie watched the whole thing unfold from the kitchen windows. *Clever*, she thought. *It takes a boy to know a boy*. That was in the Good Book.

Late in the afternoon, Sylvie opened the door to Jimmy and Joey. Jimmy pulled off his hat with a flourish, flashing her a dazzling smile. "We've come to invite you to the grand opening of the henhouse. But first, we need you to cast the deciding vote for its name."

"A name for the henhouse?"

Joey beamed. "Here's our ideas, Mem. Jimmy likes Poul-try Palace. I like Chick Inn. Get it? Chick Inn. Chicken."

"Hmmm," Sylvie said. "Is the contest closed? Can I add some ideas?"

"Sure can," Jimmy said. "Like what?"

"Like . . . Cackle Coop. Or Hen Den."

Jimmy rubbed his chin, eyes twinkling. "Okay, I see where you're going with this. You're thinking about the sounds of women yakking away at a quilting bee. Then, how about Biddy City?"

A laugh burst out of Sylvie. "Done."

"Biddy City it is."

Again, that smile with the big dimples. She got so caught up in his smile that it took her a while to realize he was still talking.

". . . I'll ask Izzy to paint an official sign. Joey, you and I need to start herding those old biddies inside."

This, Sylvie had to see. She grabbed her shawl and followed them outside. Jimmy and Joey chased after and flapped their hats at the poor hens, who refused to go near the henhouse. Finally, worried the hens would be too distraught to ever lay another egg, she slipped off to the food bucket and came back with her apron full of corn. She made clucking noises, coaxing the hens up the ramp with the corn.

"Well, I'll be," Jimmy said, as the rooster appeared to inspect the corn and strutted right up the ramp. "You sure do have a way with animals, Sylvie."

She shrugged, self-conscious under his admiring gaze. "It's nothing, really. You just have to think the way they think."

Amusement lit his eyes. So blue, those eyes. "Oh? And how does a hen think?"

She lifted the corners of her apron and shook it, so that any remaining corn spilled out. "They think about food, all the livelong day. 'Feed my lambs,' Jesus said."

"I'm not sure he was talking about chickens and corn and a henhouse."

"Sure he was. It's written in the Good Book. 'Feed my lambs.'" She gave him a sweet smile. "So that's what I do."

Jimmy gave her a puzzled look before slapping his hat against his knee to knock the dust off, then plopped it on his head. Joey, standing behind him, followed his actions precisely.

Jimmy had just finished feeding the horses a breakfast of fresh hay and was filling up water buckets when he spun around at the sound of a snarl. "Whoa." A very large cat stood in the barn aisle, glaring at Jimmy. "You might just be the fattest cat I've ever seen."

Joey stood by the open barn door with a big carrot in his hand. "You hurt Lloyd's feelings when you call him fat."

"Think so? You think a cat gets hurt feelings?" The cat stared at Jimmy with an evil look in its eyes. *Maybe their feelings do get hurt.*

"Mem says he's not fat. He's a good mouser. The best Mem's ever seen, and he can eat as many mice as he can catch. We have lots of mice for him."

That, he was in favor of. Mice could have a field day at Rising Star Farm.

"She says we're not to call him fat. He's portly."

"I stand corrected. From now on I will call him an enormously portly cat." With that, the cat let out a snarl and pounced on Jimmy's foot. He yelped and shook his leg. The cat's claws clung to his pant legs. "He's trying to kill me."

"He don't like you." Joey peered up at him. "Animals don't like you."

"That's not true." Jimmy pushed the cat's big belly off his leg and stepped back before it could attack again. "We just need time to get to know each other."

"Prince still don't like you."

"I think he's coming around." Jimmy grinned. "Helps when you feed animals. It all comes down to who's feeding them. If you feed 'em, they like you. Real fast."

"Mem says animals know if you care about them. She says God gave them a special inst . . . in-stink . . ."

"Instinct?"

"That's what I said."

69

"Did your Mem say that's in the Good Book?"

Irritation flashed. "You making fun of my Mem?"

"No! Not at all. I've just noticed that when she talks about God, she quotes the Good Book." And it was always slightly misquoted. Slightly off-kilter. Joey was still glaring at him, same smoldering look as the cat. Good grief, this farm was filled with overly sensitive types. "Joey, what'd you call this portly cat?"

"Lloyd."

"Lloyd? That's a funny name for a cat."

"It's the name he came with. Some English man drove by and dropped him off one day."

"Isn't that how you ended up with a three-legged dog?"

"Yup."

"Does your mom take in every stray that gets dropped off?"

"Yup."

"How come?"

"She says God cares about each one, whether they got a family or not. She says that maybe God cares even more about the ones who don't have someone to love them. She says we should do just what God does and give them a home. Even cats."

Even enormously portly cats. Jimmy couldn't help but like Sylvie's thinking.

"That's in the Good Book too." Joey shot him a hard glance. "Mem said so."

FIVE

Normally, Izzy was cautious around other women, slow to warm up, even reluctant to offer friendship. But there was something about Sylvie that drew Izzy to her, something that made her feel as if they'd known each other all their lives. She could see why Luke felt a special attachment to this cousin of his. Unlike most women, Sylvie didn't compete or compare. She just lived her life the best way she could.

Standing next to Sylvie as the women waited to head into the Smuckers' barn for church on Sunday, Izzy felt most aware that she was not of German descent like everyone else. Sylvie was more than a head shorter than Izzy, fair and blonde next to her own dark hair and olive skin. Luke had said once that he hoped their children would have hair like Izzy's, thick and wavy and dark. Hardly aware she was doing it, she lifted a hand to the back of her neck, tucking in the wisps that escaped her pinned knot.

No. She dropped her hand. She wouldn't think about that. Those babies would never be. Dok hadn't found any reason why she and Luke weren't able to conceive and told them not

71

to give up hope. But it looked different from Izzy's perspective, with hope shriveling each month.

She pushed aside her feelings of self-pity as she followed Sylvie into the dimly lit barn and sat on a backless bench. She tucked her chin to her chest, trying to still her heart and mind. Waiting for the Lord. That was how Luke described this quiet time of expectation. She wondered what was running through Sylvie's mind during this long drawn-out silence. Now, there was a woman who'd not had an easy go of life. Izzy asked her once how she had such a sense of herself, for she was different from most Amish women. More independent. Sylvie took a long time to answer, as if she was gathering her words before she said them aloud. "I suppose," she answered, "I suppose that I've had to learn to trust my instincts."

Maybe that was it. Izzy was full of self-doubt, constantly fighting an inner tug of war.

Teddy Zook, the Vorsinger, spun out the first long note of the hymn, interrupting Izzy's train of thought, and she joined in on the women's high reedy wobble and the men's deep guttural sound, different octaves but the same note. With that, the service got under way. One church, one voice. No harmony, so no one stood out. She loved the moment that started the service, for all the reasons she loved being Amish. She had never wanted to stand out, never wanted to be noticed. During that moment, it felt like she was part of a whole. She felt truly Plain. Not a fairly recent convert, with a radically different upbringing from anyone else in this barn.

Her second favorite moment came later, when Luke stood to read Scripture. She was so proud of him, even though surely it must be prideful to think such a thing. After all, he was reading from the Holy Book! But he had grown so much in the last few years. Even the way he read Scripture was different than when he first became deacon. For the longest time, he kept his head tucked down, his voice low, as if he knew he didn't deserve to be here. But something had changed in him, something had settled. His head was lifted up, his voice was clear, carrying to the corners and rafters of the barn. Sometimes she thought this might be what it was like for those Israelites as they listened to Moses. So confident in the words he read, so full of belief in the Lord God. Luke was never plagued with doubts the way Izzy was.

Today Luke was reading a long passage from the book of Philippians. "'. . . My God will supply all your needs according to his riches in glory in Christ Jesus.'"

All your needs. All your needs.

How could that be true? She glanced over at Sylvie, wondering if she ever suffered from doubts about God supplying all her needs. After all, she was a widow, a single mother.

How could it be best to have children grow up without fathers? Take Joey, for example. He sat on the other side of Sylvie, swinging his shoes back and forth until Sylvie gently put a hand on his knee and his legs stilled. That dear little boy deserved a father, she thought. A good father, a loving one. A man who stuck around.

So did I, was her next thought.

Izzy shook her head, pushing away those troubling thoughts. Sylvie, as far as she knew, never indulged in self-pity. She should try to be more like her. Even during the long service, Sylvie sat perfectly still, statue-like. Izzy had to shift from side to side, wiggle her feet inside her shoes just to keep them from going to sleep. Yes, she should try to be more like Sylvie.

After the fellowship meal, as Sylvie and Izzy crossed the yard to start cleaning up in the kitchen, they passed by Ruthie and her father, David Stoltzfus. Ruthie had leaned into him to tell him something. David laughed as he wrapped his free arm around her shoulder and pulled her close. Their obviously warm relationship sparked a familiar swirl of envy within Izzy, and she fought to tamp it down.

Sylvie slowed, watching them, and then spoke softly the words that were on Izzy's heart. "Imagine if all fathers were like David Stoltzfus."

"I wish my own father . . ." Izzy stopped, allowing her sentence to trail away unfinished.

Sylvie glanced over at her. "Wish what?"

"Nothing," she said. "Don't mind me." She felt her cheeks grow warm.

Sylvie turned to face her, a question on her face. "If you ever want to talk about—"

"I don't." Her stomach tightened at the surprised, slightly hurt look in Sylvie's eyes. She didn't mean to be so abrupt, but she wanted to put a stop to this conversation before it got started.

"I didn't mean to pry, Izzy. I just meant that I know all about wishing for a different kind of father."

Sylvie's voice was so full of kindness and understanding that Izzy felt a little ashamed. She wasn't the only one who came from a troubled background, even among the Amish. Lately she seemed to get constantly snagged by self-pity. She had to stop dwelling on the very things that had been denied to her. *The mind feasts on what it focuses on.* One of Fern's favorite sayings.

Izzy met Sylvie's eyes with a smile in return. "We'd better

get to work." There was an enormous stack of dishes piled on the kitchen counter. Sylvie scrubbed and rinsed, Izzy dried. Each time they made a dent in the pile, someone would arrive in the kitchen with another stack.

When the kitchen had emptied for a moment, Izzy asked Sylvie how Jimmy Fisher was working out at Rising Star Farm. While the women had served lunch to the men, she'd noticed Jimmy said something to Sylvie that made her laugh.

"He's working hard, that's for sure." She handed a dripping plate to Izzy.

"Beware," Izzy said, rubbing the dish with her rag. "Jimmy is quite a charmer."

Sylvie grinned. "There's nothing charming about Jake's junk."

"Joey likes him?"

She lifted a soapy hand to seesaw it in the air. "Getting there. It's good for Joey to be around another man."

"But Jake was good to him, wasn't he? Tried to be a father to him?"

"A father? I don't know if he tried to be a father. More like a kind old uncle." Sylvie shrugged. "And my father hardly ever spoke to him, but to bark at him for the smallest things." She rolled her eyes. "Listen to me. On a Sunday, fresh out of worship, and here I am running Jake and my father down. If you can't say something nice, don't say anything at all." She gave Izzy a knowing look. "That's from the Good Book."

It was? It sounded more like something Fern would say, but Izzy was hardly the one to ask about Bible verses. Most everything about the Bible was still new to her ears.

Not a moment later, into the kitchen came Fern, holding Katy Ann in her arms. The baby's eyes were dropped at a sleepy half-mast. These long Sundays took a toll on little ones. "Luke's staying behind to help get the benches into the wagon. I'm going to head home now—catching a ride with Edith and Hank. If it's all right with you, I'll take Katy Ann home for a nap."

Izzy set down the rag and took a few steps toward Fern. Katy Ann held out her arms for her. She loved those moments, when her little girl reached for her in a way that revealed their mother-child bond. She held her close, gave her a hug and a kiss. "Sounds good. I'll finish up here and be home soon." She handed Katy Ann back to Fern with a thank-you.

Behind Fern, Edith appeared at the kitchen door, blocking the flow of traffic as women were bringing dishes into the kitchen to be washed. People naturally stepped aside when they saw her coming. They had to—Edith would step aside for no one. The pinched expression on her face as she glanced at Sylvie was a reminder to all that she was not a favorite. "We're leaving now." She turned and left without another word, and the kitchen traffic started up again.

Later, as Izzy waited for a young boy to bring Bob in from the pasture and hook him up to her buggy, she looked at the sun, already dipping to the west toward midafternoon. The October days were growing short.

My God will supply all your needs according to his riches in glory by Christ Jesus. All your needs.

All your needs.

Down the long empty country road that led to Windmill Farm, those words kept circling in her mind. Maybe that was the heart of her problem. She hadn't prayed for this longing out of fear that, what she considered a need, God would consider to be only a want. After all, Katy Ann belonged to her, just as much as if she'd borne her. Asking for more seemed indulgent. But maybe that wasn't how God felt about the topic. Luke was always telling her that the Bible said to pray about everything.

Dare she ask?

Could she be bold enough to pray for a baby of her own? Such a prayer seemed too much to ask. How could she ask? Yet how could she not ask? It was the desire of her heart. It was her greatest need.

My God will supply all your needs according to his glorious riches in Christ Jesus. All your needs.

Dear Lord, she prayed, *help me believe that to be true.*

Jimmy ran down his mental list of jobs to do at Rising Star Farm—an endless list—and prioritized them. The garden needed tilling, but that would have to wait until the ground warmed up. The apple orchard needed pruning before the sap started flowing, so he'd get to work on those trees, doing a little each day. But first, he had something in mind that he wanted from the old barn . . . dubbed by Jimmy as Jake's Junk Shop.

He pushed a wheelbarrow through a small pathway, brushing cobwebs out of his face, almost holding his breath from the dank musty stench. He went as far into the dim barn as he could, until the wheelbarrow couldn't fit any farther in. Then he started to grab all the copper he could reach and toss it in the wheelbarrow. He wasn't sure if Jake had had any organizational sense—he doubted it—but at least the copper seemed to be heaped in the same general center area of the barn.

He carted out all that he could find and wheeled it over to Luke's Fix-It Shop. Teddy Zook was inside the shop, setting a chair leg into a vise grip.

Luke held a bottle of wood glue in one hand and gave Jimmy a wave with the other. "Come on in. This is your mother's chair we're trying to fix. The legs keep splitting."

Jimmy recognized that old chair. It was his mother's favorite kitchen chair. Over the years, every single leg had broken, but she just kept getting it fixed. One of these days, the whole thing would collapse on her. "When you have a minute, I brought a cartful of copper over. I thought you might have some use for it."

"Copper?" Luke didn't even look up as he squeezed glue into the cracked chair leg. "What for?"

Teddy looked up. "What kind of copper?"

"All kinds. Jake used to haul it home from tag sales. I'm trying to sell it."

"Sell it to me?" Luke said. "No way. You're turning into Hank Lapp. He brings me all his junk too. Look out at that trampoline in the sheep pen. Bet he got that from Jake. I don't want any more junk."

"Junk?" Jimmy said. "Oh no no no, my friend. Copper is no junk. It's valuable. Costly." So far, it was the only thing Jimmy had found among Jake's junk that was worth something.

"Only if you want it."

"People do want it. Gutters, downspouts, mailboxes, trimming for their lanterns. I've seen the trend, all over Colorado. I've seen copper sinks in farmhouses. There's a shortage of copper, right as we speak. I've even heard of copper thieves, stealing trim right off houses."

"What?" Luke said. "Copper thieves?"

"He's right," Teddy Zook said. "Folks love copper. I get requests all the time for copper trim on woodwork."

Luke and Teddy walked outside to look through the wheelbarrow. Luke picked up a long, narrow copper pipe. "But what would you do with it?"

"Hammer it down and resell it," Teddy said, as he rummaged through the wheelbarrow. "Think about all the ways to use copper. Roofs on birdhouses. Trim on mailboxes. It's a hot commodity, Luke. You need to get out more." He picked up an old battered teakettle. "A little polish, get those dents out, and this could be something Alice might like."

Jimmy gave Luke a smug smile. "See? What did I tell you?"

"How much do you want for it?" Teddy said.

"The teakettle?"

"No. The whole kit and caboodle."

Jimmy rubbed his chin. "I could part with it for, say, two hundred dollars."

"I'll give you fifty," Teddy said.

"Sold!"

On the way back to Rising Star Farm with an empty wheelbarrow, Jimmy felt pretty pleased with himself. Fifty bucks was nothing to cough at, not when he'd barely had a dollar to spare in the last few weeks. He was wrapping up his first workweek at Rising Star Farm, and he'd made a dent in getting the farm in better condition. A small dent, but it was a start.

When he handed Sylvie the wad of fifty dollars, she looked at him, amazed. "You mean, someone actually paid you for something out of that old barn?"

"Yup. Teddy Zook bought it all."

She handed Jimmy back the wad of money. "You keep it. Keep the money from anything you can sell. Keep all of it."

"I can't do that."

"Why not? Consider it as an incentive to sell more of Jake's junk."

Come to think of it, they'd never really discussed Jimmy's salary. "Well, then, only if you'll consider it as my wages."

Her violet eyes widened. "Then I hope you can sell it all. Every last bit of junk." Before she turned away, she winked at him.

Those winks! What did they mean? Jimmy was thoroughly confused by them. It was on his way across the yard that evening that he wondered if she'd agreed so readily to his offer because she couldn't afford to pay him anything at all.

<hr />

Sylvie busied herself by dicing up apricots to add to a cornmeal cake. Two weeks ago, the Bent N' Dent had an entire box of badly dented apricot cans, marked only twenty cents each, so she bought them all. Joey had already grown tired of canned apricots, so she was trying to find creative ways to use them. She glanced out the kitchen window to see Jimmy Fisher emerge from the barn leading Prince by the halter, Joey bobbing alongside him. After the construction of the henhouse, Joey could not be detached from Jimmy. He watched for him to arrive in the morning. He shadowed him as he did his chores. It pleased Sylvie and worried her, both.

Joey opened the gate to the paddock, and Jimmy led Prince in, unhooking the lead from his halter. The horse danced around inside, eager to be free, before he took off charging down to the far end, almost as if he was going to hop the fence and take off, but at the last minute he made a sharp turn to gallop back to the other end. The three-legged dog hopped over to join them as Jimmy latched the paddock and stooped down to ruffle his head.

Then she watched as Jimmy put his heel on the lower rail and leaned forward to rest his elbows on the top rail. Joey tried to copy him, but he couldn't reach the top rail, so he had both elbows on the lower rail and his bottom high in the air. It made him look silly, such a little boy trying so hard to be a man, and had Sylvie smiling through a sudden prickle of tears. She whipped the batter so hard with the wooden spoon that some spilled over the edges and she stopped suddenly. Whipping all the air out would only make this cornmeal cake as heavy as a stone.

He should have a father, Sylvie thought for the thousandth time. A boy deserved a father. Every child did.

Luke walked through the orchards to check on Amos's trees. He felt his friend's presence most keenly up on this hillside, remembering the care Amos had given those fruit trees—planted by his great-grandfather, tended by subsequent generations. Amos wasn't particularly fussy about most things—Windmill Farm had needed a lot of repairs when Luke first arrived. But when it came to the orchards, Amos babied them like they were saplings. Today, Luke was marking the branches to be pruned during the month of January, just the way Amos had taught him.

Luke missed the dear old man. Amos and David had become fathers to him, filling that seemingly bottomless hole in his life. They were the reason he knew he could love Katy

Ann as if she were his own and be the father she needed—
because Amos and David had done that for him.

As he crested the hilltop, he saw a car pull up the driveway
and park in front of the yarn shop. He winced in a grimace,
then checked himself, when he saw Izzy's mother, Grace,
emerge from the car. She had come a long way in the last year
and he wholeheartedly supported her recovery. She showed a
lot of interest in Katy Ann, which he hadn't expected of her.
She was a new and improved Grace Mitchell Miller, often surprising him in good ways, yet he had a hard time not thinking
of her as the old Grace. It shamed him to be so judgmental,
yet he was. He supposed the cause of it was feeling protective
of Izzy for a lifetime of neglect. He, of all people, should have
an empathy for someone making a fresh start.

As he watched, he saw Izzy come out of the yarn shop
with the baby in her arms. Katy Ann reached out for Grace.
Again, he winced. He disliked this routine: Grace would
offer the baby a piece of candy, something he and Izzy would
never let her eat. Too sugary, too filled with junk. He'd objected to Izzy about it and it hadn't gone well. "Why can't
your mother bring something healthy to her? Something that
doesn't cause cavities on her brand-new beautiful little teeth?
A carrot, maybe."

Izzy had rolled her eyes at that. "It's my mother's way to
relate to Katy Ann. We're not going to interfere."

Maybe not, but he drew the line at letting Grace babysit
Katy Ann.

"Luke," Izzy would remind him, "she's never even offered.
She can sense you don't trust her. So stop worrying about
things that haven't happened."

He checked himself again. He was too hard on Grace. She

was trying, after all. Imagine if he ever met Izzy's father—he would blast him for abandoning his family, for letting his child grow up in the foster care system. What kind of man was that? He could almost hear David's voice, gently correcting him. "Life isn't quite so black and white, Luke. Most people do the best they can."

Maybe so. Probably not. Not taking care of your children . . . it just wasn't enough to say you did the best you could. You had to do better.

At first light on a cold but sunny morning in early November, the low-beamed kitchen of Rising Star Farm was already humming with life. Sylvie had a tray of biscuits baking in the oven, its sweet scent competing with the sizzle of sausage, seasoned with sage and red pepper, frying on the stovetop. Upstairs, Joey was clomping around in his room, looking for clothes. The rooster let out his cry, the cat scratched at the back door, the three-legged dog got up from his warm spot near the stove to bark at both of them, then lay back down. She opened the door to let the cat in and paused for a moment. All the way from the barn, she could hear the horses start whinnying, impatient for breakfast. First one whinnied, then another answered back. Jimmy Fisher must be in the barn, forking hay into a wheelbarrow.

She smiled. A new day had begun.

After Jake died, the house had seemed so quiet. Far too quiet. She had poured all her energies into the horses. Doing so cheered her out of her doldrums.

Joey, now dressed, hopped down the stairs in his usual way and appeared at the kitchen door. "Something smells good."

"It is. Your favorite. Sausage and gravy over biscuits." The biscuits! She spun around and grabbed the oven mitt, then pulled the biscuit tray out. Not bad. Not great, but not bad.

"Just a little burned on the edges," Joey said. "Did you get distracted again?"

She laughed. "I sure did, honey. Listening to all the sounds of morning."

Some gentle taps at the front door gave her a start, but then she realized it was Jimmy Fisher's signature knock. Seven short knocks, like he was tapping out a tune. As she walked to the door, it occurred to her that she was starting to become familiar with Jimmy's ways. They were happy ways. His nature, it was cheerful. She hadn't been around a lot of lighthearted people in her life. Her mother could be happy, but only so long as her father wasn't home. Being around a genuinely happy person . . . it was quite nice.

Sylvie opened the door and saw Jimmy standing there with his hat on his chest. "Good morning, ma'am. I just finished feeding the horses and couldn't help but feel overcome by the most delicious smell, wafting down from the house."

"Sausage and gravy over biscuits," Joey said. "It's my favorite."

"Mine too."

Jimmy flashed Sylvie a double-dimple smile that was practically bouncing in his eyes, and what could she do but invite him in? Her eyes followed him as he strode past her and into the kitchen. The man did have a way about him. A dangerous way, she could almost hear her father warning her.

⌒

The lure of the scent of sizzling sausage and his empty belly proved too much for Jimmy. Each day, the aroma of

Sylvie's cooking had pulled him to the kitchen like a magnet. So far, she'd never welcomed him in. Though he'd lived near the old house most of his life, he'd never been inside. Not one single time. Jake, being a bachelor, was given a pass from hosting church, plus his mother had always warned them to stay away from the house. Jake was to be avoided and was definitely not the type to tolerate boys messing around on his property. Jimmy had never doubted her.

This morning, he caved in. When she answered his knock, he briefly wondered if he should invent a lame excuse for interrupting her breakfast. But then he got a stronger whiff—was that the smell of biscuits baking?—plus, he was a terrible liar. He just went ahead and invited himself to breakfast, and she was too nice, or maybe too surprised, to refuse him.

He took a few steps inside the house and stopped. For a building this large, the old house had a cramped front hall—no more than a stairwell, really, that received no sunlight at all. As Jimmy stood there, his eyes adjusted to the dimness: a rack on the wall was filled with old hats and bonnets; a buck's head hung close to the ceiling, its antlers festooned with sweaters.

To the right was the kitchen. He swept the room in a glance. This room held a charm and warmth that came only from a woman's hand. Neat and tidy as a well-kept cupboard, filled with the usual necessities of living. Copper pots hung off a rack above a large stove. On top of the stove were two freshly baked loaves of bread. Clean rags, neatly folded, hung on a wall rod. In the center of the kitchen table was a vase filled with some kind of flower, and a small candle.

He pointed to the delicate white flowers. "Late bloomers?"

"Early. They're narcissus bulbs. You can force them to

bloom if you keep them indoors, in a sunny spot. It's a trick my mother taught me."

"Why not just wait until spring? Why force anything to bloom before its time?"

She gazed at him for a moment. "Are you talking about flowers? Or life in general?"

He sputtered a moment, unsure of how to answer her. She did that a lot to him, turned his questions around so they were staring right at him.

"I guess because it might hasten spring along." She leaned over to sniff them. "Best smell in the world." She lifted the pot and held it to him.

He sniffed, then grinned. "It's nice, kinda perfume-y. But nothing in the world beats the smell of biscuits in the oven."

He watched as she set the vase back down, right in the middle of the table as if there were an X on the spot. The morning sun slanted through the windows, casting a paned pattern on the floor—which, by the way, was spotless, even with a small boy and a three-legged dog in the house. Clearly, this was the kitchen of an industrious woman who cared about her home. From the outside appearance of the place, he would never have guessed it.

He sat at the table's end. His plate was soon heaped with a split-open flaky biscuit, brown on the edges, just the way he liked it, slathered with sausage soaked in creamy gravy. He swallowed a bite of biscuit, nearly speechless at its goodness. Along with the delicious taste, he felt a queer emptiness. Here he sat at Jake the Junkman's table, with his wife and boy surrounding him. Was he sitting in Jake's very seat?

He raised his gaze to look into Sylvie's violet eyes. "Sylvie, this is delicious. I've had a lot of biscuits and gravy in my day, but it's never tasted like this." He sat back as she stole away his empty plate to refill it.

Over her shoulder, she said, "No different than any other Plain woman's biscuits and gravy."

"Not true." It might have looked the same, but it didn't taste the same. "The seasoning—it's different." Brighter, bolder, stronger. Like Sylvie, he realized. "Where'd you learn to cook like that?"

"I worked in a diner for a while."

"You left the Amish?"

A slight hesitation. She lowered her eyes as she set his dish in front of him, flicking away a crumb on the linen cloth. "My sister, she needed looking after. So I left with her." She lifted her eyes to Jimmy. "But I came back. I always intended to come back. I never was one to leave, not like my sister did."

"So she didn't return with you?"

Her eyes darted toward Joey. "No. She left. I don't think she'll be back. Being Amish . . . it didn't suit her. She was always restless, never happy. She said it felt like she was wearing a dress that was two sizes too small. It never did fit."

"Are you in touch with her much?"

"No. Not in a long, long time."

Jimmy never liked that side of being Amish. Depending on the bishop, once a person left the community, they were out. He didn't think David was the type to draw a hard line to those who left, cutting them off from their family. But it sounded like Sylvie's church had a different view.

At the table, Jimmy stayed for morning devotions with Sylvie and Joey before he went back to the barn, stomach full of good food. Soul satisfied with God's good Word. It surprised him when Sylvie said she had no Bible to read, so he volunteered to quote aloud a psalm by heart and she was impressed. He didn't mind seeing the glint of admiration in her eyes.

That was one thing his father had taught him—the importance of memorizing Scripture. He could hear his dad's deep voice even now, gone twenty years. "You'll never know when you're in a tight spot and you don't have a Bible handy." His dad would tap his forehead. "Best to have it stored away up here, so it's always there when you need it."

He hadn't thought about his dad for a long time, but being home, back in Stoney Ridge, had rekindled a lot of memories. His dad was a gentle man, soft-spoken, prone to ups and downs. More downs than ups, as Jimmy vaguely recalled. He remembered his dad had stayed in bed a lot, for weeks at a time. His mother had no patience for his father's low times, as she called them. She wanted him to be strong and sturdy, but he just wasn't made that way. The harder she pushed, the weaker he became. Toward the end, his low times became longer and longer, more severe. Until he just gave up the fight.

Jimmy saw how hard Sylvie worked, how lonely a life she had. What must it have been like for his mother to raise two young boys, to manage a small farm alone, while her husband was confined to bed? Not so easy.

Strange, to feel sympathy for his mother.

Six

On a gray Monday afternoon in early November, Izzy closed the Stitches in Time Yarn Shop and took Katy Ann out to the Mountain Vista Rehab Facility to see her mother, Grace Miller, who worked at the clinic. Grace had been through the program, twice, and just as she was ready to be released, she applied for a job. She worked in the kitchen, washing dishes and cleaning up. It wasn't much of a job, but it provided room and board, and it kept her clean and sober. That was all that mattered to Izzy and to Jenny, her half-sister.

Izzy found her mother in the facility's dining room, sweeping up after lunch.

Her mother smiled when she saw her. "Well, look who's come to see her grandma."

She set the broom down and reached for Katy Ann. Izzy watched the two of them for a while, feeling pleased that her mother was affectionate with the baby. Katy Ann was adopted and looked nothing like Izzy or Luke. She had creamed-coffee skin, and a headful of soft dark ringlets, and eyes as big and brown as a dairy cow. Izzy often wondered about Katy Ann's biological father, about his race, his background, his features, his personality. She guessed he was probably a high school student, like Cassidy, Katy Ann's biological mother. Cassidy had ended up at Windmill Farm for a few months while the group home she lived in was under renovations. Izzy and Cassidy had become friendly, though not so much that she confided in Izzy that she was pregnant. That news came later, after she'd left Windmill Farm and sent the social worker to ask Luke and Izzy to adopt her newborn. Shocked, thrilled, overwhelmed . . . they said *Yes!* and never looked back.

"You came at the perfect time," Grace said. "I'm due for a break." She pulled out a chair and sat down, motioning to Izzy to join her. She bounced Katy Ann on her lap, making her giggle. "She's grown since I saw her last."

"She's got two more teeth too."

Her mother gently pulled one of Katy Ann's ringlets, released it and smiled as it bounced back. "This head of hair. I've never seen anything like it."

"Cassidy's hair was straight. Or maybe she straightened it. I've wondered if her biological father had curly hair."

Grace played peekaboo with Katy Ann as Izzy gathered her courage. "Speaking of biological fathers, one of the reasons I came to see you today was to ask you a few questions. About my father."

Her mother either didn't hear her or didn't want to hear. She focused on trying to get Katy Ann to open her mouth so she could see her teeth.

"I'd like to know more about my father. Other than his name was Frank Miller and he was in the military." Izzy had only vague memories of him, and they weren't good ones.

"No, not Frank." Grace took in a deep breath. "One drum they're always beating around here is to tell the truth."

"What do you mean?" Izzy sat up straight. *Oh my gosh.* "Are you saying that . . . Frank Miller isn't my father?"

"No." Grace glanced at her, then looked away nervously. "Frank was deployed overseas when I met your father. When Frank found out I was pregnant with another man's child, he up and divorced me. He let you keep his name, though, so I could get military benefits. He was a real gentleman, that way. Not much else, though."

Izzy squeezed her eyes closed. Her mother's life was littered with broken relationships. It shouldn't surprise her, and she knew she shouldn't get pulled backward. They'd come so far, she and her mother. To think they could actually sit and have a conversation and share a love for Katy Ann. "Okay. Then what can you tell me about my father?"

Her mother kept playing with Katy Ann, as if they were talking about the weather. "Why do you want to know?"

"Is it so wrong to want to know? I watch Luke with Katy Ann, and it's gotten me to think about him. I'd like to know more about him. That's all."

"There's just not much to tell." She shrugged. "And I don't remember much from back then. Those were my drug days."

"There must be something you can tell me about him."

Grace straightened the prayer cap on Katy Ann's head. "He was married and he had good teeth."

Married. Good teeth. Izzy's stomach clenched. "So let me get this straight. You had an affair with a married man."

Her mother frowned. "It takes two, you know."

"Where did you meet him?"

Her mother squirmed. "Around here somewhere."

"So, not in Ohio?"

Grace looked at the clock. "I'd better get back to work."

"Mama, did you ever tell him about me?"

She handed Katy Ann to Izzy. "Things were complicated."

"You didn't, did you?"

She glared at her. "Don't sit there judging me. You couldn't possibly understand what it was like back then. I was having a real hard time."

Argh. They'd slipped right down the slope to where they used to be, all the time. At an impasse. Unable to move forward. *Lord, help.* "Mama, you're right. I don't know what it was like for you. I just wanted to know more about my father."

Grace's face relaxed. "He was real nice looking, if that helps. You look a lot like him, if I remember correctly."

"Did he have a name?"

Her mother pushed the toe of her shoe at her broom. "Johnny. That's what I called him."

"What did this Johnny fellow do for a living?"

"Hmm." She squinted, concentrating. "He wore a uniform. I remember that." Her face grew softer, sweeter, as if thinking about this Johnny evoked a happy memory. "I've always been a sucker for a guy in a uniform." She bent down and kissed Katy Ann. "Let me give you some advice, Izzy. Leave the past in the past. Otherwise you might stir up a hornet's nest." She picked up her broom and got back to work, leaving Izzy with more questions than answers.

And the biggest question of all: her biological father, Johnny-in-a-uniform, might still be here, somewhere in Lancaster County.

If there was a leaf left on a tree in Stoney Ridge, the storm that blew through last night would've swept it away. The sky cleared midmorning on Tuesday, and despite the bright blue sky, the air turned bitter cold. Izzy set chairs up in the yarn shop for a class of advanced knitters, hoping the room wasn't too cold for the women. Most were older, skilled in their craft. As she surveyed the circle of chairs, her thoughts kept returning to the sparse facts that her mother had told her yesterday about her biological father, wondering how she could ever track him down with such a feeble list.

Johnny. He was married and had good teeth. And he wore a uniform.

Appalling. Not much to go on, other than one big clue: Grace had met him in Lancaster County, not in Ohio as Izzy had assumed. As much as her mother's life was a tangled web of marriages and deceit, it did lift Izzy's spirits considerably to know she was not the offspring of a man like Frank Miller.

On the backs of two chairs, she spread out the baby blanket that this class would be working on, a combination of knitting and crocheting. It was complicated, yet oh-so-beautiful: a scene of a stockinette-stitch blue sky filled with puffy white clouds and a yellow pompom sun, a green and brown field below in a purl stitch, with crocheted pieces of sheep grazing on grass, a rocky fence crossing over it made of gray and brown bobble, and a tree filled with cherry blossoms. Attaching the appliqued crochet pieces would be today's assignment—to sew them into the knit stitches in a way that there was no sign of stitches on the back of the blanket. It was a good thing Edith Lapp would be here today. She was a master at such handcrafts.

Izzy's thoughts swung to Edith. She set a skein of yarn to mark Edith's spot, and far across the circle of chairs, she placed a skein for Sylvie. Those two needed to be separated.

Or rather, Sylvie needed some protection from Edith. Izzy didn't know why Edith was so hard on Sylvie, but she'd been snippy to her since the day she married Jake and had gotten progressively sharp-tongued. Sylvie could do nothing right in Edith's eyes. Last time this class met, Edith sat next to Sylvie and nitpicked at her for the solid hour, under her breath but loud enough for all to hear.

For some reason, Izzy had a pleasant relationship with Edith, and she was grateful for her help with the yarn shop, but she took utmost care to avoid getting on the wrong side of her. Poor Sylvie.

She ran a hand over the sheep that was appliqued on the baby blanket. That's how it seemed to her, as if Edith was like one of her bossy ewes, bullying a smaller ewe for no good reason. It happened all the time among her woollies.

She had chosen a soft cotton yarn for this baby blanket project, lightweight and washable, because babies did terrible things to blankets. Terrible! Katy Ann had been a spitter from the start, and the woolen blanket she'd knitted for her still had a sour formula odor embedded in it, no matter what she tried to get rid of it. Baking soda, detergent, vinegar. Nothing. It just stank.

Out the window, Izzy spotted a dash of indigo blue fly past. The mailman was heading up to the house with a package.

A mailman! Mailmen wore uniforms. So did UPS drivers, pilots, security guards, gasoline attendants . . . and garbagemen. The possibilities were endless. Izzy sighed. Her mother had said she was a sucker for a man in a uniform.

No concern for a man's character, or his faithfulness, or what kind of father he would make. Just the clothes on his back.

She reined in her thoughts as she heard a horse and buggy turn into the drive of Windmill Farm. If this Johnny fellow was in the military, he could have been Navy, Air Force, Army.

She stopped, straightened. Police. Her father might have been a policeman. Heaven only knew, her mother had plenty of interactions with policemen. She'd been arrested lots of times, and she had a way with men. There would have been multiple opportunities to get to know a police officer with an eye for a pretty woman. She rolled her eyes, thinking of her mother's taste in men. A married man with good teeth. Appalling.

Other than Edith Lapp's sharp glances at Sylvie, the class went much better than last month's, when Sylvie had ended up sitting next to Edith and heard nothing but complaints about the appearance of her grandfather's farm. Not Jake's farm, not Sylvie's farm, but Edith's grandfather's farm. She'd thought Edith was inexplicably unkind to her after she'd married Jake, but something changed after he passed, almost the moment his body was lowered in the ground. It was as if a bitterly cold wind blew in from across the creek, and never left.

Since Joey was up in Luke's Fix-It Shop, Sylvie stayed afterward to help Izzy clean up.

Izzy collected scissors while Sylvie put chairs back. "I would think Edith would have her knickers in a twist about her son working for you."

"Oh, I'm sure she does. She has a say-so about everything I do." *All wrong.*

"Is Jimmy earning his keep?"

"There's no denying he's a hard worker, and . . ."

"And . . . ?"

Sylvie brushed bits of yarn off her skirt. "And . . . I suppose it's nice to have someone cheerful around the farm." How different Jimmy was from Jake, with whom she shared a home but little else. And so very, very different from her father.

"Especially someone with bright blue eyes and dimples in his cheeks."

Startled, Sylvie froze, blushed at the thought, felt her cheeks grow warm with color.

"Why, Sylvie King, I do believe Jimmy Fisher has turned your head."

She felt her eyes start to twitch. "Don't be silly. This is Edith Lapp's second son, remember?" But she kept her chin tucked low as she said it and busied herself with straightening a chair.

⌒

Once or twice a day, Sylvie and Joey would take time to lean on the fence posts of Prince's paddock, just to watch him. He seemed to know he was being admired and often put on a show for them—breaking into a run around the paddock, kicking up his heels.

Sylvie heard footsteps behind her and turned to see Jimmy Fisher pushing a wheelbarrow past them, full of old pieces of lumber. He dumped it on the driveway. On the way back to the barn, he stopped, tilted the wheelbarrow upright, mopped his forehead with a blue handkerchief, and walked over to them.

"Any idea why Jake had that lumber? I found it piled in a horse stall."

She looked at the pile. "Someone was knocking down their barn and gave him the free wood."

"How long ago?"

"Maybe two years. Why do you ask?"

"A couple of those timbers are full of termites."

Her eyes went wide. "Think they've spread to the barn?"

"I'll be looking for them."

Joey pushed in between them. "If you're ever starving in a jungle, you can eat termites."

Jimmy looked at him. "What? Eat termites?"

"It's true. I read it in a book. They taste like . . ." Joey pulled a carrot out of his pants pocket and held it up. "Like a minty carrot." He looked up at Sylvie. "Can I go eat a termite?"

She smiled down at him, rubbing his small chin in her fingers. "No, honey. Let's save termite eating for the jungle."

Prince had spotted the carrot and nickered to Joey. He slipped through the rail to take a carrot to the big horse.

"Jake must have had a Thoroughbred for buggy riding."

"He did. A sweet mare. I sold her after he died. A fellow offered me those two broodmares if he could have her and I said yes. I was a little sorry to say goodbye to her, but I couldn't afford to keep Prince and a buggy horse. That's when I started using Prince as a buggy horse. And when I got the idea of trying to create a Partbred."

"You're pushing a rock uphill. The Amish are devoted to their Thoroughbreds."

"I like Thoroughbreds. They're mighty fine animals." Sylvie took in a big draught of air. "But for me, nothing beats an Arabian. They're eager to please. A perfect partner. They're built to run, with their big nostrils. They have an incredible presence." Prince was running around the pasture, tail flowing, as Joey stood in the center and watched him. "The sight of that horse . . . it just catches you in the heart."

"Do you happen to know how a Thoroughbred got its name?" Jimmy asked.

"Can't say that I do."

"Two hundred years ago, there were people who bred for a certain kind of horse. When they got everything they wanted in the horse, all the characteristics they were looking for, they decided they were done. The breed was thorough. Nothing more could be added. Hence the name Thoroughbred. In fact, all Thoroughbreds can be traced down to just three horses." He turned to look her straight in the eye. "It's hard to beat a Thoroughbred as a buggy horse, Sylvie. Why fix what ain't broke?"

"I never said it was broke. I said it could be improved."

"I've never seen any Amish with Arabians."

"No, not yet. That doesn't mean not ever."

"Just what are you trying to improve?"

"Endurance, mostly. They can handle the heat better than other breeds. And there's lots of other characteristics too. They're easy to handle, so athletic."

"Where'd you learn so much about Arabians?"

She hesitated, a few seconds too long. "I had a friend who had an Arabian horse."

"A friend?"

"A friend," she repeated, in a tone that ended the conversation.

He took the hint.

They stood together in silence for a while, Jimmy's gaze fixed on Prince. "Sylvie, would you let me ride him?"

"Drive him?"

"No. On saddle. Or bareback."

"Why?"

"I just want to see what kind of horse he is. I can't really tell until I'm on a horse's back."

Sylvie's eye started twitching. She looked over at Prince, conflicted, worried this was a bad idea. But it did please her that Jimmy Fisher had such a high opinion of Prince. Jake had never been overly partial to Prince or any other animal, felt nothing for them like Sylvie did. If she hadn't come into this horse's life when she did, he would've spent the rest of his days standing in a paddock. That would've been a crime. Still, what did she know about Jimmy Fisher and his judgment? Not much. "I don't know when he's last been ridden, if at all," she said, turning slightly to Jimmy, trying to hide her twitching eye. "He might toss you right off."

"I'm a skilled rider. I can handle him." He gave her his most dazzling smile. The double-dimple smile.

Still not convinced it was a good idea, she gave him a cautious nod. As he bolted into the barn to look for tack before she changed her mind, her thoughts spun with objections. Prince had only been harnessed to a heavy buggy. She had no idea what he'd do with a rider on his back.

Jimmy Fisher talked big, that much she knew about him. She would have to remember that he had a way of making her say yes to things she might not agree to in the cold light of day, had she not allowed herself to be swayed by those bright blue twinkling eyes and deep-set dimples in his cheeks.

A few minutes later, Jimmy came out holding a bridle in one hand. "I couldn't find a saddle."

Both eyes were twitching now. No saddle meant he would go bareback. "I've never seen one in the tack room."

Jimmy hopped into the paddock and whistled for Prince, holding the bridle up in the air. Curious, Prince trotted over, sniffed the bridle, and dipped his head so Jimmy could slip the bit into his mouth and the bridle over his head. So far, so good.

Sylvie and Joey stayed outside the paddock, watching. "Mem, I don't think this is such a good idea."

"How come?"

"Prince don't like Jimmy."

"Prince just hasn't learned to trust him yet. Maybe they just need a little time together."

Jimmy swung a leg over Prince's back like he'd done it a thousand times. Sylvie wondered about his life in Colorado, if this was what he did all day. Prince trotted around the paddock, Jimmy sitting on his back like he was glued there. Watching the two of them, Sylvie was impressed. Prince enjoyed working, and Jimmy knew how to ride. She heard him click his tongue to the horse and he went from a trot to a canter. Joey stayed by her side, watching the two go around and around.

Just as Sylvie was starting to relax, to even think about going to the pile of lumber to see if they could find the one with termites, Jimmy either did something or said something that made Prince stretch out. Not thirty seconds later, Prince vaulted over the side railing as if it were nothing more than a fallen-down tree log, and off they went, galloping down toward the road.

Sylvie and Joey watched them, wide-eyed. Stunned.

"Think Jimmy Fisher meant to jump the fence with Prince, Mem?"

"I don't know. That horse does have a mind of his own."

"Think they're coming back?"

"I don't know, son. I just don't know."

SEVEN

After four years in Colorado, Jimmy considered himself something of an expert on horses, but after a few weeks at Rising Star Farm, he quickly discovered there was much he didn't know. All his life, he'd watched many men handle the animals, but none had Sylvie's way with a horse. He knew all about rounding up wild mustangs, saddle-breaking them, and taking them to auction. But his experience out west had meant that everything he'd done with horses was a quick turnover. It was all about making money. It had nothing to do with building trust, the kind of trust that Prince had in Sylvie.

Prince would do anything Sylvie wanted him to. He followed her around like a trained puppy. And her touch with the horse was so oddly gentle, her words so soothing and calm. She needed no buggy switch with him, not even when she exercised him in the paddock. She would give the command to him, almost as if she was letting him choose to say yes or not, and he would never fail to do exactly what she asked of him. Sometimes Jimmy would catch Sylvie looking into Prince's eye as she whispered to him, and his ears would flicker back and forth, as if the two were sharing secrets.

Just yesterday he'd overheard her talking to Joey as they brushed Prince down. "The more time I spend with horses," she said, "the more I realize what a gift they are."

Who thought like that? No one he knew. Even the Amish, they thought of their horses fondly, but they were still beasts of burden. Certainly not as gifts. She scrambled his senses, that woman.

On a cold afternoon, Jimmy came out of the barn to find Sylvie and Joey soaking up the sunshine, resting on the top of the fence, watching Prince in the paddock. Barely glancing at him, she said coolly, "I'm going to take Prince into town to get a few things at the Bent N' Dent."

She was still mad at him for taking the horse on a joyride through town.

Not a joyride, he had tried to explain to her, but she didn't believe him. "This horse," he'd said as he patted Prince's lathered-up neck after their ride into town and back, "he is something else. He has destiny."

"I've been telling you that since the day I met you. You didn't need to risk your neck and jump over the fence to find that out."

Jimmy led Prince out of the paddock and tied him to the hitching post, then disappeared into the barn and came back out with the harness. This time, Prince didn't object; he dipped his head into the bridle, ears pointed forward.

Sylvie rolled her eyes. "Seems like Prince is warming up to you, ever since that joyride."

He grinned. "Not a joyride. Testing him out, that's what I was doing."

Sylvie harrumphed.

"Sylvie, you know as well as I do that I gave Prince what he wanted most: a chance to prove himself."

"I know," she said softly. "This horse isn't meant to spend his days grazing in a pasture."

As Jimmy buckled the harness to the buggy, he said, "Still seems odd to me to see an Arabian pulling a buggy. And not a Thoroughbred."

"Change isn't such a bad thing."

He looked at her over Prince's withers. "Speaking of change, I've got an idea that I think is better than trying to get the Amish to accept a new buggy horse."

Her fingers stopped buckling. "What's that?"

"You're absolutely right about Prince. He's made for something more than sitting in a pasture. I think if we asked him what he wanted, he'd say he's made . . . to race." He'd been working this idea out ever since he rode Prince into town, sensed the way the horse instinctively knew when to stretch out, when to pull in. His quick reflexes astonished Jimmy. Of all the horses he'd worked with, Thoroughbred or Mustang or Belgian, he'd never ridden a horse as athletic as Prince.

"Racing?" She scoffed. "Amish don't race horses."

"But you're not racing them. Actually, neither is Prince. He's going to sire horses that are destined for the racetrack." He lifted a finger in the air. "That's the angle we've been missing to promote him as a stud. Sylvie, I think you should forget the Partbred idea. Forget the better buggy horse idea. This horse is meant to be a stud for Arabians."

"But wouldn't the bishop object to that?"

"You're not doing anything wrong. You're creating an

Arabian horse farm. If that has an appeal to the racehorse community, well, all the better. And I happen to know a little bit about racehorses around here. I know they're in short supply."

"But . . ." One eye started winking at him.

She was softening, for sure. He was getting to know those winks. "If you ruffle some feathers, you can always apologize later. That's been my policy."

She pinned him with her look. "How about this? Let's run it by David, first."

Prince made a sudden dash around the paddock, and Jimmy turned to watch him, avoiding those piercing violet eyes. "I'm pretty sure there's nothing to worry about. It's all in the way we explain it. Besides, you're not doing the actual racing. From past experience as a wayward youth, I happen to know *that* is the line where you'd be sticking your neck out too far."

"Isn't this a little like Amish farmers who grow tobacco to sell?"

He hesitated. "You mean . . . horseracing is the same thing as smoking cigarettes?"

"Yes. Not good for you but not illegal."

Hmm. He would have to give that some thought, because David might bring up the same argument. "There's lots of Amish communities that race each year. I've been to buggy races in Shipshewana."

"For money?"

"Well . . . no. Winner got a new halter." He backed Prince into the buggy traces. "What kind of bloodlines does he have?"

"What do you mean?"

"His lineage."

"He's a fine horse. Anyone can see that for himself."

"Sylvie, that's not enough."

"Why would I need more than that?"

Oh boy. "Usually, when people are looking for a stud, they want to know the full lineage of the horse."

"Can't they tell just by looking at him? Taking him out for a test drive? That's how my daddy would buy his buggy horses. Checking them over, one end to the other."

"That might work for a buggy horse, but remember, this is an Arabian horse. They're not common around these parts." He watched her gaze at the horse. "How much have you been asking for his stud fee?"

"Well, no one's asked yet. Just the other day, I put an index card down at the bulletin board at the Hay & Grain. Jake used to put a lot of index cards up there of stuff he wanted to sell. Sometimes it worked. Mostly, he'd find more stuff to buy."

"How much would you think about asking for a stud fee?"

"As much as anyone would be willing to pay, I suppose."

Jimmy let out a puff of air. "Sylvie, if you can prove Prince has a notable lineage, you might be able to demand a substantial stud fee."

She whipped her head around. "Why would that matter?"

"Because the horse has to prove it's more than a flash in the pan. It's got good genes to pass on to another generation. Same as people."

She turned back to the paddock. "People are different."

"How so?"

"They have choices about how they turn out."

Jimmy wasn't sure how to answer that, because he didn't

think she was talking about a person's hair or eye color. "Do you have any paperwork on Prince? A bill of sale?"

She frowned. "Jake wasn't much for keeping track of paperwork."

Or anything else for that matter.

"There might be a bill of sale somewhere." She swiveled around to look at the house. "'The Lord helps those who help themselves.' It's written in the Good Book."

"No, it's not."

"Sure it is. You need to listen more in church." Holding her boy's hand, she made a beeline to the house.

Jimmy followed, lengthening his stride, wondering if Sylvie Schrock King was as hopeless a dreamer as her husband had been. Before she went into the house, she stopped to wait for him.

"Better prepare yourself. Jake wasn't exactly the type to organize himself."

He came to the bottom porch step and stopped. Again that uneasy feeling hovered. It still felt a little funny to cross the threshold to Jake's house, like he was passing an invisible line.

Sylvie looked at him curiously. "You coming or not?" she finally said, opening the door and walking through the house.

"I'm coming." He bolted up the stairs.

Sylvie stood in front of a closed door. "I'm doing the best I can, but there's some things I just don't know where to start on. So I just close the doors and wait for another day."

"Like the barns."

She nodded. "Brace yourself," she said as she opened the door. "This is Jake's office."

Jimmy stopped dead, pushed back his hat, and gaped. "Lord-a-mercy," he muttered. He'd seen some messes in his day, but this one took the cake.

The small room was packed, floor to ceiling, with boxes, filled with who knew what. Every square inch of space was stuffed with tottering piles of boxes. Stacks of yellowing newspapers leaned against the walls. A narrow pathway, like a goat path, led to what Jimmy assumed was a desk. It too was covered with folders, shoeboxes, cuttings from newspapers. If there was ever an avalanche from all this junk, no one would find Jimmy.

"I haven't gone in here since Jake passed."

"You really think there could be a bill of sale in here?"

"First place to look, I would think."

"Lord-a-mercy," Jimmy repeated, lifting his hat and scratching his head, imagining the chore of looking for that one small but critically important piece of paper. "Where would be the second place?" *Oh no. Please don't say what I think you're going to say.*

"The old barn. Jake spent a lot of time in there."

Just what he was afraid she'd say.

⌒⌒

It felt odd to Sylvie to have someone go through Jake's things, but she knew she'd avoided it long enough. She didn't know where to start or what to look for. Jimmy Fisher seemed to have a sense of things. If Jimmy Fisher thought the old barn was a frightful mess, imagine what was running through his mind as he tackled Jake's office.

Sylvie kept the door closed so that Joey didn't wander in and bother him. Now and then, Jimmy would haul a few boxes out to the porch, and she'd peek in to see he was making progress. The goat path was growing wider.

He wasn't throwing out important papers—only old newspapers that Jake saved to find yard sales. She knew that because she would peek in the boxes after Jimmy hauled them out. It took him a full week of afternoons, but by Saturday, he called to her.

She poked her head in the door, astounded. "Why, I can see the floor!"

"Even better," Jimmy said. "Come on in."

The room was tidy, neat as a pin. A cherrywood desk with an empty and polished top, a chair, and a filing cabinet that she hadn't even known was in the room.

He opened the top drawer of the filing cabinet. "Inside here are folders. I tried to categorize everything, so you'd know where things were when it came time to pay."

"You've worked wonders."

"I've tried." He took one folder from the drawer. "But I think . . . I might have found a problem, Sylvie."

Those words out of his mouth sent a shiver through her. She didn't need any more problems. She had more than enough problems as it was.

"There's some unopened envelopes here from the Tax Claim Bureau. They look official. Registered mail and all."

She ignored him and walked around the room, admiring how clean it was.

"I think you should open these letters."

She didn't want to know what was in them. She picked an envelope up and ran a finger behind the seal to open it. Sylvie felt a swirl of familiar stress in her stomach as she skimmed the contents. She had never bothered Jake with questions about their finances. She knew so little about money, only that it came and went quickly.

"What's an upset tax sale?" She handed the paper to Jimmy. He read the letter. "Oh boy."

"Not good news?"

"When did you last pay the property tax bill?"

"Um, pay what?"

Jimmy lifted his head. "You did pay property tax last year, didn't you?"

She felt her left eye start its annoying twitch and turned away from Jimmy so he wouldn't notice.

"Sylvie, when exactly did Jake pass?"

"In July."

"Let's see." He scanned the letter again. "Property tax is due in Pennsylvania by the end of March. Most likely, he paid this year's bill. Surely"—he waved the letter in the air—"this must be a mistake."

She kept her eyes averted from Jimmy. "Most likely." He carried on speaking, but his words weren't fixing properly in her brain.

Fear flashed through her. Had Jake paid it? She never recalled Jake saying anything about taxes, other than complaining about them and the government in general. Even if he had paid last year's tax bill, she had a new one coming up. How would she manage to pay taxes this year? She wasn't even sure how she would pay Jimmy Fisher for work. Hard work too. "What exactly does it mean? An upset tax sale."

"When a person defaults on their property tax, their home becomes delinquent."

"And?"

"They can lose the home. The Tax Claim Bureau sends out a thirty-day notice that the home will be sold at an upset tax sale."

Her stomach twisted. "Is that what the letter said is going to happen?"

"Yes." He gave her a sympathetic glance. "I'll look into it. Maybe there's a way to get it all straightened out."

"You would do that?"

"Of course."

At this came such a rush of relief she wanted to fling her arms around his neck.

Putting his coat on, he had his eyes on his buttons. "But if Jake happened to have missed a property tax payment, you have the cash to pay it, right?"

She looked away and skimmed through more folders, neatly hanging vertically in the top drawer of the file cabinet. "Any sign of the bill of sale for Prince?"

"None. I'll keep looking though."

"Maybe I should just put another index card advertisement down on the bulletin board at the Hay & Grain. For Prince. As a stud."

"Hold on a little longer," he said. "Let me just see what we can find out about Prince first."

We. He said "we." Like he wasn't going to leave anytime soon. She felt her twitchy eye relax.

"Before I commit to the horrific chore of cleaning out the old barn, could there be any more places in the house where Jake kept papers?"

As she thought about his question, Joey wandered in and stopped short with a perplexed look on his face. "Hey! This room has a floor!"

Sylvie laughed, and her stress lightened up a notch. "Jimmy Fisher cleaned out Jake's office."

Joey walked around the desk, amazed.

"It's a nice room," Jimmy said. "Windows on both sides. Lots of morning light."

"Can I have this room?" Joey asked. "For my train set."

"Jake brought home an old train set. We haven't set it up yet."

"Soon, though," Joey said.

Sylvie's heart caught. That had been Jake's response to everything: "Soon, though." "Why not? Let's set up in here, Joey." The words were barely out of her mouth and he dashed away. Moments later, she heard him huff and puff, lugging a box down the hallway from a closet. As soon as he had it in the office, he opened it up and started pulling out a wooden toy set of train and tracks.

Sylvie bent down to help and then straightened in a flash. "These trains! It was the same fellow who had sold Prince to Jake. I remember now. The man had bashed down the pasture fence and gave Prince to Jake instead of paying for a new fence. And then we were in town one day and we happened to meet up with that very man. We had Joey with us, and Jake made the man feel guilty about the fence—Jake had a way of doing that to people. It wasn't right and it wasn't fair, because I'm pretty sure that fence was already broke down—but the man looked very embarrassed. He opened up his car trunk and gave Joey the box of trains."

Jimmy crouched down to look at the address label on the box. "Think this could be him?"

Sylvie looked at the label. State senator Elroy Funk. "I think so. I remember thinking he had an unfortunate name."

Jimmy sat back on his seat. "Maybe I'll go pay Elroy Funk a visit and see if he has a bill of sale for Prince."

"It's that important?"

"It could be."

"But it might not be." Seemed like an awful lot of time was going into finding this bill of sale.

"It might not be, Sylvie. But it just might be worth it." He fixed his eyes on her and let them speak for him: *Can you trust me on this?*

His level gaze made her feel funny, like she'd been on the tree swing he'd just put up for Joey. She felt her cheeks grow warm and quickly looked away, because she knew what followed. Her eye would start to twitch.

⌁

Jimmy didn't know what to make of Sylvie's winks. He kept a careful distance from her, lest she think he was after something more than a steady job with horses. Truth to tell, he didn't deny she was pretty to look at, but no way was he about to step into another man's spot. Take on another man's child! Not a chance. The very thought of it made him feel like he had a collar on that was strangling him.

Jimmy was walking from the barn to the house and stopped for a moment to look around. The improvements he'd made were beginning to tally up. Everything looked a little better, like someone cared. Rising Star Farm had a long way to go, but it was definitely moving in the right direction. Satisfied, he headed toward the house and saw Sylvie struggling to lug ten-pound bags of sugar from the buggy. "What are you doing with these?"

"The sugar was on sale at the Bent N' Dent because the bags were torn."

Each bag was taped with masking tape. "You go through this much sugar?"

She smiled at him as she stacked one bag of sugar in his arms on top of another. "Not for us. For the hummingbirds."

Joey nodded solemnly. "For when they come back."

"What?"

"Joey and I, we feed the hummingbirds. Last year we had hundreds humming around Rising Star Farm." She pointed to the ridge way beyond the barn, just an outline in the gloaming. "They come zooming down here and fill up on the sugar drink we make for them. And in return, they eat plenty of bugs for us."

"For protein," Joey said.

"That's right, honey. The sugar gives them energy so they can feast on the flies and mosquitos. I don't think we had to shoo a single fly away last summer."

Jimmy doubted that, with the stink made from those free-ranging chickens. It was much better now, with the hens corralled in Biddy City. "Hundreds?"

"Thousands," Joey said. "Millions. I counted."

"Sylvie, do you think you should be spending money on sugar and birds when you can't pay your property tax?"

"Yes, I think I should." She spun around to head to the porch steps. "Jesus said we need to take care of the birds. It's in the Good Book."

"No, it's not." He might have said it a little louder than he needed to, because she pivoted on the first step and looked at him in surprise. "I mean, the Bible indicates we should take good care of the natural world, but there's no place I can think of where it says to feed the birds. Just the opposite. It says that the Father feeds the birds. And so we don't have to worry, because he'll provide for us too."

"Well, see?" She smiled. "Now that's just what I meant."

Jimmy shook his head. "Sylvie, you can't keep collecting animals with problems. Every farmer knows that. Animals need to earn their keep."

"Like Prince."

"Exactly like Prince."

She came down the step, closer to him, and looked him straight in the eye. "Now, who made the rule that animals with problems don't earn their keep?" She patted the three-legged dog on the head and its tail whipped around like a whirligig. "They give us lots of joy, don't they, Joey?"

When Joey didn't answer, Jimmy and Sylvie turned to see where he'd gone. The boy was seated on the top porch step, gazing up at the sky.

She went to sit down next to him. "Isn't that just like you? Always so quick to spot the wonders of the Lord. Look at that moon. Nearly full. Have you ever seen anything so glorious? Amazing, to think it's reflecting light from the sun right onto us, way down here on earth." She patted the spot on the stairs next to her. "Sit with us, Jimmy. Just for a few minutes. The sugar can wait. Even Prince doesn't mind waiting for his supper. Don't miss this." She breathed out a long, slow sigh. "An extravagant moon, illuminating the earth. Oh, it's such a sight to behold."

He nearly chuckled at her being so childlike. Here she was, studying the sky like she'd never seen it before, open wonder in her face. Then he glanced behind him and realized she was right. Rising low on the horizon, the moon was so visible he could see its craters. He set the sugar down on the porch and settled on the steps.

Somehow, sitting there beside Sylvie and Joey seemed the most natural thing in the world.

A horse nickered in the distance and Prince answered back. Joey stood up. "Someone's at your house, Jimmy."

He rose and looked over Prince's withers to see Rosemary Blank arrive at the house. Second time this week.

The spell was broken. "Tell me where you want the sugar to go. Then I'll take Prince to the barn and get him tucked in for the night."

When Sylvie didn't answer, he turned. Her violet eyes were still fastened to the night sky. Moonlight limned her cheekbones and fringe of lashes. She looked . . . stunning. "Uh, Sylvie?"

She startled, as if she'd forgotten he was there. "You go on home, Jimmy. Looks like you've got company for dinner. Joey and I, we can take care of things here."

He hesitated, then heard his mother's voice call out for him in the dusk. He tipped his hat, cowboy style, and turned on his heels to head home. He stopped at the creek, noticing the moon shining down on it. He'd grown up here but had never noticed how the moon made the current glisten. Before jumping across, he looked back. Sylvie and Joey were still on the porch steps, heads tipped upward, pointing at stars in the sky. He felt a little sorry to leave.

$\mathcal{E}$IGHT

atherless. There was that word again.

Izzy had opened the King James Bible Luke had given her and thumbed through the pages, then finally pressed her finger on a random verse. It was a little game she played each morning, a silly way to find out what God might have to say to her today. This whole notion of reading the Bible, seeking God's guidance, looking for answers . . . it was still new to her. How could words from an ancient old book jump out and give you a direction? It's not that she doubted, she'd just never experienced having God communicate directly to her the way Luke had. Or Fern. Or David. Definitely like David. He was always talking about the Bible like it was a living thing.

Today her finger landed on Hosea 14:3. "For in you the fatherless find compassion."

The word *fatherless* ran through her mind again. It was strange how thoughts had a way of circling around one's head, then settling in for a stay. Or was it God's way of reinforcing a message? She didn't know. All she knew was that she couldn't stop thinking about her own biological father,

116

where he was, who he was. If it would matter to him to know he had a daughter. A granddaughter.

Should she even try to find out who he was? Or could that only open up a Pandora's box of trouble? After all, she'd come this far in life without a father. She had no real need for one, not anymore. She wasn't seeking money, or validation, or even much of a relationship; nor did she want to disrupt this man's life.

But maybe that was good too. Maybe it was best that way, to pursue this out of curiosity, not out of neediness. She squeezed her eyes shut. She had no idea what to do or how to do it. *Pray.* She could practically hear Luke's voice, like he was right in the room with her, though she knew he was meeting with David at the Bent N' Dent this morning. She opened her eyes wide and looked up at the ceiling.

Praying didn't come naturally to Izzy, not with the practiced ease it did for Luke. She couldn't get past the feeling that God was much too busy to be bothered with her. Luke said that was faulty thinking. He said the Bible told us to pray about everything. "Everything," he emphasized to her, more times than she could count. She had read that verse too, but mostly she let Luke do the praying for both of them. That, too, was faulty thinking, and she didn't need Luke to point that out. Was she still leaning on Luke's faith?

"Well, Lord, sir, this Bible says that in you, the fatherless find compassion. Is that really true? And . . . if it is . . . what exactly does it mean?" *Because I was raised fatherless,* she thought but didn't say aloud, as if she could hide her thoughts from the Almighty. *There were plenty of times I could have used some of that compassion.*

She sat very still and listened. She wasn't exactly sure what she was listening for. Luke said he never had a doubt when God was telling him something. He said it might not be audible, but he knew. It sounded different from anything else.

But all Izzy heard were the sounds of Katy Ann stirring from her nap. Soon, she'd be calling out for her mama to come get her. Izzy closed her Bible and hugged it against her chest before tucking it away on her bedside table. She had come to love and revere the Lord God, and she appreciated this wise and holy book, but it wasn't easy for her to understand. She'd never been much of a reader, and reading the King James Version was no walk in the park. Better than Luke's Luther version in High German but still full of words and thoughts she didn't know. Sometimes she just wished God would talk to her in a loud, clear voice so she would know it was unmistakably him.

Her eyes flickered up to the ceiling. Was that okay to say, to think? *If prayer is supposed to be a two-way street, Lord God, then please, please, please . . . make your words clear.*

⌒

The November morning sky was just starting to lighten as Jimmy took the bus into Lancaster the next morning and went straight to state senator Elroy Funk's office. There was a bite to the wind, a smell of snow in the air. He was so early that he had to wait for the receptionist to arrive. She was a small, middle-aged woman, with lips pursed primly.

"Good morning," Jimmy said cheerfully as she unlocked the door to the state senator's office.

"Do you have an appointment?"

"No, I don't. I was just hoping to ask him a quick question."

"Impossible. He has a fully booked day."

"Ah, I see." Not to be fobbed off so easily, Jimmy followed her inside. "It will be very, very quick."

She flicked on the light switch and set her purse on her desk. "Maybe I can help. What's your question?"

"A while back, the state senator gave a horse, a white Arabian, to a fellow out in Stoney Ridge." He watched the woman move with military precision, hanging her coat on a coatrack, yanking a drawer open, dropping in her purse, closing it. "An Amish fellow, like me."

"What's your question?"

Jimmy smiled, but it seemed to have no effect on her. She remained stoic. "Well, you see, the state senator bashed down his fence, and in exchange for fixing the fence, he gave him the horse. I was hoping he might have a bill of sale or some kind of receipt. I can't seem to find any paperwork on the horse."

She crossed her arms, pondering. "That doesn't sound like a tax-paying constituent concern."

"Huh? A what?"

"In my office."

Jimmy spun around at the sound of a man's gruff voice. State senator Elroy Funk, he gathered, had arrived, and was glaring at Jimmy like he knew him, knew exactly why he was standing in his office, and he sure didn't like it. He marched straight to a door to the right, opened it, and disappeared inside. Jimmy looked back at the receptionist.

She shrugged, eyebrows lifted, and said, "You heard him."

Jimmy went to the inner office but stood by the doorjamb.

"Close the door behind you."

Jimmy did as he said and took a few steps inside.

The state senator sat at his desk and glared at Jimmy.

Midfifties, Jimmy guessed. Maybe older. His hair looked like it had been recently colored, his cheeks hung in jowls, and his eyes looked a tad too bloodshot for only eight in the morning. "So Jake King sent you. What does he want now?"

"Pardon?"

"Jake and I had a deal. The horse for the fence. Fair and square."

"Jake said that?"

"Instead he just keeps coming back for more. He thinks he found a pot of honey in me. Just when I think he's gone for good, he dips back in for another scoop. He promised me he wouldn't go to the papers or the police. Well, I'll deny the whole thing."

Jimmy tried not to look as confused as he felt, which was not easy. "Because . . ."

The state senator pounded his fist on the desk. "Because there's no proof that I'd been drinking that night."

"I see," he murmured. And with another glance at Elroy Funk, he thought, *Oh yes, I do see* . . . Jimmy was starting to get a full picture. Clearly, this man was not aware that Jake had passed on. "We were hoping you might have some paperwork on the horse. A bill of sale. A receipt. Anything." If he worded things carefully, it wasn't really a lie. He felt no remorse about the sin of omission. "Jake never was much of a fellow for details."

The state senator narrowed his eyes. "And just why do you need paperwork?"

"We want to try to use the horse as a stud. I just thought it might help if I could trace his lineage."

He scoffed, relaxing a little. "Young feller, you know anything about horses?"

Jimmy shrugged. "Maybe a little."

"Well, I do. I was raised with horses. And one thing I know—a horse needs to earn its keep. That horse ain't worth a plug nickel except to take a pretty picture. Hot blooded, those Arabians. Too spirited. Too hard to handle. Hay burners." He leaned back in his chair.

"Excellent points." Jimmy didn't disagree. "I wonder . . . how'd you end up with the horse in the first place?"

Elroy Funk shot forward on the desk and pointed a finger at Jimmy. "Young fella, you trying to nail something on me? Cuz I'll deny it."

"No, no." Jimmy lifted his hands in mock surrender. "I'm just interested in the horse."

"I won him in a card game that same night I accidentally bumped into Jake King's pasture fence."

"Poker?" Maybe he shouldn't have said that.

Elroy's bushy eyebrows furrowed as he wagged his finger at Jimmy. "I'll deny that too."

"And you don't have any paperwork on him? Nothing at all?"

The state senator looked up at the ceiling and scratched his cheek jowls. "I might have something." He unlocked a drawer and pulled out a metal box. From another drawer, he took a key to unlock the box. In it were all kinds of bits of papers, plus bills—big ones. Jimmy squinted to try to see more, but the state senator noticed and shielded the box from his sight line. He rooted through the papers until he finally found something. "Here. This is all I've got." He handed a folded piece of paper to Jimmy and rose to his feet. "This is the last time Jake asks me for a favor. Is that clear?"

"Yes. Crystal clear. You don't have to worry about Jake

anymore." That was the truth. "Thank you for your time."
He held up the paper. "And for this."

"Tell Jake I don't want to hear from him again. Not ever
again. I'm done. Tell him that he's dipped in the honeypot
for the last time."

"You won't be hearing from Jake again. I promise you
that." Jimmy went out the door, closing it quietly behind
him as he gave the receptionist his most dazzling smile—
yet still, no response. Outside, he opened the slip of paper.
There wasn't much on it, but it did have the official name of
the horse on it: America's Prince.

Next stop was the public library. When Jimmy arrived,
the doors were locked. Snow had started to fall, thick flakes
that stuck on the ground. He had an hour to kill before the
library opened and it was too cold to stay outside, so he
walked a few blocks to City Hall and located the Tax Claim
Bureau that managed property tax. A young woman with
frizzy hair was working the front desk, but her attention
was completely focused on a computer screen. She barely
responded when he said he had a problem with property tax
that needed straightening out. In fact, she seemed annoyed
to be interrupted from . . . what was she doing that took
such attention? Jimmy leaned over the counter. Aha. She
was playing a video game. She glanced up at Jimmy, then
did a double take. She rocketed off her chair, straightened
her skirt, then fussed with her frizzy hair. He beamed, and
whatever reservation she had seemed to dissipate.

"How can I help?"

Relieved he hadn't lost his touch, he kept on smiling. "I'm
not sure what this letter means." He handed Sylvie's registered letter to her. Before she took it, she ran her eyes down

his lanky form. He didn't really want to know what was going through her mind, but whatever it was, she couldn't have been more eager to help. She looked up the history of taxes for Rising Star Farm, printed out a copy for him, and handed it to him, leaning so far over the counter that he nearly sneezed from her heavy perfume.

As he scanned the tax history, his heart dropped to his feet. Jake King hadn't paid property taxes for the last two years.

Jimmy lowered his voice and asked, "Off the record, what might happen if this bill doesn't get paid soon?"

"Rachel. Call me Rachel." She grazed a fingertip along the tax history paper, and he noticed her long fingernails were painted red, like talons. "When the owner defaults and doesn't pay the property tax, then the property will be sold in an upset tax sale. So did you and your, uh, wife, forget to pay the taxes?" Her eyes flicked down to his left hand.

"I'm not married."

She smiled.

Jimmy offered his most charming, boyish smile. "Rachel, is there any way to stop the sale?"

Rachel was leaning so far over the counter between them that Jimmy had to remind himself to keep his eyes up, away from her well-endowed chest with its low-cut blouse.

"There might be a few things we can do." She tucked a lock of hair behind her ear in a coquettish way. "Best option is to pay the amount that's due. Maybe I can make those extra fines"—she waved her hand in the air, like a bird in flight—"go away."

"What if . . . the property owner can't pay it all at once?"

Rachel drummed her painted fingertips along the counter, reminding Jimmy of a clacking crow. Sylvie, being such a bird lover, would find that amusing; he'd have to remember to tell her.

"Four payments can be made in four equal installments, to stop the sale. The first payment has to happen right away, though. As soon as possible." Rachel ran a finger along her lips, as if she was sharing a secret. "But if you need a little more time, I might be able to help," she added with a big exaggerated wink.

Those winks! So many lately. Used to be, Jimmy was the winker.

He thanked Rachel, accepted her business card, smiled when she pointed out she had added her personal phone number on the back. "I'll put this in a safe place," he promised her, holding the little card against his heart as he walked backward to the door.

As soon as the door shut behind him, his smile faded. He used to enjoy those kinds of flirty and harmless interactions with women. Not so much anymore. This last year of defeats—losing Bethany to another man, losing ranch work in Colorado—had taken the wind out of his flirting sails.

On the way to the library, he fretted over Rising Star's property tax bill. He shouldn't be worried. This wasn't his problem. He was getting too involved with Sylvie's financial matters. It really shouldn't matter to him—he was just working as a farmhand for her. It shouldn't matter, but it did. Exactly why, he didn't know—perhaps it was because she seemed so vulnerable, so alone. Or that she wasn't looking to anyone else for help. Perhaps it was nothing more than the dismissive way his mother treated her, like she didn't belong in Stoney Ridge. Whatever the reason, he found himself wanting to do all he could to help Sylvie.

He wondered why Sylvie had ever married Jake King in the first place. Over the last week, he had tried to cobble together bits and pieces of her life without asking her directly, because he sure didn't want her getting any ideas that he was interested in her. No sir. Not after getting warned off by Hank Lapp that she was casting her web around him like a black widow spider. Sylvie's winks, they thoroughly confused him.

With the help of a librarian, Jimmy located the site for an Arabian horse registry on one of the public computers and typed in Prince's full name. He skimmed through pages and pages of pictures, until he saw one that looked just like Sylvie's Prince. He clicked a few more links and came to the names of Prince's sire and dam. More clicks to the sire's link led to a long list of notable progeny.

Jimmy's heart started to pound. *Oh wow. Lord-a-mercy.* "Jackpot."

Sylvie Schrock King was sitting on top of a gold mine and she didn't even know it.

NINE

By midafternoon, after a few hours of steadily falling snow, the ground was covered with an inch of soft white. It was cold, but not too cold, not too windy. A pleasant start to winter, Sylvie thought, as she exercised Prince in the paddock.

Jimmy Fisher came loping up from the road, jumping over the broken rails in the pasture, waving some papers over his head. "Sylvie! You won't believe what I found out today."

Joey was sitting on the top rail of the paddock fence, kicking his feet.

Sylvie pulled the lead line in to bring Prince to her, then walked over to Joey. "What do you suppose he's talking about?"

Joey shrugged.

By the time Sylvie unhooked Prince's halter, Jimmy was ducking under a rail to come join them. Prince's ears went back.

"He still don't like you," Joey said.

Jimmy grinned. "I think he'll like me better after he hears this news. Sylvie, that horse of yours . . . he's worth a mint.

His father is a champion. And his mother has great bloodlines." He handed her the paperwork. "I want to get him registered right off. As soon as he's officially recognized, then we'll be able to charge big stud fees."

"Stud fees?"

"Absolutely. Big ones."

She cocked one eyebrow and thought a moment. "You think the Amish will pay big stud fees? For an Arabian?"

Jimmy took off his hat and ran a hand through his hair. "No. Not the Amish. No way. But the English will. We need to go beyond the Amish, right to the English."

That made her feel unsettled. It wasn't the way things were done back in her church. They avoided overlaps with the English world, tried to remain self-sufficient. "You might have to be in the world but do your best to stay out of it," as the Good Book warned. "The thing is, Jimmy, I'm just thinking about improving the buggy horse."

Jimmy gave her that big smile of his, the one with the dimples in both cheeks. "Sylvie, you got to think big. You don't put a hundred-dollar saddle on a million-dollar horse."

Her face pinched in confusion. "I don't even have a ten-dollar saddle."

A laugh burst out of him. "This horse is meant for bigger things than being a buggy horse. Look, we have to be practical. The Amish are never going to be open to a new horse breed. They like their traditions. But the English . . . an Arabian stud like Prince could go far."

"Seems like the bishop would have something to say about that."

Jimmy lifted his palms in the air. "You're trying to pay your property taxes and keep food on your table. How's that any different from Izzy's yarn shop, with all those tour buses coming through? David's never objected to anyone trying to take care of their families."

"I just don't want to make a decision based on how to make money. Money is the root of all evil. That's in the Good Book."

His dark eyebrows furrowed together, then he shook his head. "Sylvie, I don't mean to frighten you, but you've got to get some income coming in. Fast. Really fast. Otherwise . . ."

"Otherwise what?"

"There's a chance . . . that you might lose the farm."

Surprise sucked the breath right out of her. She stared at Jimmy, afraid to believe him. "Really?" she finally managed. "Did you find something out today?"

"Yes."

She glanced at Joey. He was listening, trying to understand, and his little worried face kept shifting from her to Jimmy back to her. "Honey, would you go fill up that water bucket for Prince?" She waited until the boy was out of hearing distance before she said, "How could that be? How could that possibly be?"

"Jake hasn't paid the property tax for the last two years. There's an upset tax sale planned in about twenty-five days."

"But that's not fair. It's not right! Jake inherited this property. From his grandfather, he told me that himself."

"Well, sure he did, but that doesn't exempt him from paying property taxes. The tax man keeps on coming for his share. Every year."

She stared at him. She felt dumb! How could she have let this happen? She'd had plenty of examples around the farm to prove that Jake ignored things he didn't want to be bothered with. Why hadn't she paid more attention to those inklings, those little hitches in her gut, especially when it came to finances? Probably, she realized, because she didn't know what to do. She'd never owned land, never knew what it would require. And Jake was older than her too. Not so easy to challenge a man his age about his finances. But she should have at least tried to have a conversation about money matters. In a way, she was no better than Jake. An ostrich, with its head in the sand.

"I did find out," Jimmy said, "that there's an option to stop the sale, but it's going to take some money right away."

"What's the option?"

"If you agree to pay what you owe in four equal payments, then the sale can be stopped."

"Oh." It was a complicated "oh."

Jimmy wasn't going to leave it at that. "You have the money to pay those taxes, don't you?"

She kept her eyes fixed on the ground. "Um, not . . . right now." What if she couldn't make that upset tax sale payment? Sylvie felt the worry of that deep in her heart. It made her shaky and she gripped her elbows to keep herself together.

Jimmy let out a thoughtful sigh but not in a defeated way. "I didn't think so. I don't either, otherwise I'd loan it to you." He took off his hat and scratched his head. "I'm going to talk to David and Luke, to see if they might be willing to float you the money."

"Until when?" She tucked her chin to her chest, feeling her eye start its annoying twitching. "I don't really anticipate having much money anytime soon. Not as much as I'll need."

Jimmy's mouth tightened. "It's too soon to worry about that. Maybe you don't have the money right now, and maybe not for a while, but you will. Look, Sylvie, that horse ended up at Rising Star Farm, and lo and behold, he is your rising star." He looked around him and said, almost more to himself than to her, "I better get to work and get this place cleaned up. Folks are going to be coming by to see a champion. They'll keep right on driving if all they see is a junkyard, and I sure wouldn't blame them." He ducked back under the railing and headed toward the barn.

"Where ya going?" Joey called out.

He turned around but kept walking, making tracks in the fresh snow. "I want to get Prince moved into a bigger stall. That horse needs to be sleeping on a bed of goose feathers."

"Goose feathers?" Sylvie said. She shook her head. "I'm starting to think that Edith Lapp's second son is a little bit crazy." She clucked her tongue. "Feathers for a horse. Wonders never cease."

Prince pushed his way forward and nuzzled his nose against Sylvie's back. She smiled and turned toward him to rub his head. "You like the sound of that, don't you, Prince." She should be feeling all worried and tense. After all, she was facing a gigantic problem. But strangely enough, she felt as if a burden had just been lifted, a load had been taken off her shoulders. Somehow, someway, everything was going to work out. Jimmy Fisher had that effect.

It was nearly dusk and the snow kept falling. Jimmy had finished up in the barn when he saw Sylvie and Joey trudge past, wrapped up in winter clothing, holding hands. They didn't notice him watching them as they made their way up the small hill behind the old barn, dragging the lid of the garbage can that covered the chicken food. Now what was she up to?

He ducked behind a tree to watch them, rooted to the spot. Sledding. She was bothering to take the boy sledding on the first snowfall. He heard the boy's squeals of joy as he soared down the little hill, and Sylvie's laughter rang out in peals. He suddenly saw her in an entirely new light. Despite all the worry he knew she must be feeling—a farm that was in truly terrible condition, pregnant maiden mares in the barn, and now a looming property tax bill—she took care to hide it from her boy. What kind of a woman made time to go sledding with her son when she had so many other things to do? It amazed him, to think a woman could be such a tenderhearted mother.

He rolled the large barn door shut, ready to head home, and thought of his own mother, tried to remember her as a younger woman. He racked his memories for some moment of levity, of tenderness with her sons. He tried to imagine his own mother doing something so simple and carefree.

Nope. Nothing came to mind.

If Jimmy hadn't been broke and homeless, he would've put more thought behind returning to Stoney Ridge. Or rather, returning to live with his mother. And Hank. He'd forgotten the bellow of Hank Lapp's regular speaking voice. He'd forgotten how his mother still treated him like he was an eight-year-old boy. He'd forgotten how much his brother Paul had served as a buffer for him. He'd forgotten how Paul, a somewhat passive guy, had shocked everyone and married the one girl their mother had forbidden him to marry. Just a few months after the wedding, Paul moved far away to Canada with his new wife. Far, far away. Jimmy hadn't been paying much attention. Back then, he'd been more focused on himself. *What about now?* he could practically hear his mother's voice ask in her pointed way.

As he hopped the creek, he noticed a horse and buggy pull up the driveway at his mother's house. He froze, wondering if he could veer off before he was seen. Too late. Rosemary Blank waved to him as she climbed out of the buggy. He was trapped, like a pinned butterfly, to another dull dinner with Rosemary. Something that had been happening quite a lot lately.

His mother had a bee in her bonnet about Rosemary—convinced she was "the one" for Jimmy. When he'd first met Rosemary, he'd admit he liked what he saw. Tall, graceful, delicate features. Breathtakingly beautiful. She reminded him of an orchid. But the thing he'd since learned about an orchid was that it's fussy. Surprisingly brittle. You couldn't get too close to it because the petals bruised easily, and it needed just the right indirect sunlight and moderate temperature to be happy. A little bit of water, but not too much. It was very hard to know the right balance of everything, and if you got it wrong—easy to do—an orchid punished you by dying. It took a lot of work to keep an orchid happy. Rosemary Blank was an orchid. He'd told his mother as much, but did she listen? Of course not.

Nothing was ever quite right for Rosemary. She fancied herself a poet, which seemed to Jimmy to be a means to camouflage complaints. Gray clouds, she called sodden skies. Sweet birdsong, she called piercing cacophony. She picked at her food, fussed over small things. And she constantly corrected others—not just nitpicking grammar but also facts in conversation. It made for a very long evening as she tried to correct and improve Hank.

Now . . . Sylvie? That woman, she had plenty of genuine things to grouse about, yet he never heard her complain. When he'd first met her at the Bent N' Dent, he'd noticed those big violet eyes of hers, almost too big for her face. Sure, he'd thought she was pretty to look at, the way you'd notice a rose or a sunflower or a cherry tree in bloom. Nice, pleasing to the eye, forgotten the moment you turned away. But something had changed. Lately, he couldn't stop himself from watching her, noticing little things about her, like the way she made a slight gasp whenever she saw Prince kick up his heels in the paddock. Or how she clapped with delight when Joey threw a snowball at Jimmy and hit him right in the face. Or when she winked at him. He'd become accustomed to those winks and found he liked them.

A rare insight occurred to Jimmy, rare because he knew he was not a man blessed with the gift of an insightful mind: getting to know somebody made them more beautiful, or less.

Rosemary stood waiting for him by the edge of the driveway. With each step he took, dread covered him like an invisible blanket. Another long, drawn-out evening lay ahead.

As she waited for him, hands holding her elbows, feet planted apart like a sailor on a ship, he caught the look on her face and braced himself for some kind of grievance. Was he late again? Had he forgotten something he'd said he would do? He searched his mind for flimsy excuses, though he wasn't quite sure what he'd done wrong, and it dawned on him that this was how he always greeted Rosemary. With a vague sense of guilt, a feeling that he hadn't done enough. A weird déjà vu came over him. Why was that?

Ah yes. This was how he felt around his mother.

⌒

Izzy was glad Fern had offered to watch Katy Ann while she did her errands today, especially after yesterday's weather. It had snowed all day and into the night and made for a slow trip to the Bent N' Dent. She was waiting in an unusually long line at the store—a group of Englishers had come through and were stocking up on spices, and they were animated about something that had happened in the news. Izzy had been listening to their talk, trying to piece it all together, but kept her silence. Then her eye caught the headline of a newspaper in the purse of a woman just ahead of her in line.

She tapped on the woman's shoulder. "May I see your newspaper for a moment?"

The English woman looked surprised, and pleased, and handed Izzy the paper. "Keep it." Then she whispered, "You speak English so well. You don't even have a Penn Dutch accent."

Izzy smiled. "Raised in Ohio."

The woman seemed satisfied with that answer and turned around to her friends.

Izzy read the story under the headline, read it twice, as a mix of violent feelings of outrage swirled in her head. She squeezed her eyes shut.

"That's all we've been talking about this morning too."

Izzy opened her eyes to find the English woman watching her. "It's . . . it's . . ."

The woman lifted her chin. "Unconscionable."

Izzy wasn't sure what that word meant, but if it meant wrong, that sounded about right.

"Something must be done," the English woman said. "The Lord expects us to be his feet and hands to help our fellow man."

Izzy stared at her, stunned.

As soon as she reached Windmill Farm, she unhooked Bob the horse from the buggy traces as fast as she could and led him into his stall. As she ran a hand over each leg to check for stones in his hooves, she saw that her hands were still trembling. *Something must be done. Something must be done.*

Inside the kitchen, she found a note from Fern on the table, letting her know that she and Katy Ann had gone to the group home to take cookies to the girls, and they would be back by four.

The group home.

The fatherless.

"For in you the fatherless find compassion."

Something must be done.

Those phrases kept swirling in Izzy's mind like barn swallows in the rafters. She glanced at the clock. Half past three. Fern's Bible had been left open on the kitchen table, as if she'd been in the middle of reading a passage and was interrupted—Katy Ann awake from her nap, most likely. She bent down to see what Fern was reading and saw it was opened to the book of Isaiah. She ran her hand across the Bible page as though she could absorb the verses through her fingertips, and froze when her eye snagged on a word: "*den Waisen.*" Orphans. Fatherless.

Again that word . . . *fatherless.*

She read the sentence again, slower, to try to understand the German.

"*Verschafft den Waisen ihr Recht.*" Defend the fatherless.

Izzy's heart started pounding. She'd asked. Just yesterday morning, she'd asked. She'd wanted God to make himself clear to her. She didn't doubt the Lord put those words in her mind. Or in front of her in this open Bible.

Defend the fatherless.

Isn't that what David and Amos had done for her? She was fatherless, and they had defended her, helped her get off the streets and into a home. Onto a lighted path that brought a future. And such a wonderful life she now had—beyond anything she could have imagined.

She stared at the words in the Bible until they blurred on the page. Was this the answer to her prayer? *It's not about me, it's about them. Is that what you're saying, Lord?*

No words came down from heaven, but these words kept ringing in her ears: *Something must be done.*

She rose from the chair and went to the window. She saw a light in a window in Luke's shop. She had to talk to him, right now. *Something must be done.*

⌒

Contemplating a nap was the only thing on Luke's mind. He'd been called out for deacon duty last evening with a death message and didn't return home until the wee hours. Teddy Zook's grandfather had passed away unexpectedly, and it hit Teddy hard. His grandfather had taught him all his carpentry skills, had even given him his first tools.

Luke had been a deacon for only a year or so, but he still wasn't accustomed to giving someone a death message.

He'd wished David had accompanied him, because he'd seen how many times he was able to deliver those final words in a soothing manner, full of hope. Not so for Luke. As much as he tried to be soothing, the words usually blurted right out of him.

He closed his eyes for a moment, just a moment, and then a blast of arctic air jolted him awake. Izzy had come into the shop and was peering at him curiously.

"Are you asleep, standing up like a horse?" she asked.

"No!" Yes.

"I was at the Bent N' Dent today and saw this." She handed a newspaper to Luke. "Does that mean what I think it does?"

New York State Passes a Bill to Allow for Abortions Up to Birth, for Any Reason

Luke inhaled a deep breath. "Yes. David and I were talking about this just the other day."

"Luke, how could this happen?"

"Hard for us to understand, but supporters say it's about women's rights."

She started pacing around the room. "It's like that baby found in the gas station restroom last month." She stopped and swiveled around to face him. "I knew girls on the street who had abortions. The medical community . . . they use words that make it sound like . . . like it's just a procedure. Like going to the dentist for a root canal. Like it's just a thing in their uterus, not a person with a soul."

Luke was wide awake now. Izzy didn't talk much about her past and shut him down if he ever asked her questions. When she did bring something up, she had a reason for it. When she did, he listened.

"Those girls I knew, Luke. They suffered." She thumped her chest with her fist. "In their hearts, they suffered."

He wasn't sure how to respond. If he said too much, she would clamp down. "It's certainly a matter for prayer."

"Yes, prayer. And then to put feet to prayer."

He watched his wife as she stared out the window, wondering how much of this had to do with her own frustration at being unable to conceive. How must it feel to be barren? To live in an Amish world that centered on family and children like the hub of a wheel. It wasn't easy for him, a man. Imagine what it was like for her.

Izzy pressed her fingers against her temples, as if her head hurt. "With my woollies, the only time I need to separate a ewe from her lamb is when she's desperate, or fearful, or sick or hungry. A female's instinct is to care for her young. Even among animals. The maternal bond is *that* powerful."

"You're right. Among the animal world, the males have no such sense of responsibility for their young." Too often, Luke thought, among the human world too.

He saw her grip her elbows. "The girls I knew on the street, they were desperate. Not just overwhelmed with having a baby, but really, truly desperate. They had no hope. No future. And living without hope is a terrible, terrible thing."

She spun around to face him. In her eyes was a look of determination that he'd never seen before. "Luke, these women need to know there's another choice. That God has a way out of the darkness, a choice that's good and right."

"I'm not following."

She lifted her chin slightly and crossed her arms against

her chest. "They need to know . . . that we'll take their babies."

Luke stilled. "What does that mean?"

"There's no better place for a child to be raised than on an Amish farm, where children are loved and wanted. Cassidy said that very thing to us. Remember?"

"I do," he said softly. He would never forget that miraculous moment, when the social worker called and asked if they wanted to adopt one-day-old Katy Ann.

"Cassidy had no knowledge of the Amish before she came to us, but after living here awhile, she decided that this was the best place for a child to live. Luke, that was why she wanted us to adopt her baby."

"I'm still not sure what you're getting at."

She rushed toward him and took his hands in hers, her face filled with concern. "Luke . . . think! If Cassidy had been living in New York State last year, she might have made a different decision."

He swayed, the fatigue of a sleepless night and too little to eat cutting into him. He tried to make sense of what she was saying, but his thoughts were slow to catch up.

"Don't you see?" She squeezed his hands. "We need to let other women know that there's a place for their baby in this world. That God has a place for their baby to be raised. To be loved."

He'd never seen his wife like this about a cause, so riled. He'd seen her mad at him, plenty of times, but not about a cause. "Izzy, do you have any idea what you're asking?"

"I do." She nodded solemnly. "We need to let women everywhere know that the Amish of Stoney Ridge will raise their babies. No questions asked."

He stared at her for a long while. His heart skipped a beat. Now he understood. "Um, uh, how would we do that?"

"Maybe . . ." She pointed to the newspaper. "Maybe that. Take out an advertisement."

He had to bite his lip to keep from smiling. His wife was relatively new to the Amish, and although she had adopted many of their ways, even the language, there were aspects of being Amish that were still foreign to her. "Iz, honey, the Amish don't advertise. They like to keep a low profile."

"Oh no," she said, wagging a finger at him. "That's not entirely true. They might like to keep a low profile, but it's not always possible. Like, when God convicts them that it's time to act, or to move to another country. David talks about those critical moments a lot. Just last week, he mentioned the first Amish who came to the New World because of religious persecution. And I've heard plenty of stories about the Amish who went all the way to the Supreme Court to allow their children to be taught in one-room schoolhouses. This is the same kind of thing, Luke. The *same* thing. Somehow, someway, we need to care for these babies. To show the world that every single child is precious to God. Every single one."

He wasn't sure it was the same kind of thing, not to the Amish. Those examples she'd brought up were about protecting their way of life. They didn't interfere with the ways of the world. He watched her as she paced around the room, caught between admiring her convictions and feeling terrified of what this could mean for him as deacon. For Stoney Ridge. This was no small thing she was proposing.

She stopped and pivoted to look at him. "You'll talk to David?"

He nodded. David was levelheaded. He would help Izzy calm down. He glanced at the newspaper headline. Maybe Izzy was right. Maybe none of them should calm down. Not if staying calm and letting things happen as they had always happened meant what it meant.

"Soon?"

"As soon as I can."

"Luke . . . I've never felt God's voice before, the way you've described it. Like someone pushed their fingers into a loaf of rising bread dough. But . . . today, I think I felt it. I can't ignore it." She lifted her hands. "I just can't."

He nodded. "That would be it." And one thing he had learned as deacon, he knew better than to ignore the voice of God.

Sylvie had gone to bed early, exhausted from a busy day, and startled awake around midnight. Her eyes popped open. Was that Prince's whinny? But then there was silence again. It was probably nothing, she told herself and turned over.

She closed her eyes. In the stillness, she thought she heard the faint crunching sound of footsteps on snow, and her eyes opened abruptly. The squeak of a barn door moving on its tracks made her lurch upright, her heart in her throat. Her scalp prickled. A water can—someone dropped a water can. Or kicked one.

She knew she'd never sleep until she checked on Prince. She turned back the quilt and climbed from the bed, wrapping a shawl around herself and wiggling her feet into slippers. She grabbed a flashlight and crept downstairs. Heart pounding, she opened the door. Silence. She peered over the porch railing to look at the new old barn. The door was closed, no light flickered inside.

Her three-legged dog rose from his spot near the warm stove in the kitchen to join her on the porch, tongue lagging. If some stranger was poking around Rising Star Farm, surely the dog would have warned her with a bark. Or maybe she was asking too much of that poor dog?

She listened again but heard nothing. Looked again but saw nothing. Probably a skunk or a raccoon. "Go on to bed," she told the dog and locked the door behind her. Never before had she felt like she needed to lock the door at Rising Star Farm.

A few minutes later, as she lay in bed, she felt suspicion nip at her. Earlier today, when she had run an errand into town with Joey, she'd noticed a drawer in the kitchen left ajar. But maybe she'd forgotten to close it.

Maybe it was just fatigue that was causing her worries to spin out of control. When she was most tired, most over-whelmed by the work, she fretted most, worried most. At midnight, the worries always seemed biggest.

But she just couldn't shake the feeling that something wasn't right.

TEN

Jimmy came up the basement stairs and opened the door that led to the kitchen. Hank was alone, near the sink, pouring a cup of coffee. When he saw Jimmy, he took another cup off the wall hook and filled it with coffee. He took it from Hank appreciatively, cupping his hands around the hot mug. It had snowed a few more inches last night, and the light filled the kitchen with a gray-blue color.

"Hooboy," Jimmy said, "it is cold down there in the basement. I could use an extra quilt or two."

"YOUR MOTHER DON'T WANT YOU TO GET TOO COMFORTABLE."

"Yeah?" Jimmy took a sip of coffee. "Why is that?"

"She don't want you to STAY TOO LONG. She's planning for you to MARRY Rosemary and go live across the CREEK."

"Well, that's not happening. I'm not marrying Rosemary."

"Well, who, then? SYLVIE? Your mother sure won't give her blessing for THAT."

Just at that moment, Edith came into the kitchen carrying a bowl of bread dough from its resting spot on the warm top of the woodstove in the living room. He glanced at his mother, expecting her to snap at Hank, because she must have heard this entire conversation. You'd have to be stone deaf not to hear Hank Lapp. Instead, she raised her eyebrows and pierced him with a startled look. "You are NOT marrying Sylvie Schrock King."

Jimmy took another sip of coffee, telling himself to remain calm. "Not that I'm planning to marry her, but what do you have against Sylvie?"

She pulled the cloth off the bowl and started punching the dough with her fist. "All kinds of things."

"Name one."

Thump, thump, thump. "She's a cowbird." Her retort was swift, as if she'd thought this through and had been expecting such a confrontation.

"She's a *what*?"

"A cowbird. If you don't know, ask her. She seems to like birds."

"I'LL SAY. She keeps encouraging those WOODPECKERS to nest nearby. They're PECKING HOLES in our siding."

Jimmy rolled his eyes. "Hank, woodpeckers have been pecking holes in this house's siding long before Sylvie moved here. That creek draws all kinds of birds. It always has."

"Just ask her," his mother repeated. "Ask her what she knows about cowbirds."

So he did. Later that morning, he accidentally-on-purpose bumped into Sylvie in the tack room as she was getting Prince's harness. "I heard someone mention a bird I've never known. Do you know anything about cowbirds?"

"Cowbirds?" She put her hands on her hips. "Those are the laziest mother birds of all. They don't even bother to build their own nest. They just wait until they find some other poor unsuspecting bird's nest and lay their eggs in it. I've seen them lay their eggs in red-winged blackbirds' nests around the creek. Then they let that worn-out mama bird feed all their hatchlings. Usually the cowbirds' babies are bigger and louder than the other hatchlings. But those poor mama birds don't know that. They think the cowbird is theirs. Meanwhile, the cowbird parents are whistling away in the creek, growing fat and happy, all through springtime." She looked at him curiously. "What makes you ask such a question?" Then her face grew solemn and her mouth puckered in an O. "Your mother told you to ask me about cowbirds, didn't she?"

Cornered, Jimmy stammered a feeble answer. "My mother . . . she isn't the cunning type."

Sylvie gave him a pointed look, and Jimmy quickly recanted. "You're right, she is the type." He shrugged. "She does have a way of vexing people, I'll grant you that."

She tucked her chin for a moment, then looked up. "Why don't you ask your mother why barn swallows are most like the Amish."

Jimmy didn't want to get caught in a war of words between his mother and Sylvie, one he didn't really understand. He knew he'd be the one to lose that war, caught in the crossfire. "Maybe you should just tell me."

"Community. Barn swallows work together to raise their young. Everyone helps out to make sure the baby chicks are being well taken care of." She turned and lifted a foot onto the porch step, then stopped and pivoted. "It takes a flock to raise a barn swallow chick. Remind your mother of *that*."

Jimmy was not completely without self-awareness or

perception, though no one would ever say he was overly blessed with discernment. But even he knew she wasn't talking about birds.

⌒

Luke Schrock had many character flaws, but avoidance was no longer one of them. Or so he'd thought. He'd made a promise to Izzy that he would run her idea to save babies by David, but when it came right down to it, he found excuse after excuse to avoid doing so. Her grand idea seemed too far-fetched, too outlandish, too bold for a Plain church, too everything. But a promise was a promise, and besides, Izzy nagged him every single day to go talk to David. And finally he'd run out of excuses.

As he drove the buggy into the parking lot of the Bent N' Dent, he breathed a sigh of relief that there was no sign of Hank Lapp. It was a rare day when Hank wasn't sitting inside by the stove, playing checkers, or outside on the porch, drinking iced tea. He was fond of Hank, the same way he was fond of creamed onions at Thanksgiving. Once a year was plenty.

David looked up from his desk in the back room when he heard Luke's knock and gave him a warm smile. You'd think by now that Luke would be accustomed to the pleased look on David's face when he saw him, but it always hit him as new, always caught him in the heart. Even when Luke was at his worst, David had always seemed pleased to see him.

"Sit down," David said, pointing to a chair across from his desk. "What's on your mind?"

As Luke eased into the chair, he wondered how many bottoms had polished this chair seat, bringing their problems to the bishop to solve. He'd sat in this very chair dozens and dozens of times, unloading himself on David. He thought he might have Izzy paint a sign for the Bent N' Dent office: Stoney Ridge Counseling Center. "You said you wanted ideas to help the church better prepare for Easter in their hearts."

David's eyebrows lifted in interest. "Got an idea?"

"Actually, it's Izzy's idea." He passed the newspaper to David and waited for his reaction as he skimmed the story about the state of New York passing the Reproductive Health Act. "Remember when we talked about this?"

"I do." David set the newspaper down. "This whole topic heralds a darkness to me, a malevolent blackness."

"New York shares a border with Pennsylvania. You know that if it gets passed there, it won't be long until it spreads here. That's how change has happened in the past."

David nodded. "It's cause to grieve."

"Grieve, yes, and maybe to act. We're meant to be a light in the darkness. To put feet to a prayer." He had borrowed that quote from Izzy and he liked it.

"Go on."

"Izzy told me something I can't get out of my head. If Cassidy had been living in New York State, she might have made a different decision. About Katy Ann."

"Go on."

Luke leaned forward in the chair. "The world is full of girls like Cassidy. Girls and women in desperate situations. They've run out of hope."

"Is this about foster care? I'm all for that. You know that. You're welcome to encourage the church to open their homes again."

"It's more than foster care. But I do want our church to open their homes."

Now David looked completely confused. "So, what are you saying?"

"Izzy suggested that the Amish could provide an alternative to these women." He took a deep breath before he said, "She wants our church to offer to raise these babies, so that women know there's another way."

David leaned back in his chair. "I appreciate the heart of this concern, Luke. I do. But I see only problems."

"Okay, then, let's start there. What problem do you see first?"

"It's not our way. We don't get involved in political problems."

"But we're not. We're just providing an answer to girls and women who need help and hope. Just like the church did in the book of Acts. Caring for those in need."

David ran a hand over his bearded chin, pondering.

"What other problems do you see?"

"It's asking a lot of our families. Most already have six to eight children. Do you really think they would be willing to take in more?"

"Honestly, I don't know. A year or so ago, only a handful of families in the church were willing to foster children. But those who did foster have stayed connected with their foster children, even after the group home reopened. And now the group home is, well, almost like a favorite charity for our church. The girls who live there are invited to frolics and socials, and Fern teaches cooking classes once a week. Izzy teaches the girls how to knit."

"It's one thing to visit once a week. It's another thing to

openly offer a home to an infant. No strings attached. No recourse. No turning back. Like you did with Katy Ann. It's a pretty radical idea."

"All true. But isn't that what God does for us when he adopts us?"

Slowly, David gave a nod. "I can't argue with that."

"And you wanted our church to take Easter seriously."

David rubbed his forehead. "Luke, we're just a speck. The church of Stoney Ridge is just a tiny speck."

"But consider the alternative. Imagine if we saved one baby . . . just one baby. Wouldn't it be worth it?"

David was quiet for a long, long time, with his head tucked down. Luke figured he was praying, so he didn't dare interrupt, didn't move a muscle, didn't cough or clear his throat. He wanted David to get a clear word from God on this.

When David lifted his head, he said, "How would you propose communicating this to the outside world?"

Luke expelled a deep breath. David was getting on board. Or he was close to climbing on board, anyway. "About that . . . I have no idea." He scratched his head. "Izzy suggested taking an advertisement out in the New York newspapers, but I didn't think you'd go for that."

"No. No, that's not an option." David tapped his fingers on his desk. "We need to think it through carefully. Handle each obstacle one by one."

"One by one. That's it. That's what we're trying to do by giving those babies a home. One by one. We can't fix the whole world, but we can do what we can. One by one."

David looked at Luke for a long moment. "I don't mean to discourage you, Luke. What you're proposing—it's what

Christ would want his believers to do. I'm just not quite sure what it looks like for us. How it could happen."

"I'll work on that."

"No. Don't work on that. It's got nothing to do with work, only with prayer. Pray on that, Luke. Storm heaven with prayer over it. I will too. The answer will come."

Jimmy led Prince back into his stall for supper and smiled when he saw Joey slip into the barn to follow along as he did the evening chores. It was becoming a habit, this shadowing by the boy, and Jimmy loved it. They had a little game they played together. Jimmy called it "Did you know?"

Joey always started it off. "Did you know horse's teeth never stop growing?"

"Like a beaver?"

"Yup. Did you know that horses have the biggest eyes of any animal?"

"Hmm," Jimmy said. "They do seem bigger than a whale's eyes, I'll grant you that."

When Joey had run out of the day's newest horse facts, it was Jimmy's turn. "Did you know that a horse's whiskers are sensitive?"

Joey peered at him. "Are yours?"

Jimmy rubbed his chin, feeling the roughness of a five o'clock shadow. "Nope. But for a horse, those whiskers detect what eyes can't see."

Joey rubbed his chin too.

"Here's another one for you. Did you know that a horse's lips are loaded with nerve endings?"

The boy wiggled his lips, pondering that fact.

"Last one for the day. Did you know that a horse's hooves are shock absorbers?"

Joey rocked back and forth on his heels. "So they can take the pounding?"

"Exactly that." This boy, he was a smart one. "How old are you, Joey?"

"Four and a half."

"Is that half year important?"

"Yes."

"How do you know all this stuff?"

"I read. I been reading since I was three."

"No way. There is no possible way you've been reading since you were three years old."

Joey drew himself up like an injured rooster. "Ask Mem if you don't believe me. She's the one who taught me to read. She said a boy with a mind as good as mine needed books to fill it up." He narrowed his eyes at Jimmy. "Can you read?"

"Sure I can. But I didn't start reading when I was three, I'll tell you that much."

"So how old are you?"

"How old do you think?"

"Fifteen. Maybe fifteen and a half."

"Fifteen? Why, I'm a grown man! What makes you think I'm fifteen?"

He cast Jimmy a disdainful glance. "You live in your mom's basement."

"Oh, well, *that* . . ."

"And you don't have your own horse and courting buggy. If you were sixteen, then you'd have your own horse and buggy. Your dad would get it for you on your sixteenth birthday."

"My dad died when I was around your age."

151

"Hank Lapp ain't your daddy?"

"Whoa! No! No, he is most definitely *not* my father. My mother married him just a few years ago."

"I don't have a dad. I had Jake, but he died. And I have a grandpa, but he don't like me. We had to move away from him when he kept calling me by the wrong name."

"What name?"

"He called me Willie Jitmit."

"Willie Jitmit? What kind of name is that?"

"I dunno. Mem said he called me that one time too many. She didn't want me growing up with any name other than Joey." He shrugged. "So that's when we moved here." He tipped his hat back. "You know who this Willie Jitmit is?"

"Never heard of the man." Unless . . . unless it wasn't a man, a person. Williejitmit. Williejitmit. A sigh breathed out of Jimmy.

Illegitimate.

⌒

The next morning, Sylvie was alone in the kitchen when dawn lit the sky. She listened for movement upstairs, signs that Joey was stirring. He'd always been a champion sleeper and sometimes needed a gentle poke or two to get up and get going. Coffee needed making, breakfast needed starting, but for the moment she was lost in the past, an avalanche of memories. She had grown used to the sounds of Joey, but how strange they were to her in those first few weeks. He had cried so much, as if he knew his world had turned upside down, and Sylvie cried right along with him. What was she going to do? She had nowhere to go but home to her father, and that turned out to be the worst place of all.

She went to the window to watch the apricot light bathe the farm before the sun crested the ridge. Behind the farm was darkness; in front of her, a soft light had begun to paint the sky. It seemed as if the whole world was holding its breath. Waiting. This was her favorite sight in all the world, bar none. The promise of a new day.

For the time being, Sylvie felt at peace. Blessed. The house and farm, all was tranquil. The worries of the day seemed years away.

Then the morning stillness was broken by Jimmy, waving cheerfully to her as he headed toward the new old barn to feed the horses. And this, too, was becoming a favorite sight to her. For the last few weeks she'd watched his comings and goings, half amused and half admiring.

She found she could hardly wait for the night to pass, just so that she could catch a glimpse of Jimmy as he crossed the creek and strolled past the house in the morning. It was the way he carried himself, not cocky but sure. She merely gave him a slight wave in return, biting her lip to hide a smile, averting her eyes.

As she watched him head down the path toward the barn, Sylvie regarded him, her hands on her hips. For all the chatter she'd heard about Jimmy Fisher—how he could charm the spots off a leopard, how he was a flirt, and how every woman in church was half in love with him, how his mother made decisions for him—Sylvie had no quarrel with how diligently he worked. He was always coming up with ways to improve Rising Star Farm—how to make a chore easier, or how to organize things in a better way.

Yesterday afternoon, he'd spent hours gathering wood from fallen branches after a windstorm that blew through. He split the wood, creating tidy stacks of hickory and oak kindling on the porch for her to use. It spoke to her heart in a way she couldn't put into words. Wonder crept in. At long last, she had someone alongside her.

It was hard not to grow fond of that man—he was like a ray of sunshine breaking through the gray clouds. He had an easy way about him, always looking on the sunny side of things, always bringing that smile and those sparkling blue eyes along with him. Little wonder that Bethany Schrock had waited so long for him.

Waffles. She would make waffles for Jimmy today, as she knew he was partial to them. Last time she'd made them, she'd never seen a man look so delighted. As if a waffle was a wondrous thing. Making waffles would be a way to thank him for being kind to her. To Joey. How he had the patience for that boy's endless questions as he trailed behind him for most of the day, she didn't know.

She scooped a few tablespoons of coffee into the filter, then a few more because she knew Jimmy liked his coffee strong and black. Strange, the knowledge you collected about a person, without even being aware of it. No, that wasn't entirely true. She was far too aware of Jimmy Fisher.

Be careful, Sylvie, she told herself. *Guard your heart. This one, he's not like Jake.*

Jimmy watched as Sylvie whisked the batter for waffles and set the iron on top of the hot stove. She poured the batter into the greased iron with an expert hand, shut the iron, and thrust it into the oven by its long handles. She flipped the iron over, waited, then opened the iron and dumped the waffle on a waiting platter.

"Care for some coffee?"

"I would," Jimmy said, eyeing the waffle iron. How he loved waffles.

She handed the plate to Joey, then overfilled the iron, spilling batter onto the floor. As she stooped to clean it up before the three-legged dog got to it, she forgot about the waffle in the iron. Jimmy smelled the burned smell in the air and jumped out of his seat to open the iron.

"Never you mind," Jimmy said. "That's just the way I like my waffle. Crispy edges."

"Scorched," Joey said.

"Even better," Jimmy said, drizzling maple syrup over the top of his waffle, watching it run down into the small divots.

As soon as he set the pitcher of maple syrup down, Joey made a grab for it and spilled syrup all over his pants. Automatically Jimmy braced himself, ready for Sylvie to scold, the way his mother would scold if he or his brother spilled something. But Sylvie surprised him yet again. She quietly mopped up the syrup and told Joey to run upstairs to change his clothes. He watched the interaction, amazed. No scolding, no reprimanding, no cross words. Just accepting the mess as part of life with a child. What a woman.

"Sylvie, I've been wondering about this friend of yours, the one who had an Arabian horse."

Still wiping up drops of syrup on the floor, she darted a glance at him. "What about him?"

"I wondered . . ." He studied her with measuring interest, noticing a flush of pink start up her cheeks. It made her look touchingly girlish. "It occurred to me that he might have some advice about Arabians. About how to get the word out about Prince. I thought I might try and talk to him sometime."

She shook her head vigorously. "Absolutely not." Avoiding

his eyes, she sniffed the air curiously. "The waffle!" She bolted to the waffle iron and opened it. Smoke curled up above another charred, blackened waffle.

He watched as she grabbed a fork and removed the waffle, tossing it into the sink.

Moving to stand at her elbow, Jimmy said quietly, "Sylvie, is there some reason I shouldn't talk to this fellow?"

Not meeting his eyes, she scooped more batter into the iron and closed it. The pink flush crept from down her cheeks onto her neck. "I . . ."

"Is he important to you?"

She hesitated. "Does it matter?"

Jimmy shifted and said awkwardly, "I was just trying to help, Sylvie. I didn't mean to stir up anything."

"You don't need anybody's advice. You know plenty about horses." She formed a vague smile while still avoiding his eyes. "Now . . . how about a waffle that doesn't taste like charcoal?"

And with that, she redirected her attention toward Joey as he came back into the kitchen.

Katy Ann was asleep in Luke's arms as he took another sip of coffee at the end of another Sunday's fellowship meal. These were his favorite moments within a month, and it only happened twice. The church set aside their daily pressures of life, their differences amongst themselves, and came together to worship, to renew their faith and commitment to both God and community. He started the Sabbath morning in a low state of mind, discouraged and worn out, like a flashlight with run-down batteries. He ended the day recharged, ready for the work that lay ahead.

As deacon, Luke was privy to the underbelly of his people's lives. This last year had been particularly difficult, one in which he and David had dealt with issues he'd never dreamed were part of the Stoney Ridge church. Things Luke wished he didn't have to know about, because once he knew, he had to confront. That was the deacon's role. David often reminded him that God brought all things to light, all things—good and bad. The power of light had many purposes, David said. To expose, to cleanse, to renew, to promote growth, to inspire.

He swallowed the last of his coffee, ready to go find Izzy and Fern and get back to Windmill Farm, but before he set the mug on the table, Jimmy Fisher plunked down next to him.

"Out cold," Jimmy said, peering over Luke to see Katy Ann's sleeping face. "She sure is a cutie."

"That she is," Luke said in a low voice. "And it's a good thing, because ever since she started walking, she's running us ragged." He'd only talked with Jimmy a few times since he'd returned to Stoney Ridge. He felt a little ill at ease around him, because he knew that Jimmy's indecision—or was it inability?—to get married had caused hurt to his sister Bethany. She had deserved better than a waffling, long-distance boyfriend, who seemed more committed to horses than to her. She thought so too, because she finally gave up on Jimmy and married a good man, one who realized that love came with a commitment.

Still, Luke was Jimmy's deacon, and though he was ready to go home, he could tell there was something on his mind. "So how's it going for you, being home again?"

Jimmy hesitated just a few seconds too long. "Fine, just fine."

Luke shifted on the bench, uncomfortable. The arm that

held Katy Ann was going numb. "I remember when I came back after rehab, it felt pretty uncomfortable."

Jimmy's eyebrows lifted. "Yeah? How so?"

"Everybody remembered the old Luke. Assumed I hadn't changed. Or couldn't change."

He nodded, knowingly. "Does it get better?"

"I'll be honest with you, it took a long time. People don't adjust their thinking easily."

"You're preaching to the choir," Jimmy said with an eye-roll. "Ever tried changing my mother's mind on something? She's like a dog with a bone."

Luke had no doubt. Edith still viewed Luke as a juvenile delinquent. He was convinced that the reason Edith was unusually kind to Izzy was because she pitied her, married to a hapless man. "It's not easy, coming back home again."

"Yeah. Growing up, it can be hard on a man."

Jimmy's words touched a deep spot in Luke. He'd never thought of Jimmy as being particularly profound, but that phrase sounded like something David would say. Growing up *was* hard on a man, especially guys like Jimmy and Luke. Guys who took their own sweet time maturing into men. He breathed in his daughter's sweet and familiar scent. "Worth it, though. Totally worth it."

Had Luke imagined Jimmy's sharp intake of breath? He felt kind of pleased with himself, like he'd provided just the right words of encouragement that Jimmy seemed to need this morning. Words to help him find his way forward, to lean into manhood. He glanced over Katy Ann's small prayer cap and realized Jimmy's gaze was riveted on Sylvie.

LEVEN

Jimmy noticed Sylvie before she noticed him. Today there'd been no sightings of her or Joey at the house. Every so often he would pause, turn toward the house, and search for some sign of her. When she finally emerged from the house and strode across the yard, he was filled with a quiet delight. There was no denying she was a fine figure of a woman. But more than that, there was a sense of purpose to her stride that made him stand at attention. She looked up, saw him, and gave a wave, heading in his direction.

She rarely came looking for him. He was the one who sought her out throughout the day, to ask questions, to find something . . . and often to just connect with her. His heart beat a little faster as she approached him. "Looking for something?" *Someone like me, perhaps?* He wondered if her insides were stirring like his.

But she was intent, not on him, but on something else entirely. She shielded her eyes from the sun as a Cooper's hawk swooped low, letting out a raucous cry before it descended on an unlucky field mouse. As it swept up into the gray sky with its prey in its talons, Sylvie released a mournful breath. "I don't know who to root for in nature. The hawk or the mouse? One has to lose for the other to win."

"That's a result of the fall," Jimmy said, sounding a lot like the new and improved Deacon Luke, even to his own ears. "The survival of the fittest. It wasn't the way God first intended the world to be. And it'll be different in Heaven. The lion and the lamb will lie down together."

She dropped her hand from her forehead to peer at him curiously. "I never heard such a thing."

"It's in the Bible."

"Is that right?" she said softly. "I do like such a thought. I can just imagine the two of them, the lion and the lamb, sitting peacefully together in a meadow. Maybe under a willow tree." She tipped her head. "Think they'll have angel wings, like people?"

"What?"

"That's in the Good Book." The corners of her lips lifted. "Maybe you should listen more in church."

Me? She was the one who was always misquoting it. He wasn't sure if she even knew the Old Testament from the New. He braved a question. "Sylvie, have you ever actually read the Bible?"

Her smile dimmed and her eyes narrowed, ever so slightly. "I heard it read. Lots of times."

"But you never read it for yourself?"

Her eyes fixed on the empty paddock. "Where's Prince?"

"I took him in when I saw the storm clouds gathering. November's full of surprises. Snow one day, rain the next." He waited, then repeated his question. "Have you never read the Bible for yourself?"

"Reading the Bible is best left to the ministers. It's their job to interpret it."

"Who told you that?"

She shifted uncomfortably. "My father."

"Didn't you ever question the bishop?"

She gave him a sly grin. "My father was the bishop." She shook her head and held up a finger. "Not was. Is. He's still living. Loud and strong."

"And he didn't want you reading the Bible?"

"He's the appointed one for the church to know the Bible. To keep the Word safe."

Lord-a-mercy. He knew Sylvie came from a tiny clutch of a church in a very isolated area, and he shouldn't be surprised by that narrow thinking, but he was. "Last Sunday, David made a remark in his sermon that I keep mulling over. He said, 'We know too much and we know too little.'"

"What does that mean?"

"I think he meant that we're all familiar with the Bible, but we don't know it for ourselves." He let that sink in for a while, then added, "What about you, Sylvie? What do you know about God?"

"I know he's up there, looking down on us. Wanting us to do good and be humble and stay out of trouble. Don't lie and don't cheat."

"Lots of rules?"

She lifted her eyes upward. "Oh, plenty of rules."

"Sylvie, what if there's more?"

She gave him a suspicious look. "What do you mean?"

"Like, if we ask for it, God will help us find a way to make Rising Star Farm thrive."

A glimmer of amusement broke through, lighting her

violet eyes, and the corners of her lips lifted in a slight grin. "That's in the Good Book?"

"'Casting all your care upon him, for he careth for you.' 1 Peter 5:7." He leaned closer. "All your care." But he saw the doubt in her eyes. "You haven't heard that verse?"

She went still. "Jimmy, this property is my burden to untangle. It isn't your worry."

But it was. He wasn't sure why he felt such a pull toward it, toward her . . . Something about Sylvie sank into his heart and stayed there. He had appointed himself guardian of Rising Star Farm.

"Here's what I know for sure," she said in a firm tone, moving the conversation onto safer ground. "That garden is going to need plowing." She surveyed the kitchen garden, with its mass of steaming manure dumped in the middle.

"It's on my list."

"But does the list have priorities?"

"Of course."

"Or is it just a long list? Because if that doesn't spread soon, it'll freeze solid."

Hmm. He hadn't considered time-sensitive prioritizing— only whatever shouted most to him to get done. A gust of wind nearly took his hat off. "Looks like it's going to be a doozy of a storm."

As he said it, a roll of thunder resounded, making Sylvie cover her ears. Lately one storm ran into the next. He felt a few sprinkles on his face, then more. Taking her hand, Jimmy rushed her into the barn before the rain came down hard.

They stood just inside the open door, watching bolts of lightning slash the thick clouds.

"It's strange, how you can feel lightning," she whispered, her violet eyes dark. "Like it shakes the sky, long before the thunder rumbles."

Just then, it did rumble. Starting with a growl, building to an earsplitting crack so loud that she shuddered, gripped her elbows. He was standing so close to her that he could smell the scent of lavender in her hair, see the sprinkle of freckles along her nose. He resisted the sudden urge to brush a lock of hair from her forehead, only to feel tempted to put an arm around her, to take away any fear. Something about Sylvie brought out every protective instinct he had, and he hadn't known he had any.

The pound of the rain lessened, the thunder and lightning less dramatic. The intensity of the storm was moving on.

"I'm going to make a run to the house. Joey's napping, and he can sleep through most anything, but I don't want him to worry if he wakes and can't find me."

"Sylvie, hold up a minute." He swallowed, nervous as a schoolboy. "About the other day . . ."

She glanced at him with a question in her eyes.

"I asked you something that I had no business asking."

Her eyebrow lifted. "Which question was that?"

"About that fellow . . . from your past. The one who taught you about Arabians."

She looked away. "I suppose you think I owe you an answer."

He lifted his hands entreatingly. "You owe me nothing, Sylvie." And that was certainly the truth. He'd made more money selling Jake's junk in the last couple of weeks than if she'd paid him wages. He'd tried to share the money with her, but she refused him, telling him it was a "win-win."

She studied him a long, dissecting moment, as if she was trying to decide if she should answer him. Or maybe how to answer him. At last she found words. "He didn't care for me the same way I cared for him."

With that, she bolted back to the house, jumping over puddles like a schoolgirl.

His first thought: *What a fool he is! Whoever he is.* His second thought: *So this is Joey's father?* His third thought: *Hold on. Wait just a minute. Does that mean she still cares for him?*

⌒

Sylvie heard some noises coming from Jake's old barn. Slowly, she tiptoed in, saw the shadows of a man, and ducked behind a trunk. He kept rummaging through things, as if he was searching for something. As the man dipped his head to riffle through an opened trunk, Sylvie tiptoed close, then slammed the lid down on him.

She gasped. "Hank Lapp!"

Hank let out an unmentionable word. "WHAT DID YOU DO THAT FOR?" He rubbed the back of his head.

"I thought you were a thief."

"A THIEF? In this junk heap?"

"Well, what're you doing here?"

He glanced at her sheepishly. Was he embarrassed to have been caught snooping, or guilty of worse? "I'm looking for something."

"In here?"

"Jake let me poke around whenever I wanted."

That was true. Hank would lug off things Jake no longer wanted.

"He always said I was welcome to anything."

"You should've asked me first. I wouldn't have minded. And I wouldn't have hit you on the head, either."

Hank's mouth worked from side to side. "Well, then, next time I'll ask." He plunked his hat back on his head and made for the door.

Strange. Very strange. But then, Hank Lapp was strange.

When Sylvie walked back into the house, she found someone else had been there. On the kitchen table was a brown paper package, wrapped in twine. And a note tucked inside:

So you can find out for yourself.

~Jimmy Fisher

She opened the package to find a leather-bound Bible. It was brand new, with paper-thin pages. She sat down at the table, holding it in her hands, touched beyond words. Fearful too. Her thoughts were all mixed up. She could sense her father's disapproval, how he discouraged anyone from reading it because he was convinced they'd only misinterpret the Word of God. Mess it up, he'd say. Get it all wrong. And that was no small thing. It was a soul-endangering fear.

And yet she could almost hear Jimmy's voice, challenging her to think for herself. Slowly, she opened the book, breathing in deeply of the scent of ink and paper. It amazed her, to think that these words had survived for thousands of years and still had such power and impact on the world. She glanced down at the open page in the book of Deuteronomy. "He found him in a desert land, and in the waste howling wilderness; he led him about, he instructed him, he kept him as the apple of his eye. As an eagle stirreth up her nest, fluttereth over her young, spreadeth abroad her wings, taketh them, beareth them on her wings."

Her lips parted, but no sound came. This image of God as an eagle sent a chill down her spine. Eagles, of all birds, were the greatest protectors and providers for their young.

She sat back in the kitchen chair. That eagle metaphor turned her view of God completely upside down. This was no fierce and wrathful judge, wagging his finger at her like he was scolding the dog. *Bad dog, bad dog.* That image belonged to her father, the bishop.

A jolt ran through her. If the almighty God protected and cared for children in such a way as the eagles, as precious as his own eyes . . . imagine! Just imagine. Joey was no accident, like her father had insisted. This one little verse, it changed everything.

Sylvie felt a burden lift, a slate wiped clean.

After church last Sunday, Jimmy had spoken to Luke about Rising Star Farm's upset tax sale, and Luke took the matter to David. They loaned the money needed to pay the overdue quarterly tax, to postpone the tax sale for a few more months. Jimmy went immediately to the Tax Claim Bureau office to pay it. The same woman was working there and recognized him.

She brightened out of boredom as he approached the counter. "Well, hello there, handsome. 'Member me? I'm Rachel."

"Of course. How could anyone forget you, Rachel?" Jimmy was grateful she'd volunteered her name, because he'd completely forgotten. "I came to pay a quarter bill of the overdue property tax, just like you'd recommended." He handed her the tax bill.

She batted her eyelashes at him before turning to the computer. She typed away on the keyboard for a moment, then she frowned. "But this bill's been paid. One quarter's payment, at least."

"What? When? By whom?"

"Just last week. And it looks like it was paid in cash, so I can't trace it."

Baffling! Jimmy leaned forward on his elbows. "Do you remember any Amish coming in to pay an overdue tax bill?"

"I don't. I'm sorry." She leaned forward and lowered her voice. "But maybe you can help jog my memory."

"Excuse me."

Rachel stiffened. Her boss, Jimmy gathered, stood at the door.

"He can't help jog your memory because you were out sick last week. Or so you said." The woman took a few steps in. "I handled that transaction."

"Can you remember anything about the person who paid it?"

"That's confidential information."

Jimmy held up the overdue tax bill. "But I'm trying to pay it! Not take anything."

She frowned. "I recall he was an older gentleman with a very loud voice."

Oh no. "Did he have wild white hair, sticking out in every direction?"

Rachel snapped her gum, eyes pinned on Jimmy. "Sounds like Christopher Lloyd in *Back to the Future*."

Her boss sighed. "Rachel, the Amish do not go to movies."

She glanced at Jimmy. "If you have the money, do you want to pay that second quarterly installment now?"

For a moment, Jimmy considered the option. It made sense to use the church's money to make another payment. Doing so would postpone the upset tax sale a few more months and allow time for Prince to get working as a stud. But in the long run, it would mean Sylvie would only owe more money. Lord-a-mercy, now she owed one quarter's payment to his mother.

"Thanks, but as long as we have a little time, I think we'll wait," he decided, pushing himself off the counter. He barely remembered saying goodbye to Rachel, he was so preoccupied with why his mother had sent Hank to pay the past-due property tax bill.

That afternoon, he arrived home to find his mother sitting at the kitchen table, sifting through the *Budget*, cutting recipes. Hank was sound asleep on the couch.

Jimmy sat at the table and leaned forward on his elbows, hands clasped together. "David gave me the money to pay off the post-due property tax for Rising Star Farm. But when I went to pay it, turned out that Hank paid it. Last week. The day after I happened to mention to you that an upset tax sale was scheduled."

His mother closed the newspaper in a huff. "David should stop interfering in family matters."

"How is Rising Star Farm's overdue property tax a family matter?"

"That's *my* grandparents' house."

"If this was my great-grandparents' house, a family house like you're saying, why have I never been inside before? Why no family dinners, or shared holidays with Jake?"

"APPARENTLY, THERE WAS A FALLING-OUT."

Edith's smirk faded, replaced by a frown, aimed at Hank, who had woken from his nap. "The past doesn't matter. What matters is the present. And the future."

"How so?" Jimmy asked, clearly skeptical. "I was never clear on what the falling-out was between you and Jake."

"There's never been any falling-out," she said. "There's only some question of ownership."

"A problem with Jake's will?"

Hank joined them at the table. "JAKE NEVER HAD A WILL."

Jimmy glanced at him. "How would you know that?"

"BECAUSE I CAN'T FIND IT."

Edith whacked him with the newspaper.

Jimmy tipped his head. "Holy smoke! Hank, are you the one who's been poking around Sylvie's barns in the night? You're scaring her half to death!"

Hank's sparse eyebrows lifted in surprise, then he looked away, but not before Jimmy saw a look of guilt flit through his eyes. None in his mother's eyes.

"Jimmy," she said, tapping the table with her index finger, "that property is yours. It goes to the youngest male in the family. My grandfather set it all down in his will." She got up and opened a drawer, then handed him some old papers.

"What's this?"

"It's my grandfather's will."

Jimmy tried to read it, but the ink was faded, the words were handwritten, in calligraphy, in High German, and the paper was yellowed and cracking. "This must be hundreds of years old."

"It's old but not that old." Peering over her glasses, she pointed to a paragraph. "Can you read that?"

"I can't."

"Go ahead. Try to read it."

"No. I really can't. I never paid attention to High German in school. And calligraphy only makes it all the more unrecognizable."

"It says that the property carries forward to the youngest male in the family. That's you. Son, you've got to go get that land."

"You can't be serious." Jimmy leaned back in the chair and stared at her. "Do you mean to tell me that you'd kick Sylvie out of her own home?"

"Have you not been listening to me? It's not her home."

"I'm listening, all right." He got to his feet and started pacing. Then he stopped abruptly. "I'm listening, and I'm shocked by your greed."

Her eyes went wide, all innocent. "Greedy? Me?"

"YOUR MOTHER ALWAYS SEES A DIME BEHIND EVERY PENNY."

Edith batted the air at Hank. "I see nothing of the kind. It's all about my grandfather's will. He wanted that property to stay in the family. He was a youngest son, and that's how he wanted it passed down. It went to Jake, and now to you."

"Hold on a minute. You've forgotten about Joey."

"No, I have not."

"Why not? He's Jake's son."

"No, he's not." She pointed a finger at him. "That child is illegitimate. She showed up in Stoney Ridge with that boy in tow. I tried to tell you when I said she was a cowbird! And it was certainly not my grandfather's intention to pass Rising Star Farm to a child out of wedlock. It's rightfully yours."

"But it's not rightfully mine. It's rightfully Joey's."

"Have you found Jake's will? Of course not! That's because he never had one. And that means that *this* will stands."

"Why can't you just be content with what land your grandfather gave you?"

"Because that land is disappearing right before my eyes! The creek has always been the boundary between the two properties and it's practically moved right up to my front door. That woman even has nature working for her."

"And what if I don't agree with you?"

Edith stared him down. "You think about it. This land is your only inheritance, Jimmy, and it's getting squeezed down to a sliver between the road and that creek. You can't see beyond your own nose. You bolt into the day like a racehorse getting released, never looking left or right. Your future rests on that land, son. There's not much else."

"NOTHING ELSE, ACTUALLY."

She frowned. "Thank you for that, Hank."

Jimmy stared out the window at Rising Star Farm. He saw the door to the house open and Sylvie come outside, pick up a shovel, and start shoveling snow off the porch steps.

His mother came up behind him. "Find Jake's will, Jimmy. That will straighten everything out."

"Maybe I will."

He could hardly believe Sylvie had done what his mother claimed: manipulated Jake into a May–September marriage. He didn't know why he felt so protective of Sylvie, but he did. It was a curious feeling for a man who'd only thought about himself most of his life.

TWELVE

The afternoon sun was melting snowdrifts around Rising Star Farm. Sylvie had taken Joey off on an errand, with Prince leading the buggy as if he were pulling royalty. Jimmy thought he'd use the time to search through the old barn and look for more salvageable, salable junk. And maybe find the missing will of Jake King. Surely, a man his age would've thought to create a will. After all, he'd inherited this property from his grandfather—he knew the importance of a will. Surely, he would've created one when he married Sylvie. Jimmy sighed. Probably not.

He'd been working from the center out, filling wheelbarrows full of anything he thought might sell. He opened the flaps of a large box to reveal a metal safety box. As he unlatched the metal box, a waft of cool, musty air met his nose. Inside were thick envelopes, filled with yellowed papers. He had found . . . something legal looking. He sat down and started going through the papers. These belonged to his great-grandfather, and unlike Jake, he seemed to have been extremely well organized.

"What are you hunting for?"

He dropped his find and whirled, feeling illogically guilty. Sylvie and Joey were only a few feet away from him. "You're back." He swallowed. "Back so early."

"We saw a rainbow and Joey wanted to come back and show you."

"But it's gone now." Joey started riffling through the wheelbarrow. "You missed it. It was a double."

"We were worried about you when we couldn't find you. Joey was the one who saw the open door to the old barn." Sylvie looked around. "What are you doing in here?"

Jimmy lifted one corner of his mouth in a grin. "Worried I'd gotten myself worked into a corner?"

"Worried you'd gotten buried in an avalanche of junk."

A swirl of guilt filled him. She trusted him completely.

Joey picked up an old gold miner's pan. "Can I go pan for gold in the creek?"

"You go right ahead," she said. "Let me know if you find any gold."

Joey tore out of the barn, pan in his hand.

"Finding anything of worth?"

He looked at the box of papers as he considered, biting his lip. Then he turned to face her and said soberly, "Sylvie, can I ask you something?"

"Sounds serious."

"I know this is none of my business, but I heard something about you and I wanted to get it straightened out."

"Something about me," she said in a flat tone.

"About you." He cleared his throat. "About Joey." He cleared his throat again. "Did you marry Jake to get this property for Joey?"

She kept her eyes lowered. "Why should it matter to you?"

"I guess . . . I just would rather know your story from you than from hearing it from others."

She smoothed the corners of her cape a little nervously. "People will always tell tall tales, but you don't have to listen."

"Is it gossip if it's true?"

She looked him straight in the eye. "All right then. Yes, I married Jake to protect Joey, to give him a home, a place to grow up, knowing God had a special purpose in mind for him." She folded her arms against her chest, almost defiantly, though he noticed her cheeks were growing pink. "I didn't dupe Jake, if that's what you mean. I was a good wife to him. He knew all about Joey's . . . start to life."

"You being unmarried, you mean?"

"So"—one eyebrow lifted—"you are listening to wagging tongues."

"Hold on. Joey's the one who told me. He said your father called him illegitimate one too many times."

"He said that?"

"He said your father called him Willie Jitmit one time too many. It wasn't hard to figure out what that meant."

"That's true. He sure did." She turned to the door. "This is a conversation that doesn't belong in a stuffy, smelly old barn. I'm going to go check on Joey. If you're still so determined to continue it, I'll be in the kitchen."

Jimmy was in this pretty deep and sure wasn't about to quit now. He left the wheelbarrow to follow her out of the barn and up toward the house. Joey had abandoned panning for gold and was swinging on the tire swing, his favorite place, with the three-legged dog hopping in circles around the tree. Inside the house, Sylvie heated up the morning's coffee. She poured one cup for Jimmy and another for herself, and they sat at the kitchen table, facing each other.

Sylvie held the coffee mug between her hands. "Joey isn't mine. He's my sister's son. When she found out she was having a baby, she told me that she was going away, to take care of things. She kept saying she didn't want this baby. That scared me. I couldn't let her go alone, so I ran away with her. I had to make sure she was going to be all right, that she didn't do anything she'd regret. I found us a room to rent in a lady's house, and work in a little diner, as waitresses. Things were better for a while, and I felt hopeful. One step at a time, you know? But after my sister had the baby, she didn't want anything to do with him. Didn't want to feed him, or change him, or even hold him. There was a fellow at the diner who paid a lot of attention to her, a trucker who stopped in a lot. One morning, I woke up and she was gone. I found a little note that said she was sorry."

"She left her baby? Just like that?"

Sylvie nodded. "She wasn't thinking straight, that's what I finally decided."

This was a story he'd never anticipated. Jimmy was on the edge of his seat, wanting to know more. Wanting to know everything.

"I stayed for a while, hoping she'd come to her senses and return for her baby. But I couldn't afford day care or make rent. Within a few weeks, I knew my sister wasn't coming back. I could just feel that, deep in my bones. I had no choice but to go home. I took the baby with me." She rose from the table and went to look out the window at Joey. "It didn't take me more than one full minute to realize I'd made a mistake. My father wouldn't even look at him. He called him a child

of the devil." She frowned. "No child belongs to the devil."
She glanced at Jimmy. "And he called him plenty of other
names too."

"Do you know who Joey's real father is?"

She lifted one shoulder in a shrug. "All my sister would tell
me was that he was married." She looked back out the window to watch Joey in the tree swing. "Luke and I talked on
the phone now and then. He'd invite me to come to Stoney
Ridge, but I kept hoping things might change at home. But
they didn't. And one day Joey asked me why his Grossdaadi
was so mean to him. That was when I accepted Luke's invita-
tion to come here."

He watched her watching Joey. He admired her for her
steadfastness. For her sense of responsibility for her son . . .
no, not her son. Her nephew. Yet that selfless act had altered
her life, shaped and defined it. He rose from the table and
came up behind her. "Sylvie . . . why did you do it?"

A quiet moment passed. "It would have been impossible
to forsake him." Her voice wavered with emotion.

He could think of a lot of people who would never have
dared to step up to a responsibility like that. Not even for
their own sibling. "Is your sister involved with him at all?"

"No. Not a word in over four years. She's the one who's
missing the blessing."

"So then, I guess Jake did rescue you."

She took a long time to answer, and he couldn't quite dis-
cern what was running through her mind. "That sounds more
like your mother than you." She lifted her chin and looked
at him with defiance. "And I suppose she thinks I'm looking
to be rescued again."

Now it was his turn to take time to respond. Yes, it was

176

exactly what his mother had said. But he didn't want to think about his mother right now. "It's just that . . . you were years apart. It's hard to believe that you were in love with Jake." He wanted to know.

She stiffened. "Who made the rule that a marriage has to be between a man and a woman who are the same age?"

"Come on, Sylvie, you and Jake . . . we're talking decades apart. I mean, it couldn't have been easy." What in the world would they have had to talk about?

She let out a weary sigh. "Is it so hard to believe that Jake was a good husband?"

"Jake never struck me as husband material." He was known as the odd old bachelor! "Ever heard Fern's theory? 'A bachelor is a man who's too fast to be caught or too slow to be worth catching.'"

"So Jake was too slow to be worth catching?"

"Well, yeah. I guess so."

A slow grin spread across her face, all the way to her eyes. "So, then, you must lean toward the type that's too fast to be caught."

Me? Jimmy had never thought of himself in that saying. He'd never really thought of himself as a confirmed bachelor. Just a fellow who hadn't quite made it to the altar yet.

They stood facing each other as if sizing the other up.

She put her hands on her hips. "What exactly is husband material?"

"I guess I don't know." Jimmy paused, then took off his hat and scratched his head. He started feeling his neck heat up. This conversation was getting a little too personal for him and needed redirecting. "Did you formally adopt Joey?"

"No. I never thought I needed to."

"So, then, Jake didn't either?"

"No. Why would it matter? Jake told me once that the farm would go to me, and that Joey could inherit it someday."

Jimmy sighed. "Sylvie, this is like the bloodlines for Prince. There are some things you need to take care of legally. Words, intentions, they're not enough. Can't you see that?"

She turned his question around. "But why? Why is it so important?"

"Because . . . not everybody is as trusting and as good as you are."

She blinked, confused. "What is it you're not telling me?"

"Rising Star Farm is supposed to pass down to the youngest son. If Joey isn't legally Jake's son, that means the next in line has the first right to claim it."

"Who's that?"

He patted his chest, but not in a proud way. Defeated, almost. "Me."

Alone in the kitchen, long after Jimmy had left for home and Joey had been tucked into bed, Sylvie sipped a cup of chamomile tea. She felt unsettled from the conversation with Jimmy Fisher earlier today.

She knew Edith Lapp had stirred the waters, put thoughts and doubts and words in her son's head. Still, she felt startled by the accusation that Jake had rescued her through marriage.

It was true, though she didn't like thinking of it that way. Those familiar pricks of guilt started again, making her squirm in her seat. Reminders, better ignored, that she had maneuvered and coaxed and wormed her way into Jake's life until he lost his heart to her. She liked Jake, and over time, she grew fond of him, but she had never loved him.

Did she want to be rescued again? Did she need to be rescued? She had assumed Rising Star Farm would be her life, hers and Joey's. Obviously, that was a naive dream. She was on the edge of the unknown again, her dream about to crack into pieces around her. The fragile life she'd constructed here felt as if it was about to shatter like spun sugar, all because of a missing piece of paper. Jake's last will and testament.

The smell of fresh varnish smacked Jimmy in the face as he opened the door to Luke's Fix-It Shop. "Holy smoke. You're going to asphyxiate yourself if you don't get some fresh air in here."

Luke looked up. "Good point. I need all the brain cells I've got. Keep that door open, would you?"

Jimmy set a big rock against it to brace it open. He walked inside and saw the sign Luke was varnishing. "Oh wow. It's turned out better than I thought." It was a sign for Rising Star Farm. "That horse looks just like Prince." It was a black silhouette of an Arabian horse in motion, curved nose, sweeping tail. The words *Home of the Flying Horse* were written on top. That was a touch he was proud of that he'd thought to add after Sylvie commissioned it from Izzy. It briefly dawned on him that he should have run the nickname by Sylvie first, but then he dismissed that thought.

Pleased, Luke smiled. "She spent an entire afternoon over at Sylvie's, sketching the horse. Wanted to get his nose just right." He glanced out the door to see Sylvie head down to the yarn shop with Izzy, Joey trailing behind, kicking at old snowdrifts. "What brings you to Windmill Farm?"

"Sylvie needed something from Izzy." Jimmy leaned against the doorframe, crossing his arms against his chest. "So, Luke . . . what exactly is husband material?"

"Huh?"

"What makes a good husband?"

"You're asking me?"

"Yup. You're married. You're a father. So what's made you good at it?"

"Who said I was any good at it?"

Jimmy grinned. "You've got a point there. Maybe I should ask Izzy."

"Why are you asking?"

"The other day I asked Sylvie why she married Jake." He pushed off from the doorframe. "I mean, why Jake, of all men."

Luke stilled his paintbrush. "What did she say?"

"Come to think of it, she never really did answer. She sort of sidestepped it and shot a question back to me." She did that a lot when she didn't want to answer his questions. "So why do you think she married him? I mean, Jake must've been twenty or thirty years older than her."

"Well, yeah. I don't think that mattered to Sylvie. He treated her right."

"Okay, then, that's what I mean. How did he treat her that was so right?"

"I don't know. Ask Sylvie."

Well, Luke was no help. That advice only brought him full circle to where he started.

"Jimmy, why aren't you married?"

Jimmy slapped his palm against his chest. "Me?" His voice rose an octave. "Married! Me?"

"Yes, you. You're not as young as you think you are. Why didn't you marry my sister Bethany when you had a chance? I never really understood it."

Jimmy rubbed his forehead. Luke was younger than him by at least four or five years, and as a boy and teen, he was a pain in the backside. But now, he sure did spout off to offer his opinions. He sure did sound like a deacon. It was a little hard to take him seriously when Jimmy still thought of Luke as the neighborhood villain. "I just needed a little more time."

"My sister got tired of that excuse."

"Excuse? I wouldn't call it an excuse."

"Then why didn't you marry her? You loved her, didn't you?"

Jimmy nodded. "If she'd only been a little more patient . . ."

"Four years is pretty patient."

Jimmy bit his lip. Well, sure, put that way.

"You already lost Bethany. Are you going to lose another girl?"

"Huh? What do you mean?"

"Seems to me that you're falling for Sylvie."

He coughed, then sputtered. "Oh no. No way. I'm not in the market for marriage. No siree. Has Sylvie said something to you?" He felt his collar start tightening up, choking his windpipe. "Maybe I should quit working for her. I sure don't want her getting the wrong idea."

Luke dipped the brush in the varnish pot. "I thought you wanted to work with horses. I thought you were helping her."

"I did. I mean, I do."

"If you aren't there to help Sylvie—"

"I am—"

"If you're just looking after yourself, like you always do, then maybe you should go ahead and quit. Sylvie deserves better than that."

"Well, I . . ." Jimmy scratched his head. This conversation had taken a turn he hadn't expected. He was starting to feel woozy from the strong varnish odor, overheated and slightly nauseated. "Look, I took on a job, that's all. Everybody takes jabs at me about getting married, but I'm not in the market."

"Why not?"

"Because . . . I want to keep my options open."

"That's not it. You're afraid of something."

"Me? Afraid?" Lord-a-mercy, he wasn't afraid of anything. Not after the last four years of breaking wild horses.

"Yeah . . . you. Every time you get close to something that's real, you find a way to botch it up. And then you act like it just wasn't meant to be. That's what you did to my sister."

"Maybe it wasn't meant to be between me and Bethany."

"Maybe it was. Maybe you're just a coward when it comes to commitment."

"That's not it. I just . . . don't want to make a mistake."

Luke scoffed. "If every man worried that he was making a mistake, there'd never be another wedding."

Luke Schrock sure had morphed into a typical Amish deacon, wagging his finger at errant church members. Jimmy rubbed his jaw. "Can't I just have an honest conversation with you?"

"You want me to be honest?" Luke set the brush into the pot. "Okay, then. Jimmy, I see a lot of my old self in you. Selfish to the core. Always looking after your own best interests."

Jimmy slapped a palm against his chest again. "Me?" Selfish?

"Maybe you should quit working for Sylvie. Let her find someone who's worthy of her." He picked up the brush and wiped the drips on the side of the varnish pot. Before he started painting again, he gave Jimmy a very direct appraisal, not a good look. "Besides, you're not exactly Sylvie's type."

"Right." Like Jake King was? And what did that mean, anyway? *How am I not Sylvie's type? What's wrong with me?* This entire conversation had gone south. He was starting to feel drips of sweat trickle down his spine, though a brisk wind was sailing through the open door.

"Look, Jimmy, I'm not trying to badger you into getting married. Maybe you're right. You and Bethany just weren't meant to be. She's very happy with her life."

Jimmy let out a puff of air. That was a relief to hear. He wished that piece of news had been conveyed at the beginning of this sticky conversation. "There. You see? It all worked out the way it was supposed to." He smiled broadly, feeling a little better.

"I see. I see plenty. What I see is this—"

Jimmy braced himself. Another blast was headed his way.

"Your way of thinking is downright immature. Who's been more faithful in her Christian walk than Sylvie? Watching after her sister, then taking care of her baby, even though it's meant that tongues wag. Her own father treated her badly. Same with her boyfriend. The jerk broke things off with her, said he didn't want to raise someone else's child. That's why she moved here, to have a fresh start." He shook his head in disgust. "Fellows like you, they break girls' hearts right and left, without a care."

Without a care? Jimmy cared. That was why he'd come here in the first place today. He did care. Luke made him sound like he was soulless. He started feeling woozy from the varnish again and sat down on the closest stool to the door.

"Jimmy, here's my final thought on the subject."

Like Jimmy had asked. This man doled out as much unasked-for advice as his mother.

"I just wonder if you might be missing something. Someone pretty special."

Oh. That advice—it wasn't what Jimmy had expected.

Luke wasn't finished. "You don't get many second chances in life. Would be a shame if you missed this one." He gave a sly wink before turning around to look for something on his workbench, missing the smile fade on Jimmy's face.

So many winks lately, coming at him from all corners. They nettled Jimmy.

After finishing the last coat of varnish to the sign, Luke took it outside the Fix-It Shop to dry in the sun. He stood back to look at it, thinking it might be Izzy's best sign yet. She was completely self-taught and had an artistic sense about her that was startling. They'd been married a few years now, yet she kept surprising him with hidden talents. Sometimes, he thought she seemed a little surprised too. Like watching a sunset—just when you thought the colors couldn't get any brighter, the sky changed and the colors deepened.

He'd thought Jimmy Fisher had followed him out, but he seemed glued to the stool. Luke might've been a little hard on him, but fellows like Jimmy needed the two-by-four approach. He recognized male obtuseness because he suffered from it himself.

Luke had more important things on his mind than Jimmy's immaturity. He still had no guidance from God on how to get the word out that the church of Stoney Ridge would welcome babies whose mothers couldn't care for them. It still seemed preposterous, overwhelming, and even a little frightening, yet the more he thought about it, the more convicted he felt. Nearly as convicted as Izzy, and she was gung ho. The conundrum lay in figuring out how to go about it. That's what stopped him from moving forward.

A car turned onto Windmill Farm's driveway and he shielded his eyes from the sun to see a flash of red. A fire chief's car. He waited until the car came to a stop and walked to meet it. A man opened the car door and lifted a hand in a wave to Luke. He was a tall, well-built man, fiftyish, with thick dark hair, just starting to show a few streaks of gray.

"Can I help you? Any problem?"

"No. Not at all." He reached a hand out to shake Luke's. "I'm the new fire chief at the Stoney Ridge Fire Station. Transferred over from Lancaster. Name's Juan Miranda. Just wanted to meet the neighbors and let them know we're here to help. I'm always looking for ways to build a better, stronger community. Plus I wanted to extend thanks to the men in your church who are volunteer firefighters."

"Luke Schrock. I'm the deacon for our church. Yes, I'm a volunteer." He noticed Jimmy had finally come outside. "This is Jimmy Fisher. He's a volunteer firefighter too."

"I am?" Jimmy cleared his throat. "I guess I am." He shook the fire chief's hand.

"There's another reason I came by," the chief said. "I

found some damage to the roof at the station. A couple of leaks. I've got the repair money approved, I just can't find any contractors. I called around but they're all booked up. I wondered if any of your men might have some experience fixing roofs. I can get the materials if you can bring the manpower."

"Count on Jimmy and me," Luke said, ignoring the shocked look on Jimmy's face. "We'll be there tomorrow, bright and early." He tried not to grin at the way Jimmy's eyebrows shot up to the top of his forehead. He was guessing that Jimmy had no experience with roofing. But Luke had done a little roofing in his day for English homes, and he could teach him what he needed to know. It wasn't hard work, and the extra cash would come in handy.

Juan Miranda pointed to the sign Luke had just finished varnishing. "Home of The Flying Horse?" He squinted to peer at the painted horse. "Is that an Arabian?"

"Why, yes it is," Jimmy said, pride deepening his voice. "Rising Star Farm boasts the most remarkable Arabian stud in the area."

Luke gave him a sideways glance. Did he really just say "boast"?

"How so?" Juan said. "What makes your Arabian different from any other?"

"Excellent question," Jimmy said. "Conformation, athletic ability, endurance, strength, sheer beauty."

"Speed?"

Jimmy paused, cast a sideways glance in Luke's direction. "You mean, how fast can he go?"

"That's right."

Ever the salesman, Jimmy gave him a huge smile. "You'll

have to come see him for yourself." He stuck out his thumb. "Not far. Just down the road. In fact, I can take you there now."

Juan Miranda hesitated, but he did look interested. "Ah, I'd like nothing better . . . but it'll have to wait for another day. I have to get back to the fire station. See you both tomorrow."

After the fire chief left, Jimmy's smile slipped off his face and he gave Luke a look like he'd lost his mind. "You took on the fire station job without even taking a look at the roof?"

Luke shrugged. "A few leaks here and there. Easy."

"Maybe for you, but I've never worked on a roof before. Even at a barn raising. Heights aren't my thing . . ." He shuddered.

The door to the yarn shop opened and out came Sylvie, heading to the house. Jimmy watched her a second or two longer than he should have.

Luke was studying him, understanding. He put a hand on his shoulder. "Jimmy, my friend. It's time you faced your fears." He gave him a sly wink. "All of them."

THIRTEEN

The following morning, Luke and Jimmy and Teddy Zook set out to work on the Stoney Ridge Fire Station. Luke had tried to sound confident yesterday, but Jimmy's words of warning did bother him and he hadn't slept well. He'd roofed before, but it was a long, long time ago. In the middle of the night, he decided it would behoove everyone to bring Teddy in on the job. Teddy could figure out anything. And then Luke had slept soundly.

Fortunately, the leaks were contained in one corner of the firehouse, making the repair work easy. Luke was still glad he'd brought Teddy along, because Jimmy Fisher stayed firmly on the ground and handed tools or shingles up to them. That guy. Thirty going on thirteen.

They'd finished up the corner, and Teddy was inspecting the entire roof to look for any other missing shingles—which was the way Teddy did everything. Extremely conscientious, unlike Luke and Jimmy, who were packing up to get home— and along came a familiar voice.

"THERE YOU BOYS ARE! I BEEN LOOKING EVERY-WHERE."

Hank Lapp.

Izzy was with him, Katy Ann on her hip. She held up a bag with her free hand. "You forgot lunch. When Hank came looking for you, we thought we'd come too. See what you're up to."

Luke finished rolling up the roofing paper and took Katy Ann from Izzy, kissing the baby on her soft cheek. "What's up, Hank?"

"I need you boys to BUILD ME A BOX," Hank said in his overly loud, clear tones. "Edith wants one for her knitting. Sylvie's BIG FAT CAT keeps slipping into the house and MAKING OFF WITH EDDY'S BALLS OF YARN. It's the darndest thing. Edith wants a box with A HEAVY LID on it."

"You're not supposed to call that cat fat," Jimmy said. "You'll hurt his feelings."

"HUH? SINCE WHEN DO CATS GET HURT FEEL-INGS?"

Jimmy shrugged, grinning.

Teddy climbed down the ladder. "Roof looks good, but I noticed some water damage coming from an old window. I think it'll need to be replaced."

"I'll tell the fire chief," Luke said. "Maybe he'll want us to replace it too."

"HOLD ON. Before you go offering away your time, I NEED THAT BOX FOR EDDY."

"How big a box?" Luke said.

"ABOUT . . ." HANK stretched his hands out. "BIG ENOUGH FOR A BABY."

"A baby-sized box?" Izzy said, eyes wide. "A baby box." Stunned, she turned to Luke. "A baby box. Luke, think. A *baby* box."

A baby box. Luke stilled. A baby box. "Hank! That's it!" He made for the door that led into the fire station.

"HEY! WHAT ABOUT MY BOX?"

Juan Miranda was on the phone, seated at his desk, when Luke knocked on the door. His sharp dark eyes darted from Luke to Izzy, and at last to Katy Ann. He waved them into his office as he wrapped up the phone call. "Sorry about the mess." He took a box off a chair, flicking curious glances in their direction. "Everything okay with the roof?"

"Better than okay," Luke said. "Done. We're just cleaning up now."

"Ah," he said. "As for your pay, I need to put in a request. You'll get a check within a few days."

"That's not why we're here." Luke motioned to Izzy to sit down and handed her the baby. "This is my wife, Izzy. And our daughter, Katy Ann."

Juan Miranda nodded a hello. "What's on your mind?"

"Yesterday you said you're always looking for ways to build a better, stronger community."

"That's true. I'm open to suggestions."

"We . . . Izzy and I . . . we have an idea to help the community, and we're hoping you'll let us try it out at the Stoney Ridge Fire Station."

"You've got my attention."

"I'm sure you've read about the infant that was abandoned at the gas station."

"A month or so ago? Yeah, I remember," he said, his eyes darkening. "Hard to forget."

"We want to make sure that never happens again. Not here. Not anywhere."

"Go on."

"Well, you see, we want to install a baby box at the fire station. And then we want to publicize it, so that women—everywhere—know they have an option. To choose life for their baby."

Juan Miranda leaned back in his chair and rubbed his jaw, more than a little stunned. "I wish it were that simple."

"Maybe it can be."

"The state of Pennsylvania already allows women to drop infants at hospitals or police stations. Any infant under the age of one month. No criminal charges."

"Yes, I've read up on that. But the problem with dropping a baby at a hospital or police station is that a mother still has to interact with someone. The baby box takes that inhibiting factor away. It's worked in Indiana. No infants have been found left for dead since the boxes were installed."

"Even if you could get permission, who will pay for it? Those boxes are climate controlled."

"We would. The Amish, that is. We'll donate the labor and pay for materials." Luke wasn't exactly sure how to pay for it, but he'd figure that part out later. "And you've got a window with water damage. It'll need to be replaced. Maybe instead of a window, we install the baby box."

Juan seemed at a loss for words. Finally, he leaned forward to say, "Do you understand what you're trying to do? What you're up against?"

"We do," Izzy said.

Pleased she spoke up, Luke added, "At least, we think we do."

Juan's gaze shifted from Luke to Izzy. "And then what? Let's say that word gets out there's a baby box in Stoney Ridge. Let's say some babies end up in the box. So CPS steps in and scrambles to find foster families. And they're already overloaded."

Luke lifted a finger in the air. "That part might be easier than you'd think. If a baby is relinquished at this fire station, then families in our church could foster the infant. Maybe eventually adopt the baby. We have families who've been licensed for foster care." He reached out for Izzy's hand. "Like us."

Juan wasn't on board yet. "I hope this doesn't sound insulting, but you people already have big families."

"Enormous families," Jimmy blurted out.

Luke turned to the door. How long had he been standing there?

Jimmy walked into the room and leaned against the wall, like he'd been invited. "Did you know Sadie Smucker is having her tenth? Not just one basketball team but two." When Izzy shot him a look of irritation, he lifted his hands entreatingly. "Joking. Mostly joking."

"But . . . why would you want more children?"

Izzy and Luke and Jimmy looked at each other. Finally Izzy spoke up. "Do you have children?"

"No. Never did. My wife and I, we couldn't have children. She passed on a few years back."

"The Amish cherish their children," Izzy said. "We think the church needs to have an answer for desperate women, those who are having babies all alone and aren't able to care for them. To give them choices—beyond other choices."

192

"Not everybody feels that way," Juan said. "Not in this day and age. There's lots of options out there."

"Not everybody fears God," Izzy said. "That's why we need the baby box."

Juan fixed his gaze on Izzy. "You really think you'd have what it takes to raise another woman's child?"

Izzy smiled. "I already do. This little girl on my lap. Her biological mother was a teenager in the foster care system. We were the foster family for this teenaged mother."

The fire chief peered curiously at Izzy. "You remind me of someone. We haven't met, have we?"

She shook her head and dropped her eyes.

He looked at Katy Ann, and his face softened. He leaned forward and put his elbows on the desk. "Look, I'll be honest with you. I don't think you'll be able to get this approved without a rubber stamp from some government official. And I wish I had a connection for you, but I just don't."

Jimmy Fisher, who had been leaning against the wall, pushed off and took a step forward. "I might just be able to help," he said with a grin.

⌒

There were moments when looking Plain had its advantages. As Jimmy and Luke stepped into Elroy Funk's office, the state senator happened to be talking to his receptionist, caught sight of their tell-tale outfit—black hats, blue shirts, black coats—and his eyebrows shot clean off his forehead. He jabbed his thumb toward his office door and told his receptionist to hold his calls.

Standing behind Jimmy, Luke whispered, "What are we doing here?"

"Elroy owes Jake King a favor or two."

"What? Does he know Jake is dead?"

Jimmy seesawed his hand in the air. "Just let me do the talking."

Jimmy and Luke followed the state senator into his office. Elroy Funk sat down, glaring at Jimmy. "I told you to tell Jake King that I was done. No more favors. I got big problems I'm facing. A liberal millennial just tossed her name in the ring to run against me. A liberal millennial! Sounds like a disease."

"This is different."

"How so?"

"Because . . ." Jimmy's mind searched for something, anything to convince him to listen. "Because *this* might help you get reelected."

The state senator opened his mouth and closed it, opened it and closed it, like a fish out of water. "Sit down," he finally said.

Jimmy and Luke sat facing Elroy. "We want to put a baby box at one of the county fire stations. In Stoney Ridge, in fact." A slight amusement filled Jimmy's eyes. "I think you know it. Close to Jake King's pasture."

Elroy's eyebrows furrowed at that. "What's a baby box?"

Jimmy looked to Luke to explain. "It's a specially designed, climate-controlled box," Luke said, "so that a woman can leave her infant in a safe place and not face any criminal prosecution."

Elroy waved that off with a frown. "Already in place in Pennsylvania. The Safe Haven Law. Mothers can leave their babies at hospitals or at police stations."

"Yes," Luke said, "but those are both intimidating places for young women to leave an infant. Not so at a fire station."

"What's the difference?"

"Fire stations are part of communities. They're viewed as a place to go for help. And the baby box is accessible from the outside, so they can be completely anonymous for a mother. The state of Indiana has implemented baby boxes and they're working. They've had zero abandonments since the baby boxes were put in, and they've had a number of safe surrenders." Luke leaned forward. "Think of those two babies that were abandoned in *your district* in the last couple months. Just think if there'd been a better option for them. A baby box."

Jimmy was impressed, watching Luke speak not only with conviction but with authority. This was not the same Luke Schrock whom he remembered. The neighborhood villain no more.

Elroy tapped a pencil on his desk, thinking. "Seems like the more options there are for women to abandon their babies, the more babies will be abandoned."

"These women are young," Luke said. "Most are teens. They're desperate. If there is no safe place for their baby, then their baby is not safe."

"Could help bring in the conservative vote," Jimmy chimed in, and Elroy's pencil tapping stopped.

"And save babies," Luke said.

The state senator dropped his pencil and pounded his fist on his desk. "Yes! And save babies too!" He stopped pounding. "Hold it. Who's going to pay for these boxes?"

"We will. The Amish will, that is. One box at the Stoney Ridge Fire Station, for now."

The state senator smiled.

"There's something else," Luke said. "It's one thing to

offer a woman a safe surrender. But we want to go even further. You've heard about this Reproductive Health Act in New York? We want to do something about it. And we need your help."

The state senator looked wary. "My wife's been talking nonstop about that. How am I supposed to help?"

"We want people to know that we"—Luke pointed to himself and Jimmy—"the Amish of Stoney Ridge, will raise their babies for them."

Elroy Funk stilled. "Why in the world would you offer such a thing?"

"Because we believe that all human life is sacred. That every child is wanted. That their baby has a purpose and a place in this world." Luke leaned forward. "We need help, though. We need you, with your connections, to speak for us. To get the word out."

The state senator made a phone call to his wife and put her on speakerphone. "Hilda, I got two Amish boys in my office. They want something." He asked Luke to explain the situation to her. After Luke finished, there was silence on the other end.

"And these baby boxes," Hilda said, "they're really trying to address what's going on in New York?"

"Yes," Luke said, "but also in Pennsylvania. You heard about that little baby found in the gas station restroom a couple months back."

"I sure did. Someone's got to put an end to that kind of thing. I keep telling Elroy that very thing. I tell him he's in politics for a reason."

"That she does." He put the speaker on mute and gave Luke and Jimmy a mournful look. "Every single day of my life." He took in a deep breath and unmuted the phone. "So, Hilda, what do you think about what these boys are asking of me?"

"Elroy, do it."

He sighed. "It'll raise a storm."

"Storms can clear the air," Jimmy piped in, trying to be helpful.

Hilda let out a hearty laugh that filled the room. "This country needs a little clean air. Elroy, it's time you do something for your constituents. Just do it."

⌒

Sylvie fussed too long with her appearance before church, and by the time she and Joey arrived, women were already lining up by the barn door, preparing to enter for worship. When Jimmy caught her eye from across the yard and smiled, her heart beat a little harder than it should have. Delight took the edge off Sylvie's fluster.

Then she realized that Edith Lapp was watching them with shrewd eyes, instantly putting Sylvie on her guard. A strange sense of shame covered her. Why did Edith have that effect on her? She had nothing to feel ashamed about. Unless . . . Edith could sense Sylvie's growing dependence on Jimmy. That, she couldn't deny.

Try as she might to ignore her attraction, Sylvie was all too aware of Jimmy, all too conscious of an overwhelming pull toward him. Lately she had trouble looking him in the eye and answering any simple question he put to her, fearful her eye would start its twitching and a blush would redden her cheeks. Her body betrayed her.

After the service, as the women were in the farmhouse

kitchen preparing the fellowship lunch—a simple meal of cold meat, pie, and salads—Sylvie overheard Edith Lapp complain to Fern about a sermon given by Gideon Smucker, one of the ministers. "He doesn't spend enough time preparing. It was far too short."

"Now, Edith," Fern said in her no-nonsense way, "you don't need a lot of words to say important things."

Edith wasn't listening. "And I certainly didn't think it was appropriate for David to encourage the church to provide support for the Baby Box Project."

"Why not?" Sylvie said, without thinking first. "What's wrong with the project? Jesus said, 'Let the little children come unto me.'" That, she knew to be factual, because she'd just read it last night in the Bible given to her by Jimmy.

"That's not what the Lord meant."

"But it is, Edith. That's it exactly. Jesus wants those little children."

Edith gave Sylvie a smug smile. "So that's your justification for raising a love child?"

A strained silence settled around the kitchen. Women stilled in their task, turned to watch, waiting for Sylvie's response.

Oh, Sylvie had plenty to say to Edith but was afraid it would be like shaking a can of soda pop and out would come a torrent of angry words. Once said, they couldn't be unsaid. That was in the Good Book. Or was it? Jimmy had her all confused.

Unaware of the thoughts that circled round Sylvie's head like a bee to a blossom, Fern broke the silence. "Edith, I do believe I hear Hank calling your name. You'd better go find him or he'll leave without you, like he did last time."

Edith huffed and hurried outside.

Fern reached out and squeezed Sylvie's forearm. "Try not to let Edith bother you."

"But it is bothersome, Fern." Birdy, David's wife, had been at the sink, listening to the entire tense exchange. "Seems like this conflict over the creek is only getting worse." She wiped her hands on her apron. "I wonder if David needs to get involved."

The weight in Birdy's words struck Sylvie hard. It was never a good thing to get the bishop involved. She knew plenty about that.

Later that afternoon, Sylvie was in her own kitchen, getting supper on the table for Joey. Peering out the window, across the creek that looked so harmless and pretty but was the source of all kinds of trouble, she saw Rosemary Blank arrive in her buggy. Edith went out to greet her, and then she saw Jimmy walk up to them to take her horse. It looked like Rosemary was going to be staying for a while, because she saw him unhook the horse from its traces and lead it into a small paddock.

So that's why he needed to get home early today. Edith Lapp had picked Jimmy a wife.

Sylvie felt little uncomfortable pricks all over, something she knew to be jealousy. She didn't like it—recognized it as sin. But heaven help her, she felt it all the same.

FOURTEEN

On a wintery Monday morning, as Izzy drove Bob into the parking lot of the Bent N' Dent, she was pleased to see Teddy Zook's buggy. She needed to talk to him about making some new signs for her to paint. She found Teddy in the aisle of bulk goods, filling a bag with Brazil nuts.

"Alice needs 'em for her thyroid," he said, lifting the bag to weigh them on the scale.

"Teddy, I'd like to order a few more signs from you."

"Okay. Just give me the sizes you need and I'll have them for you next Saturday."

Izzy looked for a paper and pencil, but no one was at the register. She was on her way to the back, when she heard Edith Lapp's voice through the open door to David's office. Something in Edith's tone made Izzy stop abruptly, right before knocking.

"This whole baby box is an absurd notion, David. We are meant to be in the world but not of it. You're letting those two drag us right into it. And what kind of experience do they have? None! Luke is a new deacon—and I'm still not sure how in the world that happened—and Izzy is new to the faith."

Outside the door, Izzy backed up, as if she'd been slapped.

"Now hold on a minute," she heard David say. "There have been times when our people have drawn a line in the sand."

"Only when it relates to us. To how our people are being treated. Persecuted. We don't get involved with the ways of the world. That's the way it's always been. 'Pure religion and undefiled before God and the Father is this, To keep himself unspotted from the world.' That's from the book of James, chapter 1, verse 27."

"Edith, you've left out some important words in that verse. 'Pure religion and undefiled before God and the Father is this, To visit the fatherless and widows in their affliction, and to keep himself unspotted from the world.' You can't just pick and choose which parts of the Bible you like."

Izzy heard a huff out of Edith, but no sharp retort.

"These infants," David said gently, "are orphans. They have no protection under the law. What Izzy and Luke are trying to do is to protect little ones, to provide a home for them among our people. And I might add that your own son is part of this effort."

Another long pause. Izzy had a sneaking suspicion that Edith had no idea Jimmy was part of the Baby Box Project, nor that he had played a significant role in it.

"You're missing the point," Edith said, her tone more strident. "Plain People should not interfere with the laws of the land."

"I don't believe the baby box is interfering with laws. It's trying to provide a solution for a desperate mother."

"You're the one who's always preaching about long-term thinking. Have you thought about where this could lead? We'll be overrun with unwanted children."

"I highly doubt that will happen. But why would providing homes for unwanted children be such a bad thing? Look at Teddy and Alice's daughter Chloe. Or Luke and Izzy's little Katy Ann. Or Izzy, for that matter."

"They're different."

"How so?"

"They just are."

"Listen to what you're saying, Edith. You can't believe that. Every child is made in the image of God."

"A leopard can't change its spots. They are who they are. And they're not us."

Izzy had heard enough. In the back of her mind, she'd always wondered if she was truly accepted by others. Edith's sharp words underlined that nagging feeling. She swiveled on her heels and returned to Teddy, still picking through Brazil nuts. "I'll have to double-check those sizes at home and let you know."

"Okay, sure. I'm glad for the business, but why doesn't Luke make the signs for you?"

"Luke tried to make a sign, but all he got was a pile of chips and a handful of splinters. He said he was retiring from carpentry and to give you all my orders."

The big man's cheeks flushed from the praise. "He was probably working against the grain. If you work with the grain, you can shape it into anything you want."

"That's exactly what I was just telling David," Edith said. "That very thing."

Izzy and Teddy both turned to find Edith and David standing just a few feet away. On Edith's face was a look Izzy had seen before, her voice biting and cold, but it was the first time she'd been on the receiving end.

Edith pointed a finger at Izzy. "Those children you think

are going to be dropped in that baby box and raised to become Amish . . . they'll never fit in. Never. They'll spend a lifetime fighting the grain."

"Edith, did you not hear what Teddy said?" David said in his gentle but firm way. "If you work with the grain, you can shape it into anything you want."

"He's talking about children, Edith," Teddy said, as if it wasn't obvious. "And thank God for that, because our little one is wearing us out."

David shot him a bemused grin, which got Teddy chuckling.

Edith sniffed. "I don't see anything funny."

Izzy checked a smile, but just barely.

⌒

Jimmy had trouble puzzling out how his mother and Rosemary Blank had teamed up to disapprove of the Baby Box Project. He thought it was a great idea of Izzy's, and it impressed him to see David stick his neck out for her. But to his mother and Rosemary, it was a dangerous idea that crossed the line for the Plain People, infecting them with worldly ways, virus-like. They felt it was going to divide the church, split it into factions. Those two women spent most of supper last evening agreeing with each other about why they didn't agree with everybody else.

His mother, he understood. But Rosemary, she disappointed Jimmy. He objected to her assumption that Izzy didn't know what it was like to be truly Amish, and that was the reason she'd introduced the Baby Box Project.

"I don't think it has anything to do with whether anybody was born Amish or not," Jimmy said. "Izzy wants to do something to help these women and their babies."

Rosemary remained unconvinced. "I quit trying to figure everything out a long time ago and learned to trust God to work it all out."

Oh, man. How boring. An image of life with Rosemary flashed before his eyes . . . in which he would bring up interesting topics and she would shut them down with a preachy-sounding platitude.

How would Sylvie react to the Baby Box Project? He didn't really know, but he'd like to. The next day, in the barn, he waited until Joey was out of earshot and asked if she'd heard about it.

"Of course I've heard about it," she said. "It's causing a bit of controversy." She glanced past his shoulder to the open barn door, looking straight at his mother's house.

"What's your opinion?"

"I think we're meant to make a difference in the world. And maybe the best of all things we do in this world are for children."

"You know," he said with a smile, "that's just what I thought you'd say."

⁓

Early one morning, Juan Miranda drove to Windmill Farm in his red fire chief car. Izzy was in the yarn shop with Katy Ann and walked outside to see what he wanted. "Last time I was here, I saw a sign for Arabian horses. I've been looking for a sire for some of my mares. Looking for months now, but I just haven't found the one I want. After meeting all of you, I thought I'd check out that horse farm. I've always liked the kind of care the Amish give to their horses. I can't remember the name of the farm, though. I should have written it down."

"Rising Star Farm," Izzy said. "I painted that sign for my friend, Sylvie. She has an Arabian named Prince. The farm is just down the road, turn right, go left, stop at the school-house, turn left, then a sharp right at the third apple tree. You can't miss it."

Juan's eyes filled with confusion. "Well, I'll try to find it some other day."

Oh no . . . no no no. Izzy couldn't let him get away. "It's not far from here, if you'd like me to show you."

"Do you have a car seat for your little girl?"

"No need. Leave your car. We can walk." She pointed up the hill. "We can slip through the orchards and get there quicker than if you drove."

They walked up the hill and through the orchard, snow crunching beneath their feet. As they walked, Juan asked Izzy questions about sign making, and her yarn shop, and Luke's Fix-It Shop, and had questions about Katy Ann. "If I could do it all over again, I would've had a houseful of kids," he said, sounding sincere. "When I was young, I didn't realize how quickly life went by." He shrugged. "Life is full of all kinds of regrets, but missing out on having a kid or two, that's one that really stings me. The older I get, the more I regret it."

As they walked, he asked Izzy more questions about her life among the Amish, intrigued that she had converted. He seemed genuinely interested in her, and not in a weird way. She had a pretty well-developed sixth sense about weird men. It was . . . nice. Juan Miranda was a nice man.

As they came down the hill to Rising Star Farm, Prince greeted them with a loud whinny. He trotted around the paddock, tail high, as if he knew he was at a job interview. Izzy had to smile.

"So that's him," Juan said, admiration in his voice.

"That's him." Izzy wasn't sure what he was looking for in a horse, but it was clear to see that Juan Miranda had found the stud he wanted.

Jimmy thought he'd heard voices through a barn window. He finished fixing the bit on Prince's bridle and wiped his hands on a rag to go outside, but before he could, Izzy popped her head into the barn and called his name.

Jimmy met her in the barn aisle and pointed at the cat asleep on a bale of hale. "Watch that fat cat around Katy Ann. I don't trust him."

"Never mind about the cat," Izzy said, looking like she was about to burst with something to tell him. "Juan Miranda is outside. The fire chief. He's interested in hiring Prince as a sire. Juan said he's got a few Thoroughbred mares and has been looking for an Arabian stud."

"For the fire station?"

"No! For when he retires. He wants to race horses, he said." She started toward the door, waving him on. "Hurry!"

Jimmy followed her outside and saw the look on the fire chief's face as he watched Prince parade around in the paddock. He knew that look on a man. His heart started thumping. This was Prince's first big break. He wondered how much he should ask for a stud fee. Could Jimmy be so bold as to ask for five hundred dollars? Better still, one thousand? Prince had the paperwork to prove he was worth betting on, but he was still unproven. Not until he had a string of winning offspring, then he could command an exorbitant stud fee. But first he had to begin.

All these thoughts ran through his mind, plus more—thoughts like the look of shining approval in Sylvie's eyes when he would tell her he had booked Prince. The gratefulness she would feel when he told her that the overdue property tax on the farm could be paid off. The awesome recognition that he was a hero. All that and more.

"WHAT'S GOING ON?"

Jimmy's heart came to a skidding halt. "Hank, what were you doing in the old barn?"

"LOOKING FOR SOMETHING."

Jimmy frowned. "Does Sylvie know you were prowling around again?"

"SHE'S NOT HERE." Hank pointed to Juan Miranda. "LOOKS LIKE PRINCE CHARMING HAS HIS FIRST CUSTOMER."

A dozen feet away, Izzy waved at Jimmy and mouthed, "Hurry up."

"Hank, you stay here."

"I'VE HAD EXPERIENCE IN THESE MATTERS. DON'T WANT YOU MESSING UP PRINCE'S FIRST CHANCE TO EARN HIS FEED."

Exasperated, Jimmy said, "Then don't say a word. Just smile and agree with everything I say."

"HA! THAT'S WHAT YOUR MOTHER IS ALWAYS TELLING ME."

"I mean it, Hank." He grabbed the old man's thin upper arms and made him look at him with his good eye. "One word and you get sent home."

Hank swatted Jimmy's hand away and said, "DON'T KEEP THE CUSTOMER WAITING."

Prince started whinnying, as if impatient for this opportunity.

Even at rest, the horse was wound tight as a guitar string. His eyes seemed to be everywhere at once, sorting, sifting, weighing, missing nothing. Jimmy straightened his hat, tucked in his shirt, and went to make a sale.

Juan Miranda knew horses. He checked Prince out from teeth to tail to toes, bent down and examined his droppings, rode him bareback in the paddock, exercised him on a lunge line, and spent an extremely long time examining the lineage paperwork. Jimmy kept giving Hank stern warning looks when he butted in. Izzy tried to distract Hank with Katy Ann. Despite Hank, Juan seemed positively besotted with Prince. And Prince was equally taken with him. The horse was nuzzling him as Juan stroked his muzzle.

"I'll pay you five thousand," Juan said, holding out his hand to seal the deal. "Half now, half later, when a healthy foal is born."

That silenced Hank. Jimmy too.

"It's a deal." Jimmy shook Juan's hand. "When would you like to deliver your mare for servicing?"

"Soon. I'm expecting this mare to go into season any day now."

"WAIT FOR A FULL MOON," Hank said. "THAT'S WHAT MY PAPA USED TO SAY."

Oh shoot. Jimmy knew Hank would find a way to louse things up. "Don't listen to him, Juan," he whispered. "Half the time, he doesn't know what he's talking about."

"I DO TOO." Hank batted his hands in the air near Jimmy, shooing a fly. "IT'S A SOLID-GOLD FACT. THAT'S WHY THERE'S ALWAYS A BUMP IN BABIES GETTING BORN NINE MONTHS AFTER A FULL MOON."

Jimmy shook his head. "Hank, that's just folklore."

But Juan didn't seem to mind Hank. In fact, he seemed

amused by the old man. "Folklore or not, there's a lot of science behind the effects of the gravitational pull of the moon on the earth."

Jimmy exchanged a look of disbelief with Izzy. "Even on . . . um . . ." He glanced at Izzy again, embarrassed. ". . . a mare's cycle?"

Juan nodded. "Even that."

Hank did a little jig. There'd be no living with him now.

Sylvie couldn't stop staring at the check for Prince's first stud fee. "I'm not sure we should cash it. Maybe we should frame it." She held it up in the air. "So we always remember this moment."

"Oh no," Jimmy said, taking it from her. "This sweet baby needs to be cashed in. I'm going to the bank first thing tomorrow morning, and then right to the Tax Claim Bureau to pay off another chunk of property tax that you owe."

They were sitting on the house's porch steps, sipping hot cocoa, watching the sunset. It was cold, but not windy. Joey swung on the tire swing, trying to turn circles.

"I'm just sorry I wasn't here for the big moment," Sylvie said. "I leave the house for a short errand, and look at all that happened."

"Just as well. Felt like a crowd gathered as it was, with Hank adding his commentary."

Joey hopped off the tire swing. "Mem, I'm going to go count the chickens."

It was something Jimmy had taught him, to make sure every hen had made it safely into the henhouse and on her roost for the night. Safe and sound.

"Be sure to close the door to the henhouse when you're done counting," she called to Joey, then turned to Jimmy. "There's one thing I've been wanting to bring up to you. Calling Prince the Flying Horse . . . something about it seems a little . . . race-horsey."

"Exactly! The Flying Horse is what hooked Juan Miranda. He saw the caption and couldn't forget it."

She hadn't realized. "It's just that the whole notion of him being a stud for racehorses . . . I'm just not sure it's the right thing to do."

"Sylvie," Jimmy said, "you've got to stop worrying about that. I've got this."

She floundered in messy doubts while he was the king of certainty. "But you haven't spoken to David, have you?"

"No, but I will, if you really want me to. And if there's any problem, then I'll take the blame." He smiled with confidence. "I'm sure he won't object."

She wondered. She reached over to take the check back from Jimmy's hands. "Well, Jimmy Fisher, I am overcome."

"I hope this means you are overcome with delight," he said, teasing in his tone.

She turned her face toward him, regarding him in the darkness, her thoughts and emotions in such a tangle she could not summon a single coherent word and she squeezed her eyes shut. Yes, overcome with delight, with gratitude, with happiness, with a rare sense of security for her and Joey's future. This dream she had just might work, and she thanked God for bringing Jimmy Fisher into her life when he did. Not a moment too soon, it seemed.

She opened her eyes and caught him looking at her, and she felt her neck heat in mild embarrassment. "Jimmy, do you think Rising Star Farm will really be safe?"

"It's sure looking better tonight than it did this morning."

She hugged her knees with a happy sigh. "Why do you suppose this farm is called Rising Star?"

"Funny you should ask. It's probably the only memory I have of my great-grandfather. I was probably around Joey's age. I was sitting right here, and he showed me why he had given the farm its name." He pointed to the night sky.

"The moon?"

"Nope. It's not even a star, but my great-grandfather either didn't know or didn't care." Enclosing her fingers in his, he pointed toward the moon, then dropped it a tiny bit to a bright star. "It's a planet. Venus. It's most visible in the sky just as the moon is rising and also in the morning, as the sun is rising. The light from the sun and the moon can overwhelm it, but for a few minutes each day, it seems like the brightest rising star. My great-grandfather had a little bit of poetry in him for things like that."

The whole world suddenly seemed to have fallen silent. He was so close to her that she could feel his whiskers on her cheeks, his warm breath on her hair. Without daring to look at him, she said, "Jimmy, I have to tell you how much I appreciate—"

Before she could say another word, he cupped her face with his hand, tilting it up, and silenced her with a kiss.

It's strange how many thoughts can go swooping through a person's mind in an instant, as swiftly as swallows in the barn rafters. All at once her mind cast back to her first kiss from Jake. They were sitting on this very porch, not far from where she was sitting right now. She'd not responded then. Jake didn't seem to mind, nor even notice so passionless a kiss.

Her senses swirled with Jimmy's unexpected kiss, but not so much that she drew back from him. She tasted peppermint, and smelled soap from his shaving, and thought his lips were surprisingly soft to the touch. And when he had finished kissing her, gently releasing her, she reached up and wrapped her arms around his neck, pulling him down to kiss him back.

There was a path beaten down now in the yard between Rising Star Farm and Edith's house, including a jump over the creek. Walking home in the dark, Jimmy wasn't sure what had prompted him to do such a thing as to kiss Sylvie. Kiss his employer! What kind of a fool did that? He did. It was a good thing that Joey came running when he did, sure he saw a snake in the henhouse. It was only a stick, but it served its purpose—snapping sense into Jimmy. He never could think too far down the road, about how a momentary impulse might play out.

But then, what kind of a fool would he have been to miss out on *that* kiss?

Heaven help him . . . after that kiss. Jimmy was no novice at kissing, but that kiss from Sylvie sent a jolt clear down his spine.

Tomorrow, he would apologize to her, and promise her that it was a onetime thing, a joyful reaction to Prince's first stud booking, a momentary lapse in judgment on his part.

But what about her part? She had kissed him back. He rubbed his finger across his lips, thinking of how sweet and soft she was. Yup, she had sure kissed him back.

ℱIFTEEN

First came Luke's birthday in mid-December, then Christmas. All that, Izzy had prepared for. But this?! Never.

Izzy couldn't believe what her eyes were seeing. For the last couple of weeks, off and on during the day, she'd felt a little funny, as if she might be coming down with something.

She was over at Jenny's yesterday, helping to bake Christmas cookies. When she passed up drinking coffee, and then declined her favorite dessert, Jenny looked at her curiously. "I think you might be pregnant."

"No no," Izzy said, sure she was wrong.

Jenny went into her bedroom and came out with an unused pregnancy kit. "Mama bought these for me. She said we Amish don't go to the doctor soon enough, so she wanted me to know I was pregnant right away, for vitamins. You know Mama and her vitamins. Take the test home. Try it. If you're not pregnant, then you're not. But if you are . . . ," she gave Izzy's arms a squeeze, "then why waste a minute of not knowing?"

The next morning, after she knew that Fern was outside

hanging laundry with Katy Ann and Luke was down at the Fix-It Shop, she took the test. And waited. And waited.

Then, to her shock, a little pink plus mark emerged. She read the directions again, and there it was, the plus mark. It had happened. It had really happened. Hank Lapp, who was wrong about everything, might have been right about the effect of the full moon on a woman's cycle.

Izzy was going to have a baby! She sat down on the edge of the tub and wept.

Jimmy slathered a piece of bread with butter, sensing something strange in the air, the way it changed right before lightning struck. As his mother poured herself a cup of tea, he could tell she was plotting something.

She sat down in a chair across from him and fixed her glare on him. "Son, it's time you took a bride."

Ah, there it was. The lightning strike. The bee sting. He should have known, should've seen it coming. Things had been too quiet lately, too peaceful. There'd been a shocking lack of henpecking. No long, dull dinners with Rosemary. He'd noticed but thought his mother had been preoccupied with the holidays. Now he realized she'd been preparing for the final assault. Calmly, without acknowledging his mother's high-handed order, he continued to butter the bread.

"You're thirty years old."

"GETTING A FEW GRAY HAIRS, I NOTICED."

Oh joy. Hank had come in the room, eager to chime in.

Jimmy took a bite of bread, chewed slowly, swallowed. "And I suppose you've already picked the girl out for me."

When he looked up, his mother gave him a cool nod.

"Rosemary Blank. She's got a real fine character. She's a lovely girl."

"REAL PRETTY TO LOOK AT."

Rosemary was a fine-looking woman, Jimmy couldn't deny that. But there was a heap of things about her he didn't like. Didn't like at all.

"DID YOU KNOW SHE'S AN ONLY CHILD?" Hank sat down at the table and reached over to take one slice of Jimmy's bread.

"Why should that matter?"

"She'll inherit EVERYTHING. You won't have to WORK another day in your life. You can spend your DAYS with me, PLAYING CHECKERS at the Bent N' Dent."

Jimmy practically choked on a bite of bread. "Thanks, both of you. But I'll choose my own bride in my own time."

His mother slapped her palms on the table. "Son, it's time."

"PAST TIME, IF YOU ASK ME."

Forgotten memories floated through Jimmy's mind. The reason he'd left for Colorado in the first place was because his mother had badgered him, night after night. She thought he could do better than Bethany Schrock.

Jimmy had accommodated his mother for as long as he could remember, intervening in the past when she'd had problems with others, smoothing things out, averting quarrels on her behalf. He just couldn't do it any longer.

He eyed the kitchen window, looked across the creek to the house at Rising Star Farm. To the buttery glow emanating from the kitchen window. Sylvie's warm kitchen. Her warm heart. She even forgave him for the bold kiss he'd given her, told him not to give it another thought. But he had. Plenty of thoughts.

Jimmy sprang to his feet, eager to toss off the weight he felt whenever his mother started in on him. He walked to the door and spun around. "You know, you're right. I think it is time I marry."

Thunder shook the sky, or maybe it just seemed that way to Jimmy as he marched over to Rising Star Farm and rapped on the front door. The three-legged dog began to howl and yip.

When Sylvie opened the door, clutching a bowl of new peas, he stood stone still, willing the flutter in his belly to settle. Only it didn't.

"Jimmy, are you all right? You look a little . . . pale. Can I get you something? A glass of water? Or maybe a piece of pie? I just made an apple snitz pie. Shall I get you a piece?"

He looked down into her eyes—eyes as violet blue as a pansy—and it struck him that she was one of the kindest, finest persons he'd ever met. Courage mustered in his heart. Suddenly the words blurted out, "Sylvie, how'd you like to marry me?"

That's what he said. What he thought was: *And help me get my mother off my back for good.*

Sylvie looked shocked by his proposal. Truth be told, he was surprised by his own words. He rushed on before she could refuse, before he could think twice about what he was suggesting. "We'd be a good team, a great team. You love horses, I love horses. We both feel a responsibility to preserve Rising Star Farm. To make something of Prince. To build something for the future. For Joey's sake as well as ours."

She met his eyes and gave him a nervous half smile. "You ought not to tease so much, Jimmy Fisher. I'm liable to say yes."

"Not teasing. I mean it. Let's get married."

216

"I . . . I . . . ," she stammered. "I don't know what to say. This is all . . . out of the blue."

"Sometimes it's good not to overthink things." He glanced at his mother's house, and the sight of it emboldened him. He turned back to her, a determined man. "Sylvie, I know it seems sudden, but I'd make sure that you and Joey would never want for anything again. Not shelter. Not food. Not clothing." He grinned. "And I'd see to always having plenty of sugar for those hummingbirds."

She appeared stunned. And then she winked.

Sylvie had to sit down before her knees gave way like jelly. She went into the kitchen and sat at the table, head swimming with confusion. What in the world had prompted such an unexpected proposal? But Jimmy was a man who was constantly surprising her.

He entered the kitchen and slipped into a chair across from her. "I'm serious, Sylvie. I want us to get married."

She met his eyes. Trouble was, that only added to her confusion. The vivid blue of those eyes, the dark eyebrows that knit together and framed his eyes. The wide set of his shoulders, the cleft in his chin, his thick, brown, wavy hair. All together, his good looks wove quite a spell on her.

"Look, you wouldn't have to pay me if we got married."

Well, she wasn't paying him to begin with. Whatever money he was able to get from the junk he sold, she'd insisted he keep as wages. Totally worth it, to both of them. He was making a significant dent in the packrat clutter of Rising Star Farm, and she didn't care what he pocketed from all that junk.

"Joey needs a father. He and I, we have an understanding."

That was true. He'd won Joey over, and that boy was no pushover. Joey adored Jimmy, followed him everywhere. Walked like him, talked like him. He'd even asked for cowboy boots for Christmas.

Jimmy's smile had completely vanished from his face, and he'd turned solemn as a Sunday minister. "We've worked together every day for months now. You've talked with me every day, you've seen how I treat you and your boy. Your horse too. What more do you need to know?"

Jimmy made an appealing case.

He reached out and covered her hands with his. "It boils down to this, Sylvie. You need me and I . . . I need you." He kept his gaze locked on her face. "This could work, for both of us."

So he *was* in need of something. But what? He already had a legal right to Rising Star Farm. What else did he need her for? Why had he come to her door, blurting out a marriage proposal that sounded more like a business proposition?

He was waiting for her answer, shifting uneasily in his chair, but her throat felt too tight to speak. Something about him seemed markedly different and he looked touchingly unsure of her. He released the hold he had on her hands and dropped his arms to the side of his chair, though he continued to study her, every angle of his face taut and tense. "I'll understand if you tell me to leave and not come back."

She didn't want that. No, no, she definitely did not want that. Jimmy had been a wonderful help to her these last two months, in more ways than she could have imagined. She felt afraid to accept him—and afraid not to.

A bit more time passed and her thoughts took a dangerous turn. What if . . . ?

She had never been an impulsive person. Never. She'd always been sensible, levelheaded. And yet, here she sat, pondering marriage to this man. A man she hardly knew, though in a strange way, felt she knew him well. Even more than that, she trusted him. He'd been truthful about his right to inherit Rising Star Farm. Such honesty spoke volumes to her.

But did she *love* him? She felt a powerful attraction to him, but was that love? Could it be felt so early? She didn't know. How could she? She'd had no real experience with love, only with practicality.

What if . . . ?

There was something between her and Jimmy, she couldn't deny that. Moments that felt like something was blooming between them. Maybe that's how true love began, like a spark that started with friendship and mutual respect. But he'd never mentioned a word of love in this proposal. She'd already had one loveless marriage. Did she want another?

And then there was his mother. Sylvie couldn't imagine what it would be like to have Edith Lapp as a mother-in-law.

Yes, she could. It would be awful.

Was Sylvie about to jump from the frying pan into the fire, like the Good Book warned?

Edith wanted this land, no matter what it cost her. Marrying Jimmy might be Sylvie's best chance to protect it for Joey. After all, that was the reason she'd married Jake. If Edith wanted this land so badly for her son, then she could have it, but Sylvie came along with it. Was that so wrong?

Maybe she *was* a terrible person, just like her father always told her.

What if . . . ?

Something indefinable filled her, a strange yearning she hadn't experienced for a very, very long time. It felt good to be wanted again. To be needed.

She kept her eyes lowered, knowing that her tic was acting up. She kept her voice light, as confident sounding as she could feel when the truth was her stomach was pitching and rolling. "I think getting married might be a real good idea." She glanced up to see his reaction.

"Yeah?" His face brightened, and he gave her his best beaming smile, both dimples deepening, eyes twinkling. "Really?"

"But I think we should do it soon, rather than wait until next fall."

"Soon?" Slowly, the smile disappeared. He swallowed, shifted self-consciously in the chair. "How soon . . . is soon?"

"Just as soon as possible." She felt a flicker of triumph. She grabbed her bonnet off the peg and opened the door. "Joey is over at Windmill Farm. Now's the perfect time to tell your mother our news."

By the time they crossed the creek, Jimmy's confidence began to wane.

Once in the house, he was shaking in his boots. Thankfully, Hank had left for the Bent N' Dent, so they only had his mother to tell.

Lord-a-mercy. What had Jimmy just gotten himself into? If ever there was a moment when he wished he could turn back the clock, it was now. Why had he agreed so readily that *now* was the time to tell his mother they were getting married? What was the hurry? It was one thing to get engaged, another thing entirely to let others know about it. He should have suggested Sylvie take some time to think this all over before giving an answer, to pray about it. Yes, definitely, to pray about it.

He had no one to blame but himself. He had pressured Sylvie into an answer. That was his first mistake. But this was the second one.

"What's wrong?" Edith asked, looking from Jimmy to Sylvie and back to Jimmy.

Jimmy coughed. He didn't feel well. "It's stuffy in here."

Edith looked around the room, as if she could see the stuffy air. "You think so?"

He nodded, tugging at the collar of his shirt. His pulse leaped over the lump in his throat.

"Maybe you're coming down with something." She reached out to touch his forehead and he stepped back.

"No, no. I'm not sick."

"Well, then, what's on your mind?"

"Um, there's some news . . . um . . . we are . . . um . . . ." He had half a mind to call the whole thing off, to pause, step back from the cliff . . . but then he looked at Sylvie's beautiful violet eyes, shining up at him with encouragement, and he felt a spurt of renewed courage. "Sylvie and I . . . we're getting married."

A thick silence descended. Then . . . *kaboom!*

"You're getting *married*? To *that* . . . ?" Edith's gaze swept Sylvie up and down, and right out the room.

To that *what*? Jimmy could only guess what word she had in mind. Her look said it all. "Yes. You heard me."

"Oh no you're not."

"Yes, we are."

"You'll change your mind when you hear the truth about that boy. That's not Jake's son. And she wasn't married before Jake, far as anybody knows."

"Sylvie told me all about Joey."

"Oh, I heard that tale about her sister. I don't believe it. You shouldn't either."

Jimmy wrapped his arm around Sylvie's shoulder and pulled her close in a defiant move, shielding her from his mother's verbal arrows.

Edith glared at Sylvie and waved a finger in her face. "I suppose this was your idea."

"Jimmy asked me to marry him." Sylvie didn't volunteer anything more.

"You knew he was courting Rosemary. You used your"—she winked and winked dramatically to make her point—"feminine wiles to turn my boy's head."

Jimmy saw Sylvie drop her chin, as if shamed. He couldn't let her down. He just couldn't. "Hardly a boy, Mom. And I never was courting Rosemary. You were doing the courting, not me." He and his mother stared at each other for a long, long time.

Bravely, Sylvie broke the silence. "Edith, I hope, in time, you'll come to accept me as your daughter-in-law, and Joey as your grandson."

His mother looked like she was about to choke. "We'll see what the bishop has to say about this."

In a calm voice, Sylvie said, "Jimmy can go talk to him now."

He gasped, tried to smile, to breathe normally, tried to will his heart to slow down its pounding. He wondered what a heart attack felt like, and if he was on the verge of one.

Sweating profusely, Jimmy drove over to the Bent N' Dent to talk to David. He went as slow as a horse could possibly go, to the point where the horse kept trying to stop and eat grass along the side of the road. Jimmy let him. When he finally arrived at the store, he was so distracted that he'd forgotten Hank had gone to the store to play checkers. He tried to slip out unnoticed, but luck wasn't with him today.

"JIMMY! COME ON IN. David's gone out of town. SOMEBODY'S FUNERAL."

Oh, that was a huge relief. That meant he wouldn't be back for a few more days, which suited Jimmy just fine. He needed time to think this marriage idea through. He needed a lot of time. After all, he and Sylvie, they were practically strangers.

"SO, I hear you're the FASTEST PROPOSER IN TOWN." He lifted his hands in the air, like they were guns, pretended to shoot them, blew on his fingers, then returned them to the holster.

Jimmy stopped. "How do you know that?"

"YOUR MOTHER JUST CALLED THE STORE."

His mother had tried to call David, ahead of him? *Lord-a-mercy.*

"SON, WHAT WERE YOU THINKING?"

Hank was so seldom right about anything, but Jimmy had to acknowledge that he was right about this. He'd proposed too quickly.

After Luke picked up the mail, he stopped in the phone shanty to see if there were any messages. There was one from Edith Lapp, insisting that he drop everything and come to her house. Right away. David was out of town and she needed help—that's the only reason she was calling Luke. She left all that in the message.

Luke found Izzy out by the clothesline, taking down the day's dry laundry. More frozen than dry, in this cold weather. When he told Izzy about Edith's message, her first response was, "I wonder if something's finally happening between Jimmy and Sylvie."

"Like, she fires him?"

"Fires him? No." She looked at him as if he might be slow-witted. "More like . . . he wants to marry her."

"Marry her? Not a chance." Too fast, too soon. He knew Jimmy.

"Why else would Edith call in the ministers? Jimmy is crazy about Sylvie. Haven't you seen how he can't take his eyes off her?"

Yes, Luke had noticed. "But surely Sylvie doesn't feel the same way."

"Surely she does."

"Why Jimmy Fisher? Of all men, why does it have to be him?"

Izzy grinned. "Every saint has a past. Every sinner has a future."

"But what if he does to Sylvie what he did to Bethany? She's had enough trouble."

Izzy folded a towel and dropped it in the basket. "Now that's the pot calling the kettle black. What if I'd said the same thing about you?"

224

That was a hard point to argue with. "I'm glad you didn't, Isabella."

She smiled at him from behind a white sheet, and he was struck again by her beauty. It was happening a lot to him lately—being struck by his wife's stunning looks. Her dark eyes contrasted strikingly with her creamy skin, almost glowing.

"What?" she asked coyly.

"Just thinking how glad I am you married me."

"Your birthday is coming up. Want anything special?"

He leaned over the clothesline to give her a kiss. First one, then another. "Just time spent with you. That's all any man could ask for."

Fifteen minutes later, Luke stood in front of Edith Lapp's door. He could feel his heart pounding, as if he was guilty of something. That was ridiculous, he knew, but Edith had a way of making him feel like he was still thirteen and had just done something wrong.

"Luke!"

He turned to see Sylvie wave to him as she and Joey jumped across the creek. When she was closer, she asked, "What are you doing here?"

"Edith asked me to come over. Right away, she said. David's out of town, so I'm her only option."

Sylvie frowned. "She asked me to come too."

Joey tugged on her hand. "Can I stay outside? I want to make a pile of snowballs to throw at Jimmy."

Sylvie nodded, and Luke wished he could join Joey.

At that moment, Edith opened the door with a cat-that-swallowed-the-canary smile. It looked all wrong on her.

Jimmy slowed the horse as the buggy climbed the slight incline to his mother's house. He needed to get over to Rising Star Farm to feed the animals soon, but he was in no hurry to jump the creek. First time he'd ever felt a reluctance to see Sylvie.

What had he done? What had he *done*!? He was an expert at avoiding responsibility. How could he possibly be expected to be someone's husband? Be a father to a little boy? What on earth had made him think he was ready to make the giant leap from where he was to—

"Jimmy!" His mother opened the door and shouted out to him. "Son, company's here."

He climbed out of the buggy and rubbed his face, tucked in his shirt. Something went whizzing by him, but he was too preoccupied to notice what it was. When he opened the door to the kitchen, he was shocked to see Luke . . . and Sylvie. Both. Staring at him with a curious look on their faces. "What's going on?"

"You tell me," Luke said. "Your mother said you had something you wanted to say."

He glanced at his mother, who looked at him with wide, innocent eyes.

"Are you all right?" Sylvie asked.

"Yes," he grunted. "Fine. I'm fine." But he wasn't. He took off his hat and wiped the perspiration from his brow, heaved a deep breath.

Sylvie's eyes were full of concern. "Are you sure you're all right? You look kind of . . . sweaty."

He took off his coat. His clammy palms moistened his hair slightly as he pushed it back from his face with both hands. "Doesn't it seem hot in here to you?"

"No, not really," Luke said, annoyed. "Now, why am I here?"

"Jimmy has something to tell you," Edith said, a smugness to her voice. "Only because David is out of town. Go ahead, son."

Oh man. He kept his eyes glued to the linoleum floor. He wasn't ready to talk, not yet. Once the engagement was announced to Luke—the deacon, Sylvie's cousin—there was no turning back. "It just seems stiflingly hot in here." Or maybe he *was* coming down with something.

"You just need a glass of water." Sylvie's soft voice had a tremble in it.

His mother cooed, "Mm-hmm."

What he needed was fresh air. He bolted to the front door, opened it wide, held on to the jamb with both hands as he forced the cold air into his constricted lungs. Maybe his lungs were bursting. He'd read of such a thing happening to a man . . . though now that he thought about it, the man was scuba diving, eighty feet under the surface of the sea. But Jimmy had a sense of how that man might have felt, just before he combusted.

While his mother got him a glass of water, Jimmy wondered if he might throw up. He dropped his head, tried to breathe like a normal person. In with the good air, out with the bad. Sylvie's gentle voice startled him. He straightened and turned to find her standing close.

"Do you want to sit down for a few minutes?"

"Uh, no. I need the fresh air."

Sylvie handed him the glass of water and he drank it straight down. "Thanks." He couldn't look her in the eyes.

She leaned close to whisper in his ear. "Jimmy, I thought you said you were sure about getting married."

His stomach clenched slightly. "Of course . . . I'm sure."
Mostly sure.

"You don't look very sure."

How could he tell her he had doubts? That he was riddled
with them? Paralyzed by them.

"Look," Luke said, walking toward them, "maybe I should
come back another time. Or maybe I'll just send David when
he gets back."

Before Jimmy could answer, Luke pushed past him through
the open door.

"What? No, we—" Jimmy's eyes darted to Sylvie's and
she fell immediately silent.

"Another day," Luke called over his shoulder without looking back.

Jimmy's face turned a deeper red and then went to no
color at all. Finally, he said, "I'm sorry, Sylvie."

And with that, a snowball came out of nowhere and hit
him in the face.

Sixteen

ylvie's thoughts were in a jumbled mess. Disgusted with Jimmy, she had left him practically whimpering at his mother's house. The next day, she cleaned up the breakfast dishes and took Joey straight over the hill to Windmill Farm, all in an attempt to avoid Jimmy. It wasn't difficult, as he was skirting around the edges of Rising Star Farm, doing his best to avoid her.

The wind, raw and cold, twisted Sylvie's skirts around her legs, and she nearly stumbled twice on icy patches. She stopped first at the Fix-It Shop, to ask Luke if Joey could watch him work for a little while.

"Sure, of course," Luke said. "Izzy and Jenny are up at the house, making something on the stove. Take all the time you need." He gestured to his workbench, where a row of flashlights was laid out. "Joey can help me fix these broken flashlights for my brother, Sam. He's been after me to fix these for a week."

Joey picked one up and peered inside. "I think it just needs batteries."

"Ah, Joey, I wish it were that easy," Luke said in a patient schoolteacher's voice. "But some problems aren't so simple to fix."

No kidding. Sylvie patted Joey's shoulder, told him to be good, and crossed the yard to the kitchen.

Izzy met her at the door and took one look at her. "What's wrong?"

"I need advice."

The house was as peaceful and sweet smelling as always. Jenny stood by the stove, stirring something in a big pot. "Come in, Sylvie. We're making caramel today, hot and dangerous work, so Jesse's watching the children at the house."

Izzy pulled out a chair for Sylvie. "Fern was worried Jesse wouldn't survive, or maybe their children wouldn't survive, so she took Katy Ann over to check on them." She patted the chair beside her. "Sit. Tell us everything."

Sylvie removed her sweater and sat down as Izzy poured her a cup of coffee. Once she started talking, it was like a dam broke open. She chattered on, a thousand words a minute, recounting every detail of Jimmy's strange behavior. Izzy propped her elbows on the table and peered at her over one folded hand.

"One minute he was begging me to marry him, not ten minutes later he was sweating and choking and gasping for air. It was like someone had socked him in the stomach or something. Could someone get sick that fast?"

"He wasn't sick," Jenny said from the stovetop. "He was panicking."

"Panicking? Because of me? Because of us?" Sylvie doctored her coffee with milk and sugar, stirring mindlessly. "But he was the one who proposed. It's just that . . . we seemed so well suited for one another. And he and Joey, they've grown so close. I've never seen Joey so happy as he's been these last few months. And Jimmy's done so much for me at Rising

230

Star Farm. More than I could've ever expected." More than that. He'd become a pillar of strength for her. "He seemed so positive that we should marry, made such a case for it. Pressed me to accept. As soon as I did, he fell apart. Do you think he changed his mind?"

When no one answered, she looked up and saw a look exchanged between Izzy and Jenny that was pregnant with unspoken meaning.

"What?"

Izzy dipped her chin. Sylvie darted her attention to Jenny, who was suddenly very focused on stirring the sugar on the stovetop.

Sylvie straightened, staring Izzy down. "What?"

"You have to tell her," Jenny said.

Sylvie's heart dropped a few feet, bouncing around as it did. "Tell me what? Something awful, right?" She thought she was a good judge of character, but maybe her attraction to Jimmy had blinded her.

Another round of exchanged glances, leaving Sylvie out in the cold.

"Jenny!" Sylvie placed both palms on the table. "Izzy! What aren't you telling me?"

Jenny folded her arms against her chest, reminding Sylvie of Fern in that mannerism. "Jimmy's a cliffhanger."

"What does that mean?"

"He gets close to a cliff, right to the edge, then backs away."

"Runs away," Izzy added with a solemn nod.

"What?" Sylvie looked at them. "You mean . . . the cliff . . . of marriage?"

Jenny nodded knowingly. "It happened with Luke's sister, Bethany. And now with you. He's attracted, convinced he's found his girl. But as soon as things get serious, after he really thinks about what it means, that there will be expectations placed on him, responsibilities . . . he turns tail and runs."

It started to sink in. Sylvie leaned back in her chair. "I see." So, she wasn't special to Jimmy, like she thought. Hoped. "So, then, it's over."

"No!" Izzy shook her head so fast that her capstrings bounced on her shoulders. "It doesn't have to be over. All men get cold feet. Luke did."

"Jesse did too," Jenny said.

"And if I'm not mistaken, Jimmy never had proposed to Bethany. They'd talked about it, but he never did actually propose. So you're the first girl he's ever proposed to."

"Why, I think you're right, Izzy. Sylvie, you're the first."

Izzy smiled. "First and last. Assuming we do this right."

"Do what?"

Izzy covered Sylvie's hand. "Jimmy takes special handling. It's very important how you handle it, though."

"Assuming you still want him," Jenny said. "He's more flawed than most men. Maybe you don't want him."

Out of Sylvie burst, "Oh, I do." And she did. The words flew out of her mouth before she even thought about them. She hadn't known how much she wanted him until right now. She was in love with Jimmy Fisher, flaws and all.

"I thought so." Jenny grinned and clapped her hands together. "You just can't let him know that, though. As far as he's concerned, it doesn't matter to you either way."

"But . . . ," Sylvie said, and she felt her eyes start stinging, which triggered her annoying twitch. "But it does matter."

"We know that, and you know that," Izzy said, giving her a reassuring nod. "But Jimmy doesn't have to know that."

Jenny held up a wooden spoon, frowning. "Knowing and understanding is half the battle."

But this isn't supposed to be a war, Sylvie thought, turning the edges of her apron. It did feel a little like one, though. "Maybe it's just too much. Joey. Edith. Hank. Maybe it's too hard."

"Without the Lord's help, any marriage is too hard."

All three women jumped at the sound of Fern's voice. In her arms was Katy Ann, who reached out for Izzy. How long had she been standing there?

Izzy rose to get her child. "We're giving Sylvie advice about how to manage Jimmy's cold feet. She's worried it's over between them."

Jenny nodded woefully. "Before it even began."

Fern handed off Katy Ann to Izzy and went to the stove top to peer into the pot of caramel. She took the wooden spoon out of Jenny's hand, shaking her head, and stirred the mixture herself, watching the liquid stream off the spoon.

"Care to chime in with suggestions?" Jenny prompted.

"About caramel? Or about Jimmy Fisher?"

"Both," Jenny said.

"Sugar needs to boil." She turned the stove flame up a notch and went back to stirring.

"And Jimmy?"

"I don't think the situation requires suggestions. I think that if God intends for Jimmy and Sylvie to end up together, we don't need to plot and plan and connive."

Izzy and Jenny cast sideways glances at each other.

"And the Good Lord works in mysterious ways."

"But what does that mean?" Sylvie asked. "In this situation, Fern, what does that really mean?"

"To let go and trust God." Fern stirred and stirred, and lifted the spoon again. What dripped down back into the pot now was light brown, sticky, gooey caramel. "Remember," she said at last with a reassuring smile aimed at Sylvie, "that even the wind and the waves obey him."

Face pinched, Jenny scratched at her neck. "I suppose . . . we might have forgotten to add all that in."

Katy Ann wiggled to get down and Izzy scrambled after her to keep her away from the stove. Jenny and Fern were focused on pouring the caramel onto the buttered tin foil. Later, after it cooled, they'd cut it into bite-size pieces and wrap them in waxed paper.

Sylvie remained at the kitchen table, thinking over the conversation. She appreciated Izzy and Jenny's concern, but their advice made her unsettled. Fern said nothing more, but her words hit the mark.

Let go and trust God. Nothing could be harder for Sylvie. She wanted to fix everything herself. But she'd tried to do that before, many times, and she'd only made things worse. In the back of her mind, she had a nagging feeling that her fix-it intentions might have interfered with her sister's life. She might have been overly helpful and made it easy for her to abandon her responsibilities. She might have interfered with Jake's life too. He'd been content with his bachelor life and hadn't felt a need to change things, not until she came along and made him fall in love with her. What about now? Yes, Jimmy had started this whole marriage idea, but he clearly wasn't ready for marriage. There was much at stake here. Yet was she interfering again?

She *was* a terrible person, just like her father had always said.

Prince needed a large pasture to graze in, bigger than that small paddock near the new old barn where he spent his days. Jimmy had noticed broken rails on the far side of the pasture, close to the road, jerry-rigged together with a rope. If the horse wanted out, all he'd need to do is scratch his back on the broken rails. Despite the cold, Jimmy had spent the day fixing the railings, a task that was long overdue and kept him away from the house and barn . . . and from bumping into Sylvie.

"YOU LOOK SADDER THAN A MULE WITH A BIT THAT PINCHES."

Hank's loud voice startled Jimmy. He straightened and turned. "Pardon?"

"I've been WONDERING how you're doing. YOU LOOK LIKE MY DOG WHEN SHE'S OFF HER FEED."

"Hank, do you think you could try to talk without shouting?"

Hank seemed shocked by that remark, as if he'd never heard it before. He tried to whisper, which came out like a normal person's speaking voice. "Feeling overwhelmed? Heart pounding? A little"—he poked out his tongue and feigned choking, sort of like a cat coughing up a hairball—"short on breath?"

Jimmy tilted into half a shrug. "I guess."

"I SEE THIS ALL THE TIME. Wedding jitters."

"This . . ." Doubts. Despair. Heart palpitations. Sheer panic. "*This* is normal?"

"WOULDN'T BE NORMAL FOR A FELLA TO NOT EXPERIENCE COLD FEET."

Cold, sure, but Jimmy had frostbite.

Hank sat down on a few stacked railings and leaned up

against a post to scratch his back. "What is it that's EAT-ING at you, SON?"

Jimmy leaned against the fence post. He really wasn't sure that Hank was the person to talk to about his doubts, but David was still out of town, and Luke was fed up with him. As Hank continued to watch him from his good eye, Jimmy realized Hank's wisdom was all he had to rely on, which was a little sad. "What if God has one woman out there for me, and I just haven't found her yet? What if I end up making a mistake?"

Hank peered up at the sky. "With that kind of THINK-ING, if one fella made a MISTAKE, then so would the NEXT ONE, and the next. Every man on earth would BE MAR-RIED TO THE WRONG WOMAN."

"Like a game of dominos."

"EXACTLY." He folded his arms. "And that CAN'T BE TRUE because your mother and I have found TRUE WED-DED BLISS."

Wow. True bliss?

"Son, marriage is the BEST THING that could ever happen to a man. LIFE ONLY GIVES YOU SO MANY CHANCES. I wouldn't want you to reach the grave FULL OF NEAR MISSES."

Jimmy straightened, struck by the words. Always before, if a woman was mad at him, he moved on. This was differ-ent, Sylvie Schrock King was different. He had been given a chance to love again with Sylvie. Was he going to blow this, like he'd done so many times before? No. No, he wasn't.

Hank, for all his irritating ways, could turn profound. "Thanks, Hank."

"THAT'S WHAT FATHERS ARE FOR." He gave Jimmy

a solemn, tender look, which was not a good look on Hank, because one eye or the other was always floating off. "SON, I THINK IT'S HIGH TIME YOU CALLED ME DAD."

Jimmy dropped his chin to his chest. *Lord-a-mercy.*

The talk with Hank had bolstered Jimmy's courage and he knew he needed to face Sylvie. He'd made a complete fool of himself the other day. He dreaded looking into Sylvie's eyes now with no idea what to expect. Would she still be peeved at him?

He finished replacing the last broken fence rail. As he picked up his tools, he saw her walk Prince into the barn. Joey was swinging on the tire swing he'd made for him. If Jimmy wanted to clear the air with her, now was the time. He stalked along, studying the ground.

Inside the barn, he found Sylvie in the center aisle. She had Prince on crossties and was combing out his long mane. "I fixed the pasture near the road."

She popped her head over Prince's neck. "Thank you. Now I can finally get this horse into a pasture that's big enough for him." She disappeared again, currying burrs out of the horse's tail. He came around the back side of the horse and laid a hand on her arm, stilling her. "Sylvie . . . I don't blame you for being angry with me."

"I'm not angry."

He tucked his chin, and raised his eyebrows, giving her a doubtful look. But she didn't sound mad at him. She really didn't. She moved away from him to comb out the horse's mane and he came closer.

"About the other day," he said softly.

She turned around to face him, and he felt any lingering trace of doubt wash away as he gazed into her violet eyes. All he wanted, all he would ever need, stood right there in front of him. He was certain of it. This was the girl for him. "I'm sorry about the other day. It was a momentary lapse."

"There's no need to even talk about it," she said, squeezing his arm before she turned away to unclip the crossties. "But I have been giving it some thought. It seems wise to slow things down."

He snapped his head up. "But you said you wanted to marry sooner rather than later."

She led the horse into his stall, taking her time answering him. "Really, we have all the time in the world."

We do? Jimmy tried not to reveal his confusion. "All the time in the world?" When had he and Sylvie ever not rushed? They met at the Bent N' Dent, she offered him a job on the spot, he took it, he created a new business plan for Prince, got his first customer. Sealed, that very evening, with a kiss between him and Sylvie. They hadn't slowed down yet.

"There's no need to rush. We can give this a lot of thought."

A strange feeling of alarm rose. "Sylvie, is something wrong?"

Sylvie was quick to answer. "Oh, not at all." She hung the harness on the hook and turned toward him. "With Prince bringing in cash money, the farm is safe. That's the important thing. Don't you agree?"

Jimmy's mouth went dry, and he narrowed his eyes and leaned forward. He took her hand in his. "Sylvie, do you . . . still . . . want to marry me?"

She fell silent for a moment, her eyes fixed on their joined hands. The silent moment stretched. And stretched. It went on so long that Jimmy's stomach swirled and dipped. *Lord-a-mercy, she's changed her mind.* A new kind of panic swept in. He couldn't lose her!

Just then, into the barn ran Joey, wailing for Sylvie because he'd fallen off the tree swing and scuffed his knees and elbows. Sylvie carried him to the house to bandage him up, leaving Jimmy alone with the horses. The three-legged dog hopped down the barn aisle and sat in front of him, tongue hanging out. Looking down at that silly dog, another thing occurred to him. Sylvie hadn't winked at him. Not once.

An hour or so later, Sylvie heard a knock at the door and hurried to open it, wondering if Jimmy might drop by before he left for home. They hadn't finished their conversation in the barn, and there was more to say. Both of them had more to say.

Her mouth dropped to an open O when she saw Hank Lapp standing there. When Jake was alive, the two were often together, rummaging around in the barns, dragging junk in and out. She always knew when Hank was around, because he made an infernal noise wherever he went. But since Jake had passed, Hank didn't come to the house much, and the few times he did, he certainly never bothered to knock.

"SO YOU DID IT! Figured out a way to outfox the fox."

She sighed. Hank Lapp could talk a jaybird off a tree limb. Edith Lapp resembled a sturdy little bulldog, complete with jowls. Sylvie never understood how those two ended up together.

"TWO BIRDS. ONE STONE."

She crossed her arms, gripping her elbows. "What are you talking about, Hank Lapp?"

"MARRYING JIMMY! IN ONE FELL SWOOP. TWO BIRDS. ONE STONE."

She began fanning herself, whether from the heat of the kitchen or the shock of Hank at her door, she didn't know. "I'm not following."

"You turned the TABLES on Edith. She's been lighting into Jimmy like a BEAR CUB AFTER A BEE'S NEST. But so far he's REFUSED TO BACK DOWN. Said he's going to MARRY you no matter what she says." He scratched his forehead. "WHY SHOULD HE? After all, he got what he was after. TWO BIRDS, ONE STONE." He laughed like it was all a big joke.

She hesitated, knowing that Hank had a tendency to talk overmuch. To talk too much, too loud, and take what bits and pieces he knew, make up the rest, and tell everybody in town before nightfall. "What's that?"

"IT'S ALL SPELLED OUT IN EDITH'S GROSSDAADI'S WILL. Tiny little print. No one can OWN that property OUTRIGHT until he up and MARRIES. Same story with Jake. Once Edith found THAT LINE in the will, told him it was HIGH TIME he'd have to move out since he couldn't find a BRIDE, well, he up and married the FIRST GIRL who said YES to him. Tried to, anyway. He'd asked every OLD MAID in Stoney Ridge, and they all REFUSED him. I know that for a SOLID-GOLD FACT." He pointed to two old rickety wooden chairs on the porch. "We sat RIGHT there and drank iced tea and made a list of EVERY SPINSTER we could think of." He turned back to Sylvie. "Then, along came YOU and that little tyke of yours." He snapped his fingers. "BINGO! Jake nailed down the property. Oooeee! Edith was MADDER THAN A WET HEN, I don't mind telling you that."

Too stunned to speak, Sylvie's mind started spinning. Jake hadn't fallen in love with her. He didn't love her. She'd felt such guilt over trapping him in a marriage in which she didn't love him, yet she was the one who had stepped into the trap.

"And now Jimmy's PLANNING to do the same thing." He touched his hat with a smile. "THAT BOY DON'T EVEN OWN HIS OWN HAT. Had to BORROW one of mine before the deacon got after him."

Sylvie stared at him, nearly forgetting she'd been in the midst of baking biscuits in the oven. It seemed an icy hand gripped her heart. She wasn't special to Jimmy. Not to Jake, not to Jimmy. She was just a means to secure Rising Star Farm. To both men.

"Come to think of it, maybe EDITH got a BIRD with that STONE too. She always said this property is meant to be ALL TOGETHER. Kept in the FAMILY. Not parceled out to outsiders."

"I may be an outsider to Edith," Sylvie said, fighting tears, "but I know that Jake intended this land to go to Joey. I'm not about to just hand it over—"

Oblivious to her upset, Hank blathered on. "THREE BIRDS. ONE STONE. MAYBE EDITH OUTFOXED EVERYONE, AFTER ALL. Wouldn't put it past her." He tapped his forehead. "She's clever that way."

Sylvie was so angry her knees shook.

"OUTFOXED THE FOX," Hank repeated. "BUT WHO IS THE FOX?" He chuckled to himself as he went on his way, walking down the porch steps to cross the yard, though Sylvie could hear his loud voice booming like he stood right next to her. "WHO'S THE FOX?"

SEVENTEEN

Luke stood at the bottom of the stairwell that led into the kitchen, watching Izzy as she grated carrots into a bowl. He enjoyed watching her whittle those poor carrots down to a nub, and was almost sorry when she caught him doing it.

She looked up at him and flashed him a smile, before swiveling around to set the bowl on the counter. "I'm making your birthday cake."

When he'd first laid eyes on her, his first thought was that she was gorgeous. But lately? She seemed stunning, almost glowing. He took a few steps closer to her, wrapping his arms around her. "We haven't had much time alone lately," he said softly, pausing to breathe in the distant shampoo fragrance of her hair.

"Tonight," she said. "We'll celebrate your birthday dinner, and then I have a special surprise for you later tonight."

He bent his head to kiss her neck. "How about a birthday gift now?" The house was quiet. Fern had taken Katy Ann on an errand to the Bent N' Dent. Why not now?

"Can't," she said. "I have too much to do for your birthday

242

dinner." She wiggled out of his arms. "Did I tell you that my mother is coming?"

He groaned.

⟜

Just as Luke left the house, Izzy slipped the cake into the oven. She had his birthday supper all planned out. Silly, probably, to make such a fuss over a man's birthday, but she had missed out on so many birthday celebrations in her childhood that she felt a bone-deep need to make each one special, to not waste a single one. She was making Luke's favorite carrot cake, just the way he liked it, with cream cheese frosting. And later tonight, after they'd put Katy Ann to bed, she planned to tell him about the baby. She'd been greatly tempted to tell him so many times over the last week, but she held off, wanting it to be a perfect moment. She ran through different scripts in her mind, trying to settle on just the right words, said in just the right way. It still astounded her, still seemed like a dream, to think she was pregnant. There were signs, though, that even she couldn't deny. Her breasts were tender, her stomach twisted and turned at certain smells. She used to love the scent of brewing coffee in the morning. Now, it made her gag. Yesterday, she ran for the door to gulp in fresh air. Fern noticed and watched her curiously. She must know. Fern must know. She knew everything. But she didn't say anything, and Izzy was grateful.

She didn't mind the discomfort. In fact, she welcomed it. It was a sign that something was happening, deep within her, in the secret places, just like King David had written in that psalm. Psalm 139. "My substance was not hid from thee, when I was made in secret." It was the first Bible verse that Izzy had memorized. It spoke to the miracle that was going on within her.

And then, around noon, she'd felt an odd stitch on the left side of her abdomen. First one, then another. Sharp pinpricks. She ignored them, reassured herself that it was something she ate, or maybe she'd tweaked a muscle. By midafternoon, she noticed a swelling start in her belly. *Oh no. No,* she prayed. *Please, God. Let this be nothing. Please let the baby be all right. Please, please, please.*

She'd had no bleeding. Jenny had miscarried once and told her that the bleeding and cramping were the first signs of a miscarriage. Fern was at a quilting, and Luke had gone to see the fire chief about installing the baby box. The buggy was gone, the horse was gone. Katy Ann was napping upstairs.

The sharp pinpricks disappeared, but the swelling increased. She could put a hand on her stomach and move it around like Jell-O, the way Jenny's stomach jiggled after delivering a baby. Something wasn't right, but Izzy kept hoping and praying that whatever it was, it didn't involve the baby. *Please let me keep this baby,* she prayed, over and over and over. *Let this be nothing. Let this be nothing, Lord.*

By four o'clock, she knew she had to get help. She bundled Katy Ann up and they went down to the phone shanty. With shaking hands, she dialed the doctor's office. When she heard Ruthie, one of David's daughters, answer the phone, she started to choke up and could barely get the words out. "I need help."

"Who is this?"

"Izzy. Luke's wife. I'm in the phone shanty at Windmill Farm and I need help."

"What's happened? Is it Katy Ann? Was there an accident?"

"No," Izzy said. "It's just that . . . I think I'm miscarrying. And I'm alone at the house. Down in the phone shanty."

There was a pause on the other end, and Izzy heard her say something to Dok.

Ruthie came back on the line. "Dok wants to know what symptoms you're having. She wants to know if you need an ambulance."

"My stomach. It's . . . it's filling up like a balloon."

"Stay right there, Izzy," Ruthie said calmly, but firmly. "Stay right in the shanty. Don't go anywhere. Keep Katy Ann with you. Close the door to the phone shanty so she can't get out to the road, and sit down on the floor. Help is on the way."

Hands shaking, Izzy hung up the phone, closed the door to the shanty, and slid carefully down to the floor, her back against the wall. She pulled Katy Ann into her lap to sing to her, trying to make a game of this moment, when it was no game. *Jesus Loves Me, This I Know.* That was the song Izzy sang, voice trembling. That was the last thing she remembered.

Luke was in Juan Miranda's office, discussing plans for the baby box to get installed, when the call came in for an ambulance to get to Windmill Farm. He listened to the loudspeaker, stunned, as if he were hearing it underwater. Garbled and slow. Windmill Farm? A woman, aged twenty-three, experiencing a possible hemorrhage.

He watched dumbly as the paramedics went into action. As the garage door opened for the ambulance, something clicked in his head. "That's my home! My farm."

Juan Miranda grabbed his helmet off the wall and turned to look at Luke. "Your place? Could that be your wife?"

Running through Luke's mind were all kinds of possibilities: A customer at the yarn shop? But the tourist buses weren't running in winter, and today was Tuesday. Izzy didn't teach any classes today. Could something have happened to Fern? No, couldn't be. He heard the dispatcher say the woman was aged twenty-three. He looked at the fire chief. "I don't . . . I don't know."

"Well, get in the truck. You can get the horse and buggy later."

Luke's heart pounded as the ambulance sped down the quiet country lane with the siren blaring. The truck came to a stop at the phone shanty and as soon as the siren stopped, Luke heard Katy Ann's cries. The firemen jumped out of the truck and opened the door to the phone shanty. Izzy was unconscious on the ground, and Katy Ann was curled in her arms, crying for her mama. One fireman lifted Katy Ann and handed her to Luke as two more surrounded Izzy.

Oh God, he prayed, heart pounding, hugging his hysterical little girl tightly against his chest, trying to calm her down. *Oh God, please help.* Katy Ann was so cold. How long had she been there? Was Izzy alive? Was she dead? *Oh God, oh God, oh God.* It was all his mind could manage.

Luke waited with Katy Ann in the emergency waiting room of the hospital, a cold, sterile room with hard plastic yellow chairs and a huge television screen.

Juan Miranda joined him after a while, bringing a cup of vending machine coffee for Luke and a candy bar for Katy

Ann. "I sent the ambulance back, and one of my men at the fire station will take your horse and buggy to Windmill Farm. Is there anyone who can help with the baby?"

Luke took the candy bar and unwrapped it for Katy Ann. She took one bite of the candy bar and looked like she had just tasted heaven. Luke tried to take it from her and she squealed. *Fine*, he thought. *Take it*. Never before had he given her a candy bar, but for now, his normal rules were thrown out. This was no normal moment. "Fern Lapp. She lives at Windmill Farm. She's kind of Katy Ann's grandmother."

"I could have one of the men bring her here. Assuming she's at the farm when the horse is returned."

"Thank you," Luke said, nodding. "I appreciate your help."

"Well, sure. That's what we do."

But it was more than that. Juan Miranda cared. Luke could see it in his eyes. He was a good man, this fire chief.

Dok came through the door with a grim look on her face. "Hi, Luke." She nodded to the fire chief, as if she either knew him or recognized him. "I have some news. Izzy has had a miscarriage."

A miscarriage. Izzy was pregnant? Pregnant? Luke flopped down on the chair, Katy Ann in his arms, grasping on to her candy bar. He swallowed, expelled a ragged breath, and sputtered, "But she'll be all right, won't she?"

There was a troubled look in Dok's eyes that sent a chill down Luke's spine.

"Unfortunately, it wasn't a typical pregnancy. It was something called an ectopic pregnancy. The fertilized egg rooted in the fallopian tubes, and as it grew, it burst the tube. Izzy has been hemorrhaging for the last few hours, quite severely. She's going to need a transfusion."

"But then she'll be OK, right?" *Please God, please God, please God.*

"There's another problem we're facing. It turns out she's a rare blood type. The hospital doesn't have a compatible blood for her."

"What do you mean? You're out of her blood?"

Dok sighed. "We've called the blood bank, but there's a severe shortage of this particular blood type."

Luke bolted to his feet, jostling Katy Ann, who kept a tight hold on her candy bar. "Our church. I can make some calls. Get everyone here to donate blood. Someone must have her blood type. I know they'd do anything for Izzy."

"I wish it were that easy, Luke. It's a very rare blood type. I doubt you'd find this blood in the entire state of Pennsylvania. We're going to have to go ahead with the surgery. She's getting prepped now."

"Surgery?" Luke's knees gave out and Juan helped him back to a seat before he dropped Katy Ann. He looked up at Dok. "Can I see her?"

"She's drifting in and out of consciousness."

"I need to see her."

Dok nodded. "And after that, you get on the phone with your people and tell them to pray. I don't mean to scare you, but the next twenty-four hours will be critical."

Juan Miranda looked at Dok. "Hold up one minute. Just what blood type does Izzy need? I donate blood a lot."

"Unfortunately, Izzy can't accept blood from any other type but the one she has." Preoccupied, Dok glanced at her pager.

"Any chance it's called golden blood?" Juan said, eyebrows raised, a smile forming on his lips.

Dok's head snapped up. "Yes, that's right. Rhnull." She tipped her head. "How did you know?"

"The universal blood donor," Juan said.

Dok fixed her eyes on Juan. "There are no positive or negative antigens on it, so anyone can receive it, whatever their blood type. It's a blood in extremely high demand, but the flip side is disastrous. When a person with Rhnull needs a transfusion, it's nearly impossible. Less than fifty known people in the world have golden blood. In the *world*."

"And one of those fifty is standing right here." Juan pulled a card out of his wallet. "Card-carrying member of the Golden Blood Club."

Dok blinked, stunned. "You're . . . Rhnull? You've *got* to be kidding." She examined the card, front and back.

"Not kidding," Juan said. "A bona fide member. In this line of work, your medical background is pretty thorough. Once they found out I had golden blood, I've been part of all kinds of studies. Blood banks, medical schools, scientists . . . they're always after my blood. I donate as often as I can." His eyes flicked from Dok to Luke and back to Dok. "I want to help. I want to do what I can to help Izzy."

The troubled look left Dok's face and was replaced with surprised relief. "Well, first let's get you tested," she said, caution in her voice. "If you really are a match for Izzy, you might just save her life."

When Luke heard those last few words of Dok, he passed Katy Ann to Dok, swooped his head down between his knees as the room swirled around him. *Don't pass out, don't pass out*, he told himself, sucking in big gulps of air. *Breathe in, breathe out, slow and steady.*

How could life change so fast? Just a few hours ago, Izzy was in the kitchen at Windmill Farm, grating carrots to put in a cake, telling him her mother was coming to dinner. Just an ordinary moment in an ordinary day.

How in the world could life change so fast?

Grace. Luke had completely forgotten to call Izzy's mother until Fern showed up at the hospital to take Katy Ann home and asked if Grace was on her way. He whacked the palm of his hand against his forehead. Not again! He was always forgetting about Grace. That wasn't right, it wasn't fair. She'd made progress over this last year, and he, of all people, should be acknowledging and encouraging her. As soon as Fern left, he found a pay phone and started to dial, then paused. He leaned his forehead against the cool metal phone, eyes stinging.

As a deacon, he'd delivered some very difficult messages to families. Being the bearer of bad tidings was part of the job, but it wasn't easy for him. He could never sleep well after he brought someone a death message, or some other sorrowful news. Participating in a family's grief, or walking through their anxiety about the unknown future—it was gut wrenching. And afterward, he never failed to wish he had a more graceful way to deliver bad news. David had reassured him, had told him that there was no ideal way to say what had to be said, or if there was, he had yet to find it.

Still. How do you tell a mother that her daughter was in surgery? That her life might be in danger? It wasn't like

Grace had been much of a mother to Izzy, but she was making amends. Grace was clean and sober, and she was a doting grandmother to Katy Ann. She and Izzy were more comfortable with each other than they'd ever been. But there was no evidence of faith in her life, and as Luke sucked in a deep breath, he realized that even in this situation, he needed to be a deacon. A servant of the Lord. Even to Grace Mitchell Miller.

Oh God, please give me the words, he prayed. *Control my tongue. Let me say just enough, but not too much. Let me be strong, let my voice not wobble, let me be a light to Grace.*

He dialed again, and waited for her to answer. "Grace," he said, "it's Luke. Something has happened this afternoon. To Izzy."

He heard her gasp. "What do you mean? What's happened? Is it the baby?"

Luke paused, winced. Izzy had told Grace she was having a baby? But not him. That stung. That really stung. *Not now*, he felt the Lord instruct. *Be the deacon.* "She's had a miscarriage. I'm down at the hospital. Could you come down? Tonight?" He paused. This was hard to say. "I'm sure she'd like her mother with her."

For a long moment, he heard nothing, and then he realized she was crying. Finally, through a voice choked with tears, Grace said, "Tell my baby girl I'll be right there."

"Grace."

"What? What else?"

"Pray."

"I will." The words were barely a whisper.

As Luke turned the corner in the hospital, he saw orderlies wheel Izzy's gurney down the hall and ran to catch up with her. As he walked alongside the gurney toward the doors that led to the surgical center, he held her hand and squeezed. Izzy's eyes flickered open, then focused on his face.

"It was going to be your birthday surprise," she said, tears running down her cheeks. She swallowed, once, twice, before saying, "But I lost the baby."

"But our baby isn't lost," Luke whispered to her, eyes filling up. "Not lost at all. Our baby is safely in God's presence."

And then he had to let her go as she was wheeled into surgery.

$\mathcal{E}$IGHTEEN

Luke wasn't sure what kind of reaction to expect from Grace, but he hadn't expected calmness. So calm that he offered to let her take a turn to sit by Izzy's bed in the ICU room. He sat outside, watching as Grace stroked Izzy's free wrist, the one that didn't have the tube of precious golden blood hooked into it.

But he didn't go far, just in case Grace started to cry. The last thing he wanted was for Izzy to wake up and see her mother wailing away, as if she was dying. She wasn't. She couldn't. He needed her. Katy Ann needed her.

He glanced at the clock, eager for Jenny to arrive. On the telephone, she said she would put the children to bed and come right down. He could let Jenny handle Grace; she had a way with her mother.

Dok turned the corner and saw him, then came down the hall and sat next to him. "Cheer up, Luke. That fire chief's blood is going to get her through this."

Dare he ask? "Dok, are you sure? She looks so . . . pale." So lifeless.

She smiled. "Watch and see."

Luke looked through the glass window at the bag of blood—Juan Miranda's precious golden blood—hanging on the tripod, slowly dripping life into Izzy, his precious wife.

Dok leaned back in the chair and rubbed her face with her hands. "Luke, do you realize what a miracle has occurred here today?" She dropped her hands. "No, not just one. More than that. That Izzy got to the phone before she passed out. That Katy Ann was safely with her in the phone shanty. That help arrived before she'd lost too much blood. Then . . . the fire chief . . . being *here*, at just the right moment. And another miracle . . . Juan Miranda said he hadn't given blood this month. He was scheduled to do it tomorrow. If he'd given blood, we couldn't have taken more from him, not without jeopardizing his own well-being." She crossed one knee over the other and folded her arms against her white coat. For a split second, she reminded Luke of David, her brother. Certain mannerisms seemed to be part of a person's DNA.

Luke was sorely missing David's presence. Whenever he was around David, he felt a sense of peace, of calm. All would be well. That was the effect David had on him, on everyone. Luke needed him here, more than ever, but he and Birdy hadn't returned from somebody's funeral in Berks County.

Juan Miranda came down the hall with two Styrofoam cups of coffee. He handed one cup to Luke and offered the second to Dok. "Would you like it?"

"No thanks," Dok said. "And you shouldn't be drinking coffee after giving so much blood. You should be eating a steak dinner. Drinking lots and lots of water."

"I will. I promise. I just wanted to check on Izzy before

heading home." Juan looked at Luke. "I thought you'd be in there with Izzy."

Luke took a sip of coffee. It was terrible and wonderful. Both. "Her mother is in with her."

Juan walked to the ICU glass window and peered in for a moment. "That's her mother?" When Luke nodded, he said, "She doesn't look Amish."

"She's not," Luke said. "Long story." Very long.

"Juan," Dok said, "there's something that keeps niggling me."

Juan turned and walked back to Dok and Luke. He took a sip of the coffee and made a face. It was terrible coffee. "What's that?"

"Rhnull blood—it tends to run in families."

At that moment, Grace walked out of the ICU room and took off her face mask. As she tossed it in the open bin, she glanced over, then did a double take and froze. Color drained from her face. Luke saw it happen, right before his eyes, like a stopper had been pulled.

After a long pause, she said, "Johnny?"

Juan swallowed, eyes wide. "Gracie? Is that you?"

"Do I look so very different?"

Juan's face softened into a gentle smile. "No, no. You haven't aged at all."

"No? Well, maybe a little." Grace dropped her gaze and fussily checked the hair at the back of her neck. She flashed him a brief, nervous smile. "Your hair. You kept it. Most men, they lose it."

Whoa. Luke had a weird feeling swirl through his gut. "How do you two know each other?"

For the moment neither Juan nor Grace moved, or spoke.

They stood rooted by surprise and curiosity, staring at each other.

It was Dok who broke the awkwardness with a gasp. "Oh my . . . ," she said. "Oh my, oh my." She pointed to Juan. "Golden blood. The odds are one in a million. A trillion! Unless . . . you're related to Izzy. Could it be? Is it possible?"

Juan let out a laugh, more like a fake cough. "No, unfortunately. I never had any children."

"Well, actually," Grace said slowly, face reddening as she spoke. "Actually, Johnny, you did."

Too much. This was too much. Too much change, too much happening. Too fast. Luke plopped down on the nearest chair, dropped his head between his knees, and gulped in air. *Don't pass out, don't pass out.*

Carefully, slowly, Izzy sat up in bed, wincing at the pain in her abdomen. Dok wanted her up and walking around as soon as she could, but told her not to get out of bed without help. At least she'd been moved out of ICU this morning, sooner than expected, and had been able to see Katy Ann.

No. She shouldn't even think in terms of *at least*. Not *at least*. Dok had said she was their miracle patient. *Golden blood.* She had no idea she had such a rare blood type. She'd never heard of such a thing as Rhnull. When Dok made her rounds this morning, she asked her, "Do you think this rare blood type is why I've had trouble getting pregnant?"

Dok chewed her lip, eyes troubled. "I don't know enough about Rhnull to answer that, Izzy. It could be the reason. I just don't know. But here's what I do know. You have one less fallopian tube now, and that means the chance to successfully conceive is even more difficult."

"But not impossible?" Izzy asked softly, not meeting Dok's eyes.

She paused. "Miracles do happen."

"Yes they do." *Just look at me*, Izzy thought. *Just look at me.*

<hr>

Luke came to the hospital later that afternoon. Izzy's heart rose to see him at the doorjamb, but the lift she felt was quickly dampened by the look on his face. "What's wrong? Katy Ann is fine, isn't she?"

"Yes, she's home with Fern." He came in and took her hands. "Nothing's wrong, honey. It's just that . . . something was revealed because of your . . . rare blood type. Something very unexpected."

Izzy's mind started to reel. "What are you saying? Am I sick?" Dok would have told her, wouldn't she?

"No, nothing like that. You're fine. In fact, you're . . . golden." He gave her a weak smile. Bad joke. "This blood type you have is rare. Really rare. Incredibly rare."

"I know. Dok told me."

"So rare that only fifty known people in the world have golden blood."

She nodded. "That's just what Dok said."

"They don't know much about this blood—"

"Luke, just say it. You're making me nervous."

"I'm trying. This isn't easy to say." He took in a deep breath. "What they do know is that it runs in families."

"Grace? Jenny? Chris? Do they have it?"

"No. No, they wouldn't."

She was getting more confused. Then it dawned on her. "Wait just a minute. You mean . . . my father?"

Luke nodded slowly.

"I don't understand. Are you saying that you found him? Had you been looking for him?" Her heart started pounding. Luke had been the one to find her mother. Had he tracked down her father too?

"Well, let's say we found each other. Because of your need for golden blood." He went to the door and opened it. Standing at the door was her mother, Grace, wary, as usual. Next to her was the fire chief, Juan Miranda, with a sheepish, nervous look on his face.

"Izzy," Luke said, "meet your father."

⁓

Luke rubbed the back of his neck. He'd been leaning against the wall so that Grace and Juan could sit in the chairs next to Izzy's bed. It was a surreal moment, watching his wife connect with *both* her parents for the very first time. How could anyone not believe that God answered impossible prayers? What Luke was witnessing right now was a miracle.

He'd always thought there were some resemblances between Izzy and Grace, especially certain mannerisms, but seeing Juan and Izzy side by side, the resemblances between father and daughter were uncanny. They looked alike, both tall with straight shoulders. Thick, dark, wavy hair, olive skin, dark almond eyes. They even gestured their hands in a similar way. But there was something even more that wove them together, and Luke had only realized it because he'd gotten to know Juan Miranda through this Baby Box Project.

They both shared a quiet reserve, keeping themselves at a distance from others, almost imperceptibly.

Juan was amazing under pressure, Luke thought, though that shouldn't surprise him. He was a fire chief, after all. Luke listened carefully to Juan's explanation that he had never known he had a child. Yet he said it without blaming Grace for deceiving him or cheating him. If Luke were in his shoes, he'd feel angry. Deceived and cheated, both.

"Had I known, Izzy," Juan said, "I would have done right by you. I'd always wanted a little girl."

But Izzy wasn't ready to let her mother off the hook. "Why didn't you tell him?"

Grace looked away. "He was married. So was I." She rose and walked to the window. "Plus, to be brutally honest—because my counselor is always yapping at me to tell the truth—I thought I'd just have it taken care of. I didn't think there was any reason to tell him about it."

It. Grace was talking about Izzy. As an it. Not as a beautiful, lovely woman, who was now a beloved wife and a mother, who had a depth of faith that inspired him, and who made the world a better place in so many ways.

"I had an appointment scheduled at the abortion clinic." Then she swung around. "On the way there, I was at the bus station, looking for the right bus to take to get to the clinic. Right on the sidewalk at the bus station was a little girl, playing hopscotch. Right there on the sidewalk. She had thick dark brown hair and big almond brown eyes, and as I walked past her, she stopped me and asked me to play hopscotch with her. I looked around and there was no adult around, anywhere. No mama, no babysitter. Just this beautiful little girl, all alone. 'What's your name, honey?' I said to her.

"The girl smiled at me. 'You know me, Mama. I'm Isabella. Your little girl.'"

Grace clutched her elbows, as if her stomach hurt. She turned to look at Izzy. "I felt . . . stricken. Gobsmacked. I could hardly breathe. I got on the next bus and took it, not even caring where it was going. It ended up being the express bus to Ohio."

Silence fell over the room. Luke and Izzy exchanged a look of shock.

"Mama, was that girl . . ."

"You. Izzy, she was you. A dead ringer." Grace shrugged. "I can't explain it. I don't know if that little girl was an angel, or my imagination running wild, or pregnancy hormones, or what."

Luke couldn't help but interject here. "'Thou hast covered me in my mother's womb. I will praise thee; for I am fearfully and wonderfully made: marvellous are thy works; and that my soul knoweth right well. My substance was not hid from thee, when I was made in secret, and curiously wrought in the lowest parts of the earth. Thine eyes did see my substance, yet being unperfect; and in thy book all my members were written, which in continuance were fashioned, when as yet there was none of them. How precious also are thy thoughts unto me, O God!'"

Grace looked at him, baffled. "Something like that. I guess."

"It's from Psalm 139. Grace, in that moment, that baby you were carrying was no longer an *it* to you. No longer just a growing mass of reproductive cells. She was a little girl, with a personality, and a beautiful face, and a future to live. 'Fearfully and wonderfully made.'" He looked at Juan.

"That's what we're trying to do at the fire station. To help women like Grace. To save these precious babies."

"I get it," Juan said, tears streaming down his cheeks. "I get it."

They talked awhile longer and shed a few more tears, until Luke could see that Izzy was wearing out. "We should let Izzy rest. There will be plenty of time later to talk."

"Will there be?" Juan said, eyes fixed on Izzy. Tears brightened his eyes and his stern chin trembled. "I've already missed so much. Is it too late?"

"It's never too late." Izzy reached out and covered his hand with hers. "There's time enough."

Luke knew this moment was a significant step for Izzy, as she was slow to trust—men in particular—and always reluctant to show affection. He hoped Juan realized what a gift he'd been given.

Luke smiled. From the tender look on the man's craggy face—a sweet mélange of gratitude and relief and joy and love—Juan knew.

Nineteen

Sylvie had come to Stoney Ridge with little and was leaving with even less. After she finished packing the last suitcase, she asked Joey if he would stay put on the tire swing while she went to give Edith Lapp a list of instructions about feeding the animals.

"Do we have to leave, Mem?"

"I'm pretty sure we do." Walking across the yard, she prayed for the Lord to give her the right words. Jimmy had taught her that kind of prayer was all right. "The Bible says to pray about everything," he had said, and showed her where it was in the book of Philippians. *So, Lord, what should I say?* A gentle whisper came, so quiet that it couldn't be heard, yet she heard it all the same. *Speak peace.*

She had barely started to knock on the door as Edith opened it, as if she'd watched Sylvie come across the yard. Probably, she had. Sylvie swallowed past the tightness in her throat. "Edith, can't we both be on the same side?"

"Depends. What is it you're after?"

"You love your son. I love your son." Sylvie saw the alarm in Edith's eyes, sensed her bone-deep loyalty to her son.

While she might bear Sylvie a grudge, she did love her son. For the first time since they'd met, Sylvie sensed some common ground. "You love Rising Star Farm. So do I. Does it have to be one or the other? Can't we both be on the same side? Can't we both want the best for Jimmy? For the farm?"

"I know what's best for my boy . . . and I know it's not you."

Edith's eyes narrowed to suspicious slits, snuffing out the last thin thread of hope that Sylvie had yet to release. "That's what I thought." She let out a sigh, her shoulders lifting in one last shrug. "We're leaving, Edith. Rising Star Farm is yours."

Edith started to speak, then clamped her mouth shut.

"Here is a list of all the animals, what they eat, how often." She held out a folded paper to Edith. "I think Jimmy knows it all, but just in case, I wanted him to be sure."

Edith opened the page and stared at it, then looked up at Sylvie, a victorious look in her eyes. "I suppose you want money."

"No, Edith. I don't want your money." Exasperation rising, she forced a calm she wasn't feeling. "Do you think I care about the house? About the money? No, I do not. Just like you, I care about my boy. And my animals."

A smile pulled at Edith's dour mouth. "Rest assured. The animals will be well tended." Her eyes shifted past Sylvie. "I see your taxi has come, so I'll say goodbye." And the door shut.

⌒

Jimmy had been in town all morning, buying lumber to fix some rotting fence posts at Rising Star Farm. The moment

263

he returned to the farm, the very instant he drove the wagon onto the property, he could sense a change. The same way he felt when a cloud passed in front of the sun. Everything felt cold, empty. The tree swing hung still, the kitchen rang silent.

Slowly, he climbed down from the wagon, his gaze sweeping the property, looking for a sign of Joey, of Sylvie. He'd had Prince with him. How could she have left Prince? Left *him*?

A sick regret gripped Jimmy. He'd done it again. Burned another bridge. Let a girl he loved slip away. The realization that he loved Sylvie nearly toppled him, and he had to put a hand out on the horse to steady himself. He'd lost her. He'd lost Sylvie. Even Prince knew. He turned his head, ears pinned back, fixing a terrible accusing stare at Jimmy.

What was wrong with him? Why did he get so close to love and marriage, toy with it, only to run in the other direction?

He saw his mother make her way across the yard toward him, holding a paper in one hand. He met her halfway. "Sylvie's gone, isn't she? You chased her away."

"If she really loved you, she wouldn't have left." She shrugged, like it was no big deal, yet it was. "If she loved you, she couldn't have left."

"Mom," he said, his voice trembling.

"Son, she's not the one for you. She and that boy of hers, let them be someone else's problem."

Until this moment, Jimmy hadn't realized how hard his mother was, or how hard the years had made her, or maybe he had such little confidence in himself that he hadn't ever seen her clearly. His mother was always so sure of herself, like a tree that wouldn't bend, even in a gale. Now he realized that if a tree didn't have deep roots—to accommodate the wind while keeping it firm and steady and strong—then its trunk could snap.

He didn't want to be that kind of a man.

She handed him the paper. "Here. She left you a list of feed for all those animals." Eyes fixed on the house, she seemed pleased with herself. "At long last, this place is rightfully yours. It's not much to look at, but the land's always been the best in Stoney Ridge. I always knew, someday, it would come back to us." Her gaze swept the property. "Won't take long to get the rest of Jake's junk out of here. Then we'll all move in. Fix it up real nice."

"No."

Her chin jerked up. "What did you say?"

"No. I said no." He locked eyes with her. "I'm going to move in here alone."

She held his gaze for a very long moment, then nodded. "If that's what you want." She turned and took a step, then stopped. She smiled. "Actually, I think that's a real good idea. Get it all fixed up to bring home a bride."

Exactly, Jimmy thought. *Just not the bride you have in mind.*

Izzy had always assumed that Frank Miller, her mother's third husband, was her biological father. She had only some vague memories of him. He wore a blue Izod shirt, had sandy blond hair, a gap between his two front teeth, smelled of beer, and whenever he looked at her, he seemed slightly bewildered.

Juan Miranda could not be more opposite, in every way. Confident, bold, handsome in a George Clooney way. And he looked at Izzy not with bewilderment, but with such tenderness. Sadness, too, for lost years. He'd always wanted a daughter, he told her so last night, after everyone had left the hospital to go home and he remained. "And when I met you, Izzy, my first thought—my very first thought—was how much you looked like my mother. Her name is Isabella." His eyes grew shiny as he spoke. "I don't know how or why Grace named you Isabella. I don't remember ever telling her about my mother, but maybe I did."

Probably, he did. Izzy was getting to know her mother well enough to know that she did remember odd little details. And forgot plenty of other ones, like birthdays.

"I called my mother in Puerto Rico and told her about you." He squeezed her hands. "She says to tell you that she already loves you, Izzy. That she's been waiting her whole life for you." He took out his wallet and showed her a picture. "See the resemblance?"

Izzy smiled. First smile in a couple of days. Even she could see the resemblance. "So what's she like, this mother of yours?"

"She's an artist. Loves to draw, to make things. Her sense of color and style is . . . ," he kissed the tips of his fingers, "legendary." His eyebrows lifted. "I told her that you're an artist too."

"Me? I'm no artist."

"Oh, but you are. Think of the Flying Horse sign. That was what brought us together."

Imagine that. Izzy Miller Schrock had found her father, a kind and good man, who actually wanted her. She had a grandmother, too, for whom she was named. For all the mistakes Grace Mitchell Miller had made, and those stacked up to the sky, she had done a few things right. Of all the names, she had chosen Isabella for her.

Imagine that, Izzy thought. *I have a father who wants me. I have a grandmother whom I resemble. And she is an artist.* She'd never had a grandmother before. Or a father. First time for both. First time for a lot of things. *If anyone doubts that miracles still exist, just look at me. Look at me.*

She shifted in the bed, felt a cramp in her tummy, and rubbed it away. Empty again. She'd hardly had time to work through grieving the loss of this little one. A boy, she sensed, though she really had no idea. One thing she knew—the baby she had miscarried had served a profound purpose in his short life. Something came to mind that David had said, a year or so ago, at a funeral for a stillborn baby: "His life was complete." At the time, such a thought shocked her. Now, she understood it.

She turned her head to look out the window, at the stars in the night sky, tears filling her eyes. "Lord, thank you for our child. Thank you that he is not lost, but with you." She hadn't realized how much she'd been holding the sadness in. Now she let it overcome her. Tears streamed down her cheeks. Sad tears at what she'd lost, happy tears at what she'd found.

⌒

Sylvie had the taxi stop at the hospital so she could tell Izzy face-to-face that she was leaving. Izzy deserved that from her. Luke, too, but she couldn't face him without bursting into tears. She left Joey in a chair outside of Izzy's room, across from the nurses' station, and told him to stay put. She popped her head in the door in case Izzy was sleeping but saw a smile fill her friend's face. Izzy looked tired, with shadows under her eyes, and yet she was entirely lovely. Even more appealing, she had no idea of how beautiful she was.

Sylvie pulled a chair up to the bed and reached out to hold Izzy's hand. "Fern told me all that's happened in the last few days." She squeezed her hand. "I'm so very sorry."

"So am I," Izzy said, eyes growing shiny, "but I'll be all right. Better than all right."

Sylvie smiled. "I have no doubt of that." She looked down at their joined hands, startled by how different they were—Izzy's olive skin, fingers long and tapered. By comparison, her own hand was so small, so white. They couldn't look more different, yet it mattered not. From the first time they met, they felt a bond. Kindred spirits, true heart-to-heart friends. Had it not been for Luke, Sylvie might not have ever known her. And now she was saying goodbye to a friend who had grown dear to her. Choking back tears, she explained why she felt she needed to leave Rising Star Farm. "I just can't stay, Izzy. Please don't try and change my mind."

"I won't," Izzy said with a disappointed sigh. "Though I wish you'd stay. Jimmy or no Jimmy, Stoney Ridge is your home. It's where you belong. It's where the people live who love you."

"I thought it was. I wish it were. But life doesn't always turn out the way you hope it might."

Izzy bit the corner of her lip. "I feel as if Edith Lapp is running you out of town."

Sylvie took in a deep breath. "She's a big part of it, that's for sure. But Jimmy is part of this too. He doesn't know what he wants. Or who." She shrugged. "It just seems best if I go. Start over." Again. "You'll tell Luke? Jenny and Fern?

Tell them I'm sorry. Let them know I'm grateful for all they did for me."

"You have nothing to be sorry for. I'll tell them what you said." Izzy tipped her head. "Just remember what Fern always says. 'The Lord works in mysterious ways.'"

Sylvie smiled. "Think that's written in the Good Book?"

"I don't know where exactly, but I think so." Izzy looked Sylvie straight in the eyes. "If he asks, should I tell him you've gone back to your father's?"

"Only if he asks." She was fairly confident Jimmy wouldn't ask.

The sun had almost set by the time the bus delivered Sylvie and Joey to the small town where her father lived.

"Are we there yet, Mem?" Joey asked for the hundredth time that day.

"Not quite yet." She'd felt a barb of alarm each time he asked, nearly reconsidering her decision to return, because she had no idea how her father would react when they knocked on his door. It was entirely possible that he would close the door in her face.

They walked a few blocks, lugging suitcases along the bumpy road, until a horse and buggy drove up alongside her and came to a stop.

"So, then, you've come back."

Sylvie startled at the familiar deep voice of her father. "Hello, Dad." She locked eyes with him, surprised at how much older he looked. His beard was entirely gray now, so were his bushy eyebrows. Had she been gone such a long time? Just two years. He seemed to have aged a decade in that time.

Her father studied her for a long while, then turned his gaze to Joey, then back to her. "Looks like you've had a long day."

"Very long." She felt her eyes start to sting, then twitch. If he drove off without them, she knew what that would mean. What would she do next? Where could they go? If the bishop turned his back on his own daughter, who would dare take them in?

But he made no effort to drive off. In fact, it was significant that he had even stopped to talk to them. When it came to holding on to grudges, her father was a champion. It seemed . . . that something had changed between them. Some thawing. Some door cracked open. Some light broke through. Or was it only wishful thinking?

"Well, it's getting dark," he said in his gruff way, staring straight ahead. "You'd better hop in."

Jimmy led Prince into the barn and hooked up his harness to the crossties. "Stop looking so sad, you big baby. You've got a pretty good life here. Besides, she's the one who left. Not us."

Prince swatted his tail from side to side, as if to say, "Right. Tell me about it."

Jimmy had never been the type to miss people, not so much. Not his brother Paul, not even Bethany. Wherever he'd gone, he'd made it a point to not let the past encroach on his present. Until now.

Jimmy's remedy to the recent upheaval in his life was to push harder, to be so preoccupied with chores and tasks on the farm that they drove out any thoughts of Sylvie.

Impossible.

Every inch of Rising Star Farm reminded him of her. Every single inch. Conversations they'd had about plans to upgrade the farm, moments when he'd watched her walk from the house to the barn or clothesline. The snowman he'd built with Joey. It was still there. The base of it, anyway. Most of the rest had melted.

And then there was the house. He'd set up a cot in Jake's old office because he couldn't bear to go upstairs, to sleep in her bed. Sitting at the kitchen table brought up endless memories, so he avoided it. He ate his meals standing up at the counter, like a horse.

And then there was Prince. Beautiful Prince.

Jimmy still couldn't believe that Sylvie had left Rising Star Farm without him. She was crazy about that horse. Obviously, she couldn't cart the big horse along with her, and to be fair, this was Prince's home. Added to that . . . Juan Miranda had booked Prince for three more mares. Five thousand dollars a pop. Half now, half when the foal was born. And Juan had told Jimmy that if all went well, he'd be back. So it made sense that Prince was left behind, but it pained him. He knew, more than anyone, what this horse meant to Sylvie.

The worst time for Jimmy was the end of the day, just as the sun was setting and the moon was rising. Evening was unfolding. That had been *their* time. He and Sylvie used to sit on the porch steps together, sipping hot cocoa, Joey swinging in the tree swing, and they'd talk about the farm. She'd point out the winter birds—the Northern Cardinals, the Pine Siskins, the Downy Woodpeckers—and then she told him about the birds that visited the feeders come spring. Birds he'd never heard of, yet she seemed to know them all. Even their calls. She taught him that the first thing you learned as a bird-watcher was to listen well for birdsong. Such a concept was new for him: to listen well.

Except for the most bitter, blustery days of winter, they'd wrap up in blankets and sit on those steps. Those minutes spent on the porch steps were some of the finest in Jimmy's life. Sometimes, he missed Sylvie so much, it actually hurt.

Last night, he woke up, heart pounding, as he remembered there'd been a man in her life before Jake. The man who had first introduced her to Arabian horses. Most likely, he'd still be there. Folks in the Hillbilly Amish didn't move around much. He felt a queer churning. Of all the emotions he'd been facing lately, jealousy was hardest to stomach.

He bent down to pick up a hoof pick to clean out Prince's hooves and ran his hand down the horse's front leg until he shifted his weight and lifted it. As Jimmy cleaned each hoof, he dared a tentative, heartfelt prayer. For forgiveness. Direction. Wisdom. For another chance. Pulse drumming in his chest, he hardly expected an answer. He dropped the hoof pick in the tack box and picked up the currycomb, then started rubbing circles on Prince's withers.

"Jimmy, are you listening?"

Jimmy jerked like a fish on the line. He looked over Prince's neck. "Luke Schrock." He stood just a few feet away.

"Man, what is wrong with you?"

"Nothing. I just didn't hear you come into the barn."

"Oh yeah? From the far-off look on your face, you must have been tuned in to something. Whose voice were you listening to?"

Jimmy stilled. Interesting question. Whose voice had he

been listening to lately? For most of his life? His mother's shrill voice came immediately to mind.

"So Sylvie's left."

"Yup."

"Your mother must be happy."

"I suppose so."

"And I suppose you're happy too. You've got the farm, after all."

From the strident, sarcastic tone in Luke's voice, Jimmy could tell where this was headed. "Save me the lecture. I've already given it to myself. Yes. I blew it. I lost the woman I loved. Again."

"So, then, you're going to just keep floating along in your stupid life?"

"I'm not floating. I'm trying to get this stud farm going."

"Okay, that's a start. But what other plans do you have? I meant, besides taking care of this horse and a three-legged dog?" He squinted, noticing something big ooze down the barn aisle and into a corner. "And a very fat cat."

Jimmy stopped currying, midbrush. "Are you asking as a friend or as a deacon?"

"Fair enough. As a friend."

He went back to brushing Prince's big neck. "It's just . . . the truth is, I'm a little stuck."

"Stuck because you let the girl you love slip away? Stuck because you let your mother call the shots? Stuck because you don't know how to make your stupid life count for anything?"

"Wow. So this is what it's like to be your friend?"

"Yup. A real friend tells you straight up."

Jimmy scratched his head. "I'm stuck because . . . I can't seem to think beyond the needs of a day."

Luke nodded knowingly. "Long-term thinking. Counselors say the lack of it is at the core of most problems they see."

Jimmy rolled his eyes. "And there you go. Sounding like a deacon again."

"Nah. I understand it because I spent most of my teens and early twenties with a serious lack of it. It's still something I have to work at. I just can't see how things will play out, down the road. Izzy can. I can't."

"Sylvie could. In most things, anyway." She was never comfortable with the idea of using Prince as a racehorse stud. She never felt comfortable with calling Prince the Flying Horse. He'd ignored her objections. More than once, Sylvie had said that just because something wasn't wrong, it didn't make it right. Was that one of the reasons she left?

"Let me ask you something. Do you even know what you'd like life to look like, down the road?"

Jimmy stopped brushing Prince's neck. He dropped his hands to his sides and rested his forehead on the horse's big neck. He was quiet for a moment, eyes squeezed shut. "I think I do. A well-managed horse farm, buildings in good condition. So clean and tidy that you couldn't even find a spiderweb. A house with buttery lights glowing from every window, to welcome a man home. Joey swinging on the tire swing. Sylvie in the kitchen, cooking supper for the three of us." He opened his eyes. "I can see it. All of it. I just don't know how to get from here to there."

Luke grinned. "Well, well. Jimmy Fisher. That might just be the first intelligent thing I've ever heard you say." He clapped his hands together. "So let's start from there and go backwards."

TWENTY

With a fork, Izzy dripped melted chocolate over the top of the brownies. She'd already spread a layer of pale green peppermint icing on top of them, so this chocolate was just a nice touch. It mattered, those little touches.

The mint brownies were going to be part of the potluck at the fire station later this afternoon, and fortunately, it was a sunny day, not too cold for January. It started out as a celebration for the installation and passed inspection for the Baby Box. The Amish church was invited, and the firefighters' families. Then Elroy Funk got involved, and he sent out press releases, and invited the high school band to attend, and now a news crew was sending a reporter and a cameraman.

That part of the celebration, Izzy would avoid. But she would definitely be celebrating the occasion. It still amazed her to think that the Baby Box was now a reality. It might not save every baby, but it might save a few. She prayed so.

And there was another piece of this day that was cause for celebration. All of the firefighters' families were coming.

She was one of them. So was her mother. Juan Miranda had invited Grace himself. For the first time since she'd been in the hospital, she and her mother and her father would be together. When she was a child in the foster care system, if someone had told her to hang in there . . . That even though her childhood wasn't easy, it wasn't the whole story. That there'd be lots of chapters ahead. Good ones. Happy ones . . . If someone had told her that, she never would've believed it. And yet, it was true.

Sometimes, her life seemed like one miracle after the other. And in this next chapter of her life, she wanted to help make miracles for someone else.

Jimmy carted out the final wheelbarrow of junk from the old barn and dumped it by the wagon. The last one. The old barn was still old, but at least it was empty. He sat down in the shade next to the hose bib and turned it on, squirting his hair, his face, his shirt with tepid water. He couldn't remember March in Pennsylvania being so hot. It's like the weather had gone from winter to summer, skipping spring. Or maybe he'd just been so distracted and preoccupied and depressed that it felt to him like spring had been skipped.

"The place looks . . . amazing."

He looked up to see Luke Schrock standing a few feet away. "I didn't even hear your horse and buggy."

"That's because I came by foot. Such a nice day, I thought I'd just walk it." Luke sat down next to Jimmy, back against the building. "Have you seen much of your mother lately?"

"She knows where I am."

"Hank says you're holding a grudge."

"He'd be right."

Luke grinned. "Just don't hold on too tight."

"Oh, I've already forgiven my mother." He took a swig of water from the hose and turned it off. "I just haven't told her yet."

"Maybe by the time Easter rolls around, you need to let her know." He brushed his hands together. "Jimmy, you've done a great job cleaning out Jake King's junk. Are you ready for phase two?"

"Phase two?"

"Getting Sylvie back."

"What? I thought cleaning out the farm was the way to get her back. Show her how serious I am about her."

"No, that only shows her you're serious about the farm. Now it's time to get serious about Sylvie."

"How do I do that when she's living hours away?"

Luke took in a long-suffering sigh. So dramatic, this deacon.

"Jimmy, you and Sylvie, you hardly knew each other. You were attracted to each other, but did you really know each other?"

"We worked together every day since October."

"What's her favorite color?"

Jimmy had no answer.

"Favorite season? Favorite food?"

Jimmy lifted a finger in the air. "Well-done waffles." He wiped a water drop off his chin. "No, hold it. That's my favorite."

Luke's eyes squeezed shut, as if he could barely tolerate Jimmy's denseness.

Jimmy leaned his head against the barn. "So how do I get to know her when she's living . . . who knows where?"

"Now you're starting to ask smart questions. I've been waiting a long time for that." He picked up a sack by his side that Jimmy hadn't noticed. Opening it, he said, "You start with this." He pulled out a box of stationery. "I trust you have a pen."

"You mean, write Sylvie a letter?"

"Every day. Until you win her back."

"And you think a letter a day will do that?"

"It will if you do it right." Again, that look. Like Jimmy might be the most dim-witted man in Stoney Ridge. "You need to court her."

Jimmy went completely still. To court a girl. Court Sylvie.

Luke rose to his feet and patted the tops of Jimmy's bent knees, before he started ambling off toward the road.

"Luke!"

Almost at the creek, he swiveled. "What now?"

"I don't even know where she lives!"

"Izzy does. Ask her." He lifted his hand in a wave as he hopped the creek.

Jimmy stayed in the shade, leaning against the barn, for a very long time, thinking. It dawned on him that he had never really set out to court a girl. Never. The girls courted him. Even Bethany, who had a firm backbone, she was the one who was waiting for him. He'd never had to wait for a girl, not until Sylvie.

He walked over to the new old barn to start feeding the horses . . . and stopped when he heard something odd. A creaking sound. Then another, and another. Like someone was pulling rusty nails out of wood. He spun on his heels, turning in a circle, trying to figure out where the creaks were coming from. Then he realized what was happening. The walls of the old barn were caving in. He stood there, stunned, as the entire building began a slow collapse. The sound was immense, so loud that Luke shouted to him from the hill. He turned to Luke, hands raised in the air, as if to convey a message of "What can I do but watch?" and then turned back as the old weathered building came crashing down. Jimmy stood there, stunned, as the air filled with a dust cloud.

Luke ran back down the hill to his side. "Man! Did you see that?"

Speechless, Jimmy could only nod.

"What happened to it?"

Jimmy blew out a breath he hadn't even realized he'd been holding. "All the stuff inside, it had been keeping the walls up."

"Wow. Do you realize how close you came to getting buried alive in that old wreck?"

Lord-a-mercy, he hadn't even thought about *that*. Luke was right, though. Jimmy had spent all week pushing the wheelbarrow in and out of that flimsy matchstick of a barn. The more he thought about what a close call he'd just had, the more his chest started to pound.

Luke gave him a pat on the back. "Not sure what plans you had for the wood, but Teddy Zook might be able to use some of those posts and beams."

"No," Jimmy said, still shaky. "Termites. Everywhere." In fact, the collapse saved him the trouble of tearing it down. But he'd nearly lost his life! This was the closest he'd ever come to meeting his Maker, even after four years breaking horses in Colorado.

Luke grinned. "In that case, we're going to have us a good old-fashioned bonfire."

A familiar pang began in Jimmy's stomach. He could just imagine the delight on Joey's face while watching the bonfire of the old barn. Man, he missed that boy.

After Luke left, Jimmy walked around the heap of the old barn, tossing stray boards into the center pile, hearing them clack. Contemplating mortality made a man think about things he might have put off.

Luke was right. Jimmy needed to court Sylvie. Woo her. Make her his. But how?

He pondered the idea of courting Sylvie like he was preparing for battle, determined to win her. With the Lord's help, he would court her. With the Lord's help, he would love Sylvie as she ought to be loved.

Another question pulled at him, burned a hole inside of him. Was it too late?

Dear Sylvie,

Greetings from Stoney Ridge.

I asked Izzy for your address. When she told me that you were living with your father, I felt more than a little concerned. I hope your father has stopped calling Joey the name Willie Jitmit. I also hope you are doing well.

Not long after you left, I moved into Rising Star Farm and have continued to clean it out. I even emptied out the old barn. Luke stopped by and said the place looked amazing. Minutes after he left to head back to Windmill Farm, the old barn collapsed. Completely imploded. All those termites had been having a field day. We had a bonfire to burn the infested wood. It was quite a sight. I was sorry Joey missed it.

Prince is happy as a sire. The maiden mares' bellies are growing round. This time next year, Lord willing, there will be a little Prince (or Princess?) running around the pastures. I hope to pay off the full amount of overdue property taxes due this year . . . thanks to Juan Miranda. He is partial to Prince.

By the way, Juan Miranda is spending a lot of time at Windmill Farm, getting to know Izzy. She sure seems happy to have a father in her life. She says fathers are undervalued yet just as important as mothers.

Just the other day, I stopped in the Sweet Tooth Bakery and there was Juan Miranda and Grace Miller, having coffee and cinnamon rolls, laughing over something. They didn't notice me watching them. They were pretty fixed on each other. I decided not to tell Izzy that piece of information. Maybe I'm getting a little wiser in my old age?

Well, that's about it for now. Please tell Joey howdy from me.

I guess I'd like to ask: Do you want me to write again?

Your friend, Jimmy Fisher

P.S. What is your favorite color?

Sylvie returned home from helping an elderly neighbor set up hummingbird feeders all around her backyard, with hopes of controlling the mosquito population. She enjoyed it, and so did Joey, but it seemed like the majority of her time was spent with people in their sunset years. She'd forgotten how old most of the people were in her father's church. Most of the young people had left.

She stopped at the mailbox and opened it, then stilled when she saw a letter addressed to her. She knew instantly who it was from. She knew because she loved his distinctive handwriting. No cursive, all print.

She set the letter aside, tucked in her pocket, until a time when she wouldn't be interrupted. Later that evening, after she got ready for bed, she held the unopened letter in her hands. Her thoughts spun out, wondering why he had written. What did he want to tell her? Her first assumption was that Jimmy was explaining his engagement to Rosemary Blank. Edith Lapp was a determined woman, and she'd made up her mind about Rosemary. How many times had Sylvie seen Rosemary's buggy roll up for supper at Edith's house? At least a dozen.

How would he tell her? How would he put an end to her meager hopes, the ones she couldn't quite relinquish? She tried to imagine it, tried to prepare herself. He would say that he appreciated her as a sister in Christ and hoped they could always stay friends and blah, blah, blah.

Okay. Get it over with. She tore the letter open before she lost courage.

She scanned it. Then she reread it. And then she hopped

out of bed, found a piece of paper and a pen, and she wrote him back.

> Dear Jimmy,
>   Greetings in the name of Christ.
>   It was quite a surprise to get your letter today. My first thought about that old barn was that it was a blessing it collapsed when no one was inside. My second thought was, good riddance to it! It was an eyesore.
>   To answer your questions: My father has not been unkind to Joey. After both daughters have left his home, he seems softer. Older. I think he's been lonely. I worry he is not well, though he refuses to see a doctor because he thinks they are all quacks.
>   I've told him that I read the Bible for myself now. He grumbled, said I was full of pride—probably there's some truth in that—but he hasn't stopped me.
>   I suppose I wouldn't mind hearing from you. ~~When I first got your letter, I thought you might be telling me news about Rosemary Blank.~~
>
>   Sincerely, Sylvie
>
> P.S. My favorite color is pink.

Jimmy's return letter came in two short days.

> Dear Sylvie,
>   Greetings.
>   I am just getting ready to paint the house.

White, I think, with black shutters. Unless you think blue shutters would be better?

Your father is wrong to say you are full of pride. You are the most humble person I have ever met. Maybe too much so.

Your old friend, Jimmy

P.S. There is nothing to tell about Rosemary Blank and me. Nothing at all.

P.P.S. The three-legged dog desperately needs a name. What do you think of calling him Hop-a-long?

~~P.P.P.S. Have you seen much of your friend who taught you about Arabian horses?~~

Once again, Sylvie found a piece of paper and wrote Jimmy back. She stuck a stamp on the envelope and took Joey into town that very afternoon to mail her letter, before she lost her nerve.

Dear Jimmy,

Greetings to you in the name of our Lord.

Hop-a-long is an ideal name for a three-legged dog. I should have given him a name, but he came to us in poor condition and, honestly, I didn't think he would live very long. I thought it might be easier on Joey if he didn't have a name when he passed. Then that silly, wonderful dog surprised us and survived. Love can work wonders.

Green shutters are my favorite. With pink azalea bushes out front, along the porch.

My friend who taught me so much about Arabian horses married a woman with an allergy to horses. They have two sets of twins, under the age of two, and I heard that they are expecting another clutch. He works long hours for his mother-in-law at her bakery. He looks a bit worn out, so much so that he fell asleep in church last week, snoring loudly, and the deacon called him out on it in front of everyone.

Cordially, Sylvie

P.S. Joey talks about you often. He wants my father to put up a tire swing, but my father says rubber wheels are of the devil.

Luke woke, disoriented. He rubbed his eyes, blinking at the bright March sun coming through the window, wondering what time it was. He'd been out late to deliver a death message to Sol and Mattie Riehl. A favorite cousin had died of cancer, and it hit Sol hard. Luke hadn't returned until past midnight.

He turned over and realized Izzy's side of the bed was empty. He heard a voice he recognized downstairs. David's. Was he here on a deacon duty? He jumped out of bed and hurried to dress. He opened the door and was about to call down to say he'd be coming, when he stopped, curious. He thought he heard David mention his name to Fern. He crept a little closer to the top of the stairs and listened. Something had happened, something good. He could hear the jubilance in David's voice.

"Fern, today is one of those rare moments in life when it all feels worthwhile. All those years of patiently trying to redirect him. We've seen a miracle of God unfold right before our eyes."

"I have to give you credit," Fern said. "You saw his potential when few others did. You and Amos. Frankly, you more than Amos."

Luke leaned his head a little farther down the stairwell. What in the world were they talking about?

"And you, Fern," David continued. "You saw it too, back when he was one of your wayward boys. I think you and I both always had a hunch about Luke. That if the passion he had for disrupting life could be used for good, there would be no stopping him. These last few years, as he gained strength in his recovery, then became deacon—despite how difficult that first year of being a deacon was. He's never given up. He reminds me of Saul in the New Testament, converted into Paul. All that destructive energy has turned into constructive energy. With the Holy Spirit guiding him, Paul became a remarkable leader among men. That's what's happened to Luke. Guided by God's Spirit, he has become a remarkable leader. I'm blessed we are leading together. Our church is blessed to have him as deacon."

Luke stepped back into his bedroom and quietly closed the door. He sank to his knees, his emotions overcome by such affirming words. Tears streamed down his face. It felt as if he'd been waiting his entire life for something like that, not for pride's sake, but for a sense of meaning and purpose. "Lord, let my life count. Let me be a light in the darkness."

When he felt he had a handle on his emotions, he wiped the tears off his face with the back of his hands and took in a deep breath. He opened the door and went down the stairs. David was still there, having a cup of coffee at the kitchen table.

"Morning," he said, bending over Katy Ann's high chair to plant a kiss on her head. He tried to act nonchalant, but the words he'd overheard still warmed his heart, made him feel close to tears. Chin tucked, he said, "Where's Izzy?"

Fern looked to David. "Do you want to tell him?"

"Izzy's over at Dok's office." David took a sip of coffee, maddeningly slowly.

Luke's heart started to pound. "What's wrong? Has something happened?"

Fern waved her dishrag at Luke. "Nothing's wrong. Just the opposite. Tell him, David."

David grinned. "There was an infant in the Baby Box early this morning. A little boy. Dok is checking him out. Izzy is over there now."

"A baby," he said softly. "A baby?" Tears stung Luke's eyes.

"There was a little tag tied around the baby's ankle. It gave the child's birthdate." David cleared his throat, and his eyes seemed a little shiny. "And it said he was from New York."

Luke covered his face with his hands. It took him a long moment before he could speak, before he could get words past the clog of tears in his throat. He blew out a puff of breath and dropped his hands, looked at David. "It's working."

"It's working." David's eyes glistened. "One by one, we are making a difference."

It was working. If Luke thought his heart was starting to pound, now it was thumping wildly. It was working! One by one.

In one month's time, Jimmy was getting and sending a letter every single day. He watched for the mailman's arrival each day and rushed to the box. He wasn't sure what had filled his mind before the letters started. They absorbed him completely, even to the point where he would stop whatever he was doing so that he could jot down something on a notepad to tell Sylvie in the letter he wrote each night. Her letters were longer, far more interesting, and far more clever than his. He spent long hours late at night writing, tearing up, and rewriting letters to her. He'd never worked this hard to get to know a girl before, to understand her better. And it was worth every minute. In a strange way, it was almost easier to get to know her without being physically close to her. He'd been so attracted to her, there were times he could hardly concentrate when she was near.

He hoped Sylvie enjoyed the letters as much as he did. He thought so, but just in case, he ended every letter in a question. Knowing Sylvie as he did, she would feel a sense of responsibility to answer him. That girl was all about responsibility.

Dear Sylvie,

Greetings from Stoney Ridge.

The house is painted. Green shutters have been put up to frame each window. Pink azalea bushes are planted out front, though they won't bloom until next spring.

I put up a new tire swing today because the fat cat has taken up residence in the old tire and he hisses at me if I get too close to him. Sometimes I think he is plotting to kill me. Or at the very least, to shred me. Tell Joey I read recently that if a housecat were as big as a person, it would kill its keeper.

Fondly, Jimmy

P.S. What is the best part of your day?

~

Dear Jimmy,

Greetings in the name of Christ.

The best part of my day is when Joey is asleep, and I have some time to myself in the evening.

Last night, I woke to the sound of a flutter of feet in the hall and suddenly there was Joey, standing in my room. "Mem, ask Jimmy if there might be kittens in the old tire swing."

I told him I'd ask you and please could he go back to sleep.

Warmly, Sylvie

~

Dear Sylvie,

Greetings.

Would you believe that Joey was right? That fat cat made a nest of kittens in that tire swing. Turns out he isn't a fat he but a fat she. We need to change its name from Lloyd.

The best part of my day is when the

mailman arrives and there is a letter waiting in the box from you.

Fondly, Jimmy

P.S. Seems like we should change the name of the fat cat. What do you think of Jezebel?

Dear Jimmy,

Greetings in the name of Jesus.

Joey has suggested the cat's name be changed from Lloyd to Lulu. It occurred to me that the cat might seem like it is trying to kill you (I don't think it would truly kill you, though who knows what goes on in a cat's mind?) because you keep calling it Lloyd. Try Lulu.

My father surprised me yesterday by asking Joey if he would like to go fishing. Joey didn't answer for the longest time, and I held my breath, afraid he might say no. If he said no, chances were my father would not ask again. But I needn't have worried. Joey said he would like to go, but he didn't like putting worms on a hook because he was afraid it might make the worms cry.

My father looked at him, befuddled, and then he smiled. More like a rusty grin. Hours later, they came home with two small fish and I fried them up for dinner.

Blessings,
Sylvie

TWENTY-ONE

David stopped by the Fix-It Shop one evening in late March to pick Luke up for a deacon-duty errand. "Easter is only a few weeks away," he told Luke, "and there's something I've put off too long. I was hoping it would take care of itself."

Luke hopped in the buggy, sensing this wouldn't be an easy visit. Normally, David didn't talk much on the ride if he felt burdened. Luke knew enough by now to remain quiet. He figured David was spending the drive time in prayer.

Luke wasn't sure where they were headed, but he had a hunch what was on David's mind, at least in a general way. The month preceding Easter was always a sobering time. Two weeks before Easter came Communion, a day in which the entire church was asked if their hearts were prepared for the coming Holy Week. All debts should have been repaid, all relationships mended. If even one person held a grudge against another, Communion would be postponed.

Maybe Luke shouldn't have been surprised when David turned the buggy into Hank and Edith Lapp's driveway, but he was. Enough so that his stomach started churning.

291

Confronting Edith Lapp was no small thing. He planned to say nothing. Nothing at all.

Hank warmly welcomed them in. Edith was far less welcoming, but that was no surprise. Always dour, she seemed even more fierce and forbidding than usual, almost a look of battening down the hatches before a storm.

They faced each other, sitting at the kitchen table. "SUCH SOLEMN FACES," Hank said. "Eddy, if I didn't know better, I'd say the bishop had come to LAY A SIN on us."

David didn't correct him. "Hank, you're not wrong."

"What has he done?" Edith looked at Hank. "What have you done now?"

"Not him," David said. "You."

Edith's sparse eyebrows rose to the top of her head. "*What* are you talking about?"

"I think you know."

"I have no idea."

"Edith, when sin enters our life, our conscience grows hard."

"Sin? I'm sure I don't know what you're talking about."

"No? Let me see your grandfather's will."

"Why?"

"I'd like to read it."

Feigning disinterest, she said, "There's no need for that."

"I'LL GET IT." Hank rummaged through a drawer and brought back a roll of yellowed paper, edges cracked with age. "HERE YOU GO."

As David gently unrolled the paper, he read through it, slowly and carefully. Luke wondered what was going through his mind. He had no idea. Nor did he have any notion of what Edith was thinking, or feeling. She sat there like a statue.

Lamplight reflected off the sheen of her face, giving off an odd glow. Or could she be perspiring?

Then David set the papers down and lifted an old leather satchel from his lap. He pulled another set of papers from it and laid it on the table. "This is a copy of the same will." He placed it on the table, each will side by side. "Your grandfather wanted the property to pass to the youngest son in the family."

"That's right. He was a youngest son himself, so he felt things should be fair."

"BUT ONLY IF HE BRINGS IN A BRIDE." Hank let out a yelp and rubbed his shin. "HEY! EDITH! What'd you do THAT for?"

"Hank doesn't know what he's talking about," she snarled.

"YOU TOLD ME THAT VERY THING!" he said, offended, still rubbing his shin.

David tilted his head. "Edith, did you tell Jake that he needed to marry to keep that property?" When she didn't respond, he continued. "Because I read it through, twice. I never found that direction. Not in either will."

"It was his *intention*. To keep the family going. To keep the land in the family."

"Maybe so," David said, "but he never put it in his will." When she didn't object, he added, "Edith, did you lie to Jake? Tell him he needed to marry so you could force him out of the house? So you could save the land for Jimmy?"

"Oh, now I see!" Luke blurted out. "Now I get it. But then Jake married Sylvie. Botched up the plan."

Edith looked at him. "Don't you have someplace else to be?"

Luke didn't really mind her sharp tongue. He'd gotten

used to it, but this outright deception shocked him. What made her do it? Who knew what—other than a misguided need to provide for her son and keep him close—made her cross the line into spinning a lie? Who knew why?

"Edith," David said, in a tone that amazed Luke with its gentleness, "you're going to need to make a confession."

"WHOA-HO! Eddy!" Hank seemed impressed.

"Oh no. I was only upholding my grandfather's intentions." She rapped her palms on the table as she said the words. "I'm the one who knew him. I remember him. No one else does. I did not do anything wrong."

"Yes, Edith, you did. You lied. You assumed no one could read High German in calligraphy . . . and you lied about what was in the will."

Luke was moved by the sympathy in David's expression, in his voice. He took no pleasure in this.

She remained stony faced. "Giving words to a man's intention is not a lie."

"Words are a funny thing," David said. "They can make big things little. And they can make little things big."

The air was taut with tension. Luke, who normally had little sensitivity to such matters, sensed it was about to snap and crackle.

"If you didn't have an ulterior motive behind it," David said, crisp and clear, "I might be able to see your point. But what you did, Edith, was to engineer a situation to suit yourself. Each of those individuals—Jake, Jimmy, Sylvie, Joey—they belong to God, they're precious in his sight. Each one—frankly, everyone—is here for some purpose. It's not up to us to decide the fate of another."

Hank slapped his palms on the table. "I'LL SIT ON THE

SINNER'S BENCH WITH YOU, EDDY. I'm sure I can think of SOMETHING I might have done wrong."

David rose. "Before Communion, Edith," he said with sudden finality. "Or . . ."

"Or what?"

"Or we hold up Communion for the church, until you're ready. We will only partake Communion when our hearts are one, under Christ." He took in a deep breath. "And we'll have to talk about what to do in the meantime."

Under the bann, David meant. Cornered, Edith looked stricken.

Luke, as deacon, had seen David handle all kinds of circumstances, but he'd never known him to put anyone under the bann. He'd given a warning, and that was all it took. This was a last recourse, a drastic step. A means for the Lord to break through that hard shell that sin created. From the look on Edith's face, a threat of the bann rattled her.

"We'll be off, then." David packed up the copy of the will.

"Where'd you get that will?"

He looked regretful, sorry for her. "Your son Jimmy gave it to me. He found it when he was cleaning things out of the old barn."

On the way back to Windmill Farm, Luke chewed on something. It was a humiliating thing to sit on the sinner's bench. He knew. He'd been there plenty of times. But it was a good thing too. After you confessed, when you rose to your feet, it felt like your sin was washed away. No one spoke of it again. They might have thought about it, but they didn't say anything. "David, will it really be a sincere confession if Edith's heart isn't in it?"

"For most folks, intention follows feelings. In someone like Edith Lapp, feelings follow intention."

That, Luke thought, was if Edith Lapp actually sat on the sinner's bench. She hadn't said she would.

⌒

Dear Sylvie,

Greetings from Stoney Ridge.

I'm sure Izzy has told you the news about her baby. A little boy. The first baby in the baby box. I don't know if they were planning to adopt babies from the baby box, but apparently Izzy took one look at him and fell in love. He looks a little like Luke, I think, with a headful of jet-black hair.

Something shocking and wonderful, both, happened last Sunday. My mother sat on the sinner's bench and made a confession in church. It had to do with something in her Grossdaadi's will, an area where she'd over-stepped her bounds. David found out and called her on it. He's all about letting folks carve their own path, stumbles and all. He says that when people come to the end of themselves, that's where they'll find God. I do believe he's right.

Here was the wonderful part. When my mother knelt to confess, she started to choke up, and then tears started spilling down her cheeks. I'd never seen my mother cry. Not even after my father died. It seemed something of a miracle, and soon everyone was in tears. Including me.

And then an interesting thing happened.

Alice Zook rose from her seat and crossed the room to apologize to her husband Teddy about something—I'm not even sure what. Then another man did the same to his wife. David stopped the service, as one person after the other rose to make amends. And when it seemed like all the fences had been mended, he resumed the service. Afterward came Communion, and it was the sweetest one we've ever had.

Love, Jimmy

P.S. Would you consider coming to Stoney Ridge for Easter Sunday? You could meet Izzy and Luke's baby. I've enclosed bus fare, just in case.

Dear Sylvie,

Greetings in the name of our Lord.

It has been brought to my attention that I might have created some mis-understanding about Rising Star Farm. If so, I hope you have it in your heart to forgive me. A mother can't help but take care of her son, that is what I know. But there is also something else I know.

On the day that Jake passed, I hap-pened to see him cross the creek with a large rope looped around his neck, cradling a large rifle under one arm. I stopped him and asked what the Sam Hill he thought he was doing. He said he was on a hunt to catch a deer. I asked him why, because I'd never known that man to hunt—why, he couldn't even catch a big fish in a small pond if his life depended on it—and he said it was because you loved venison. He wanted to surprise you on your wedding anniversary.

   I never thought to tell you that story, but I mentioned it to Hank recently and he was insistent that I should let you know.

Yours truly,
Edith Fisher Lapp

Dear Jimmy,

   Greetings in the name of our Lord.

   Izzy has written and told me all about little Amos. About your mother's confession too. And Izzy also had already invited me to come for Easter. We plan to come next Friday afternoon and stay through Easter Monday. Joey would like a turn or two in the new tire swing, if that might be all right with you.

Love, Sylvie

P.S. Thank you for the bus fare.

P.P.S. People can surprise you, can't they?

Dear Sylvie,

   I will be waiting at the bus stop on Friday afternoon for you. Tell Joey he can plan on swinging on the new tire swing. The fat cat still won't let me near the old tire swing.

   Love, Jimmy

Jimmy was at the bus stop in Stoney Ridge at twelve o'clock on Friday, freshly bathed, shaved, and laundered. He had no idea when Sylvie and Joey would be arriving, but he wasn't going to miss their bus's arrival. He wasn't going to make them wait for him. He would wait for them.

At three o'clock, the bus finally arrived. Joey saw him first and jumped out of the bus, leaping over the steps to hurl himself into Jimmy's arms.

"Hey, buddy! You've grown a foot or more!"

"Where's Prince?" Joey asked.

"In the shade, under the tree."

Joey sprinted over to the horse as Sylvie came into view at the opening of the bus. She gave the bow of her bonnet a straightening tug, then smoothed her hands over her skirt . . . garb that was no longer Lancaster Amish. The sight of her took his breath away, and he felt his eyes start to sting. Their eyes held for several beats until finally she stepped off the bus and drew close to him, so close he felt himself swept away by those violet eyes of hers.

"What's this?" she asked, concerned. "Why the tears?"

This wasn't the way he had things planned. He was going

to talk to her about a future between them on Monday morning, as she got ready to return to Big Valley. After he'd had time to show her Rising Star Farm, and the freshly painted house, and the fixed-up barns. But all those things seemed less important and sudden misery led him to ask, "Tell me it's not too late for us." His voice was choked with tears, but he didn't care. He had to ask. "Tell me I haven't spoiled things between us forever."

She took her time answering, so long that he felt his heart start to pound with worry. Her gaze shifted past him to Joey and the horse, then she took a deep breath and looked Jimmy straight in the eyes. "There's some things that stand between us." She tipped her head. "Big things."

Not a single wink. That worried him too. He'd missed those winks. "Go ahead," Jimmy said, wiping his cheeks off with the back of his hand. "Shoot."

"I don't feel right about using Prince as a stud for racehorses. And I've never felt right about calling him the Flying Horse."

"I know, I know. I steamrolled you into that, and I'm sorry. We can paint over the words *The Flying Horse*." He lifted his shoulders in a shrug. "But as for the stud fees from Juan Miranda . . . those have already been applied to the overdue property taxes. You want me to return those fees?"

"Is Rising Star Farm's tax bill squared up?"

"Yup."

"And Juan Miranda's mares are due to foal?"

"Yup."

Some of the tightness in Sylvie's face softened. "Well, sounds like everyone's got what they needed."

He relaxed, but just a little. "You want to go back to your original idea? Use Prince to create a Partbred?"

"Yes. For the Plain People."

"Sylvie . . . it's not gonna be easy."

A little smile started in her eyes. "My father wants my first trained colt."

Jimmy's eyebrows shot up. "Your father?"

Her smile spread. "People can surprise you."

"Ain't that the truth?" He turned amused eyes on her. "Who wrote the rule that a Hillbilly Amish can't try something new?"

She smiled briefly, then it faded away as she crossed her arms, gripped her elbows. "Jimmy, I'm going to stay in Big Valley. In my father's church. He's not well, not well at all. I'm needed there, more than I am in Stoney Ridge. For now, at least." She looked over at Prince and at Joey. "And I'd like to take Prince with me, if you'd let me have him."

Sylvie wasn't coming back? Jimmy drew in a quick hitching breath. She wasn't coming back. Joey wasn't coming back. Prince was leaving. He couldn't lose them, none of them. "He's your horse, Sylvie. He's always been your horse." He swallowed, trying to clear his throat of his wildly thumping heart. *Jimmy Fisher*, he told himself, *think! For once in your life, man, look beyond today and into the future.* He squeezed his eyes shut. Was he really going to say this? Was he sure he wanted to do this? Oh yes. Yes, he was. "You can have Prince," he swallowed down his inhibitions, "but I'd like to come along with him. The fat cat, he can stay."

"What?" She stared at him. "What about Rising Star Farm?"

His eyes lit with amusement, and he felt his heart settle, his whole self settle. "Just like Prince has always been your horse, I think Rising Star Farm has always been my mother's true home. It's where she belongs." He grinned. "Besides, after the big storm we had in January, the creek seems bound and determined to swallow her house."

"Jimmy, my father's church . . . it's still the Hillbilly Amish."

"Who wrote the rule that a fellow can't go to a more conservative church?"

"It's more than conservative, Jimmy." Her face pinched. "Outdoor plumbing. No running water."

"Yeah, I figured." He gulped. Then he grinned. "But I'm no featherbed. I spent four years in Colorado on the back of a horse."

A soft smile curved her lips. "We do have featherbeds. Goosedown pillows too."

"Well, that changes things." He took a step closer to her. "What else stands between us?"

Her smile slipped away. "Your waffling."

Oh, that. "Sylvie, I will waffle no more. I won't even eat waffles anymore."

"Jimmy, are you sure? Really, really sure."

"I'm sure about this one thing. A life without you is no life at all." He took her hands in his. He searched for a way to express all that was in his heart. "Can you forgive me? Can you trust me despite how many times I've blown it? Have faith in me that there are better things to come?"

She smiled. "Here's something I'm sure about. 'Love doesn't keep score of wrongs.' That's written in the Good Book. I can't remember where, but I know I read it."

Love. She had said she loved him.

He wrapped his arms around her and kissed her. Once, then twice more. And when she pulled away, she winked.

Discussion Questions

1. In *Two Steps Forward*, there is a theme of protecting those who can't defend themselves. How did you see this theme play out in the novel?

2. Sylvie was wired for taking on responsibilities. Jimmy? Not so much. Which character changed more throughout this book?

3. Sylvie was raised in an ultraconservative Old Order Amish church. Jimmy called it "Hillbilly Amish." How did her past shape her life? Why do we care so much about Sylvie?

4. How would you describe Sylvie's faith? How did it grow or change? Compare Sylvie's faith journey with Jimmy's.

5. Edith Fisher Lapp was domineering of her son, yet also protective. What does motherhood mean to her?

6. Jimmy's relationship with his mother wavered between avoiding her (off to Colorado for four years) or buckling to her wishes (dinners with Rosemary Blank). How

does their dynamic shift after Sylvie leaves Rising Star Farm?

7. When Jimmy gave David the copy of his great-grand-father's will, it created a crisis for Edith. Was it the right thing for Jimmy to do? Why or why not?

8. There's another theme in this story—the importance of having a father. A loving, steadfast father. Izzy, for example, grew up without a father and keenly felt his absence after she became a mother. At one point, Luke asks Izzy, "Aren't I enough? Can't we be enough?" Should it be enough? And if not, why not?

9. Here's a sobering statistic: today, more than one in four children live in a home without a father. (https://www .fatherhood.org/fatherhood-data-statistics)

   Is there a child in your life who needs a father figure—a nephew, a niece, a grandson, a neighbor's child? What can you do to try and fill that void?

10. While it sounds pretty far-fetched, Rhnull blood is the rarest blood type of all—one that fewer than fifty people in the entire world have—which is why scientists have nicknamed it "golden blood." The type, whose scientific name is Rhnull blood, was discovered in 1961. Since then, there have been a total of forty-three reported cases. Its rarity and unique properties combine to make it potentially dangerous, should someone with this type ever need a blood transfusion.

    What was the significance of golden blood for Izzy? For this story? How does it symbolize the valuable and costly love God has for each of his children? "How precious are also thy thoughts of me, O God! How great is the sum of them" (Ps. 139:17).

11. "Words are a funny thing," David said, when he told Edith she must make a public confession for her deception. "They can make big things little. And they can make little things big." Discuss some ways in which little things became big in *Two Steps Forward*.

12. Edith and Hank Lapp, more than any other characters, play a role in most every book set in Stoney Ridge. Complete opposites, yet happily married. Sort of. Why are they good for each other? And why are readers so drawn to them? Who in your life reminds you of Hank or Edith?

13. The Easter season is a significant time in the Old Order Amish Church. It's a time of solemn reflection before the community partakes in the sacrament of Communion, and prepares their heart for the full and complex meaning of Christ's Resurrection—forgiveness, wholeness, and new beginnings. A good example to us all to take Communion seriously by keeping short accounts, making amends, mending fences, before we accept the symbolic food and drink of the Last Supper. "If it is possible, as far as it depends on you, live at peace with everyone" (Rom. 12:18 NLT). As Easter season approaches this year, which fences need mending in your life?

Read on for a Sneak Peek of
Suzanne Woods Fisher's Next Story from
THREE SISTERS ISLAND!

$\mathcal{O}$NE

Just before Maddie unlocked the door to her office, she straightened the name plaque on the wall: *Madison Grayson, Marriage and Family Therapist.*

Her career was finally under way. Today was the starting day of her first real job, and she actually had clients. An engaged couple, who had made an appointment on the very day Captain Ed helped hang her shingle.

She opened the door and walked inside, smiling. The space she had rented was in the basement of an old house on First Street, just around the corner from the Lunch Counter, the hub of Three Sisters Island. Peg Legg owned and ran the diner, and advised Maddie to not rent space right on Main Street. "You won't get any customers if they think folks see them coming and going from the shrink's office."

Maddie bristled at being called a shrink, and her clients were not customers, but she was grateful for Peg's local savvy. The ways of locals were still new to her despite living on the island this past year. She doubted she'd ever truly understand them, but she hoped she could shed light on the problems in their lives. Problems, she understood.

She flipped on the light and smiled. On her desk was a

bouquet of a dozen red roses, her favorite, and a little card. "Good luck today. Love, Cam and Cooper, Blaine and Dad."

This was Dad's doing. He was over-the-moon pleased that she'd completed the hours required for her to be fully licensed. Over. The. Moon. He really needn't have worried about her. Maddie finished what she started, even if it took a little longer than expected. Blaine was the daughter he should save his worry for.

She opened a casement window to let in fresh air, for the May morning was unseasonably warm. Her gaze swept the small room, looking for any pillow that needed puffing up or wall frames of her diplomas that were slightly askew, but she couldn't see anything to improve. In fact, it couldn't be any more perfect. It wasn't large but she didn't need much space. Just privacy.

Cam had helped her decorate the basement and turn it into a professional office. For once, her older sister hadn't overridden Maddie's preferences. Instead of the couch and desk that she had picked out, as well as an accent wall of a boldly patterned wallpaper—she deferred to Maddie's choices. Comfortable upholstered swiveling armchairs instead of a couch. A palette of subdued colors for paint and fabrics—cool tones with warm pops—that invited one to relax, to linger. Not too feminine, not too masculine. Against the back wall was a tiny service kitchen with an expensive coffee machine that made single coffees. Customized coffee. Maddie wanted everything here to tell a client she respected their individuality.

She heard the stomping sound of someone up above, someone on the portly side, and assumed it was Tillie, the church secretary, who took her volunteer job very seriously.

The spacious house had been rented to the tiny little church on Three Sisters Island, a small fellowship that had finally found a pastor who was willing to move to an island on the edge of the world for a pittance of a salary. The house would serve as his living quarters, plus his office, and it was near the building they could use on Sunday mornings—a huge upgrade from meeting in the Baggett and Taggett shop down the street. It was hard to sing worship songs about creation when a moosehead on the wall was staring down at you. Accusingly.

She tried to remember what Seth had said when he recruited the new pastor. Richard Something-or-other. She squeezed her eyes shut. He was freshly out of the military. He loved Jesus and extreme sports, in that order. Oh, and he had tattoos. That's all she could remember Seth had said. She'd been so distracted with starting her practice that she hadn't paid much attention. She had a lot of faith in Seth Walker's judgment. He had started the little church a few years ago when he became the island's schoolteacher, so he knew what kind of a pastor would best fit the role.

Maddie took out a blank notepad, a periwinkle blue Flair pen, applied fresh lipstick, straightened her skirt, said a little prayer, and waited for her clients to arrive.

Outside the open casement window, she heard a commotion of excited shouts and footsteps pound down the street. Curious, she left her office and went to the street to see what was causing the fuss. She stood at the top of Main Street and shielded her eyes from the bright morning sun. Behind her came the stomp-stomp of Tillie's Bean boots and then the sound stopped abruptly as she stood right beside Maddie. "Oh my word," she said. "He said he was going to parachute in today, but I didn't think he meant literally."

There, floating down from the sky, right in front of Boon Dock, was a brightly colored parachute with a man dangling underneath. "Tillie, is that our new pastor?"

"Indeed it is."

"What's his name again?"

"Richard O'Shea."

"That's right." Wait. Hold it. *Oh no.* She jerked her head down. "Not . . . no, it couldn't be . . ." Her heart started to pound. "Does he happen to go by the name of Ricky?"

"No."

Maddie blew out a puff of air. *Phew.* It couldn't the same guy. No way. It couldn't possibly be the same Ricky with whom she grew up. Not a chance.

"Rick, he calls himself."

A queasy roll started up in Maddie's stomach. *No, no, no, no, no.* How could this world be so big and yet so small?

Tillie patted her on her shoulder. "I'd better get down to the dock to greet our new pastor. And you'd better see to your customers. They got confused and came upstairs to the church office. I sent them down to wait in the basement."

Maddie gasped. No! This wasn't the way the morning was supposed to go. She should be in her office, waiting to welcome her clients. And Ricky O'Shea should remain far, far away, a distant, unpleasant, suppressed-if-not-forgotten memory. Like a root canal.

⟵⟶

After dropping her eight-year-old son Cooper off at school, Camden Grayson stopped at the Lunch Counter to exchange hellos with Peg Legg, the diner's owner. Peg's round merry face lit up when she spotted Cam coming in through the door, and she enveloped her in a bear hug before hurrying to fetch her a mug of hot coffee. No matter how busy the diner was, Peg would stop and give Cam a warm welcome.

Cam not only enjoyed Peg, she admired her. Peg was the one who, last August, when the last member of the Unitarian Church at the top of Main Street passed away and the church building was donated to the town, came up with the idea of using the empty church building for the school, moving it off Camp Kicking Moose's property and into town where it belonged. That one swift action brought great relief to her dad, as a school bus full of children arriving each morning wasn't mixing well with vacationing campers.

Cam sat on a red stool at the counter, sipped a mug of very mediocre coffee, and reviewed details about a new government grant she'd found, making notes in the margins. All winter and spring, she'd been toiling away on lengthy grant applications—with the hope of making Three Sisters Island run entirely by renewable energy, thereby eliminating dependency on the extremely unreliable public utility grid.

If Cam's plan worked, Three Sisters Island would become completely self-sufficient with an off-the-grid electric system powered by water, wind, and solar. It would be an economic boost to this little island that suffered from disruptive, inconvenient brownouts and blackouts throughout the year. Summer as well as winter, with windy storms that knocked out power and canceled the Never Late ferry—its lifeline to Mount Desert Island, and then to the mainland.

Each grant took an enormous amount of time to complete, scads of paperwork. So far, she'd had ten rejections. She needed at least three grants to cover the scope of the project she had in mind. Even three might not be enough.

The rejections worried her, but Cam turned worry into action: pursuing more grants. She was determined. Partly to help the island, partly to help her dad.

Camp Kicking Moose, her dad's passion, could be a year-round destination, but that would remain a distant dream if stable energy remained elusive. The winters in Maine were long and dark, bitter cold, and if the island was cut off from the mainland for more than a few weeks like it was this past winter, it became nearly unbearable. It wasn't just the lack of supplies that started to wear thin, it was the isolation that everyone felt. Peg mentioned recently that the Alcoholics Anonymous group that met early in the mornings at the Lunch Counter doubled in size during the winters.

"Cam, come on out! You gotta see this."

Cam's head popped up when she heard Peg call to her. She hadn't noticed that the Lunch Counter had emptied out. A crowd had gathered on Main Street, staring up at the sky. Cam hesitated a few seconds, reluctant to be interrupted from her work, then set her pen on the notepad and hurried outside to see what everyone was looking at. There, high above them, floating down from the sky, was a man attached to a billowing parachute.

Standing next to Cam, Peg shook her head in disbelief, fists planted on her generous hips. "I thought I'd seen everything around here. This is a new one."

Cam tented her eyes to peer at the man who dangled underneath the colorful canopy. She thought it was a man, anyway. "Who do you think it is?"

Tillie marched past them. "He's our new pastor," she said over her shoulder, as if it were the most normal thing in the world for a person to drop out of the sky.

"How about that?" Peg said, clapping with delight. "Sent to us from above!"

As the Never Late ferry chugged toward Boon Dock at Three Sisters Island, Blaine Grayson watched a skydiver come in for a landing on the small ribbon of soft sand that bordered the harbor. Whoever was under that umbrella of bright colors seemed to know what he was doing—it was a pinpoint landing. She smiled as the man gracefully bounced feet first on the sand and immediately bolted forward to run up the beach, in such a practiced way that the parachute drifted down to the ground behind him, as gently as a leaf in the wind. He seemed oblivious to the many eyes watching him. Calmly, he unbuckled the harness around his chest and set about methodically folding up the canopy.

What must it be like to skydive out of an airplane? To stand at the open door and look down? That was exactly how Blaine felt with the announcement she needed to give to her family as she finished up her first year of culinary school. She knew she would have to be prudent about the time to tell them. There was no hurry, not until Cam and Seth's wedding date was set in stone. Mostly, it was her father's reaction, in particular, she dreaded.

As she watched the skydiver trudge up the beach toward the gathered crowd on Main Street, she thought that she could actually imagine how it would feel to jump from the plane, trusting the parachute pack to unfold at just the right moment. Everything, all of her trust rested on that one hope. A tiny little cord of hope. Of understanding.

Acknowledgments

Special thanks to Lindsey Ross, who read through this manuscript and offered guidance and wisdom. Your insights take my books to a new level. I couldn't do this without you.

To my husband, Steve, who tolerates my early rising (really, really early!) as a deadline draws near. I become an ostrich with her head in the sand, and the sand is my computer.

Heartfelt thanks to my wonderful editors, Andrea Doering and Barb Barnes, and the entire team at Revell—Michele Misiak, Karen Steele, Brianne Dekker, Gayle Raymer, and so many others who go above and beyond on my books. To Joyce Hart of Hartline Literary Agency, for opening the door for me and being such a faithful cheerleader.

To my readers near and far—you've enriched my life in countless ways through your encouraging words. You are the reason I write. That the Lord brought us together is a continual blessing to me each and every day.

Bless you all.

Suzanne Woods Fisher is an award-winning, bestselling author of more than thirty books, including *Mending Fences*, as well as the Nantucket Legacy, Amish Beginnings, The Bishop's Family, and The Inn at Eagle Hill series, among other novels. She is also the author of several nonfiction books about the Amish, including *Amish Peace* and *Amish Proverbs*. She lives in California. Learn more at www.suzanne woodsfisher.com and follow Suzanne on Facebook @Suzanne WoodsFisherAuthor and Twitter @suzannewfisher.

"There's just something unique and fresh about every Suzanne Woods Fisher book. Whatever the reason, I'm a fan."

—SHELLEY SHEPHARD GRAY,
New York Times and *USA Today* bestselling author

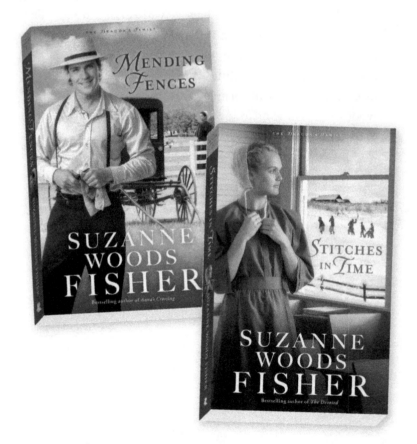

"*On a Summer Tide* is an enduring tale of
love and restoration."

–DENISE HUNTER, bestselling author of *On Magnolia Lane*

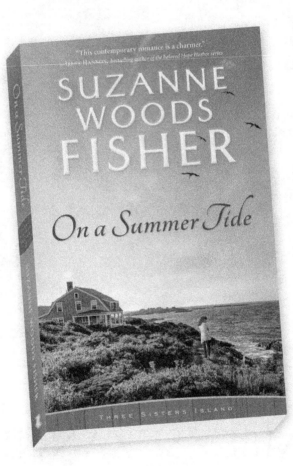

MEET SUZANNE

www.SuzanneWoodsFisher.com